The Lola Quartet

EMILY ST. JOHN MANDEL

UNBRIDLED BOOKS

The Lola Quartet

Unbridled Books

Library of Congress Cataloging-in-Publication Data

St. John Mandel, Emily.
The Lola quartet : a novel / by Emily St. John Mandel.
p. cm.
ISBN 9781609530792
1. Crime—Fiction.   2. Family secrets—Fiction.   3. Psychological fiction.
I. Title.
PR9199.4.S727L65 2012
813'.6—dc23
2011042381

1   3   5   7   9   10   8   6   4   2

BOOK DESIGN BY SH · CV

First Printing

To Kevin

"The novelty of our adventure was wearing thin, but not because our feet hurt and we were constantly blaming each other for the forgotten sunscreen. There was some other thing that we could not clearly explain. The farther we ventured, the more everything looked the same, as if each new street, park, or shopping mall was simply another version of our own, made from the same giant assembly kit. Only the names were different."

SHAUN TAN

Tales from Outer Suburbia

"One of these mornings
You're going to rise up singing
Then you'll spread your wings
And you'll take to the sky
But until that morning
There's nothing can harm you…"

GEORGE GERSHWIN

Summertime

Part One

One

A nna had fallen into a routine, or as much of a routine as a seventeen-year-old can reasonably fall into when she's transient and living in hiding with an infant. She was staying at her sister's friend's house in a small town in Virginia.

The baby always woke up crying at four thirty or five a.m. Anna got up and changed Chloe's diaper, prepared a bottle and bundled her into the stroller and then they left the basement where they were living, walked three blocks to the twenty-four-hour doughnut shop for coffee and across the wide empty street to the park. Anna sat on a swing with her first coffee of the morning and Chloe lay in the stroller staring up at the clouds. They listened to the birds in the trees at the edges of the park, the sounds of traffic in the distance. The climbing equipment cast a complicated silhouette against the pale morning sky.

There was a plastic shopping bag duct-taped to the underside of the stroller. It held a little under one hundred eighteen thousand dollars in cash.

. . .

THAT MORNING at a music school in South Carolina a pianist was sitting alone in a practice room. Jack had been playing the piano for four and a half hours and under normal circumstances his hands would have been aching by now, but he was high on painkillers and couldn't feel it. There was an east-facing window in the practice room and the morning light had long since entered. The piano was illuminated, sun caught in the varnish and gleaming in the keys, the whole room shining, he was dizzy, his skin itched and he hadn't slept all night. His roommate had gone to Virginia to rescue a girl whom Jack had imperiled and everything was coming apart around him, but so long as he kept playing he didn't have to think about any of this, so he closed his eyes against the shine and launched once more into Gershwin's *Rhapsody in Blue*.

Two

Ten years later, in February, the showerhead in Gavin's bathroom began to leak. The timing was inconvenient. His editor had assigned him to a story about Florida's exotic wildlife problem, and he was leaving New York the following morning. Gavin stood in the bathroom watching the steady dripping of hot water, at a loss. It seemed to him that this was the sort of thing Karen would have taken care of, before she'd moved out, and he realized at the same moment that he wasn't even sure where the landlord's phone number was. On a piece of paper somewhere, but pieces of paper had taken over his desk and spilled over onto the living room floor in the three weeks since Karen had left, a sort of avalanche. After a half-hour he came across a box of baby clothes that he'd forgotten to take to Goodwill and after that he didn't want to look anymore, so he retreated into the bedroom and resumed an earlier search for clean socks. He could call the landlord when he got back.

WHAT GAVIN had wanted was to be an investigative reporter, a newspaperman, but nothing about his career was as he'd imagined it would be. When he'd graduated with his journalism degree he'd thought that this would be the moment when his life would finally begin. In idealistic daydreams he'd thought he might help change the world or at least improve it, and in shallower moments he'd just wanted to be a star reporter. He'd wanted to extend his hands and feel the weight of the Pulitzer with the crowd applauding before him, step up to the podium and clear his throat in the spotlight. He'd managed eventually to land a job as a reporter at one of the city's best papers, but coming to the *New York Star* was like stepping into a drama in which all the major roles were already taken, or perhaps the play had already closed. There were veteran journalists at the *Star*, men and a woman who'd brought down titans and gone into war zones and propelled the paper to a point only just beneath the *Times* in the New York City newspaper pantheon, people who didn't have to imagine what a Pulitzer felt like, but even the veterans seemed adrift in the changed world. The paper was sending out fewer and fewer correspondents on faraway stories. There were no more bureaus overseas or even in Washington. The paper was covering local news, relying on Reuters and freelancers for everything else. Too many of the stories seemed more like entertainment than news to him.

"You have to put in your time," his editor had told him, but Gavin feared more and more that his time had passed. On two or three occasions he'd managed to get invited along for drinks with a couple of the veterans, and their stories mostly concerned a time that seemed better and more glorious than now and ended with some variation on "those were the days." He'd come home from the bars leaden with disappointment.

"You know what your problem is?" his friend Silas said one night when they were drinking together at an Irish bar near the paper. "I just figured it out." Silas was a copy editor and had been at the paper longer than Gavin had. Their desks were side-by-side in the newsroom.

"Please," Gavin said, "tell me what my problem is."

"Look at you. Jesus. The fedora, the trench coat. You want to run around the city with a flashbulb camera and a press card in your hat band."

"How is that a problem?"

"Your problem is that you don't really want to work at a *newspaper*, per se. You want to work in 1925."

"I don't disagree," Gavin said. It had been clear for some time that he was in the wrong decade. All of his favorite movies were older than he was. His camera was a 1973 Yashica. He'd seen *Chinatown* a dozen times.

He suspected his editor was sending him on his first out-of-town assignment to make him feel better about not being senior enough to be sent into a war zone, or perhaps to make him feel better about having missed the days the veterans drank to. He knew she was doing him a favor, but the assignment itself seemed depressingly symptomatic: he was being sent to his hometown. He'd gone in a circle. He wanted to scream.

"Aren't you from there?" his editor asked, when she called him over to her desk.

"I am," he said. "But—" and he realized as he spoke that of course there was no way of evading the assignment, of course he couldn't tell her that the weather in his hometown had sent him to the hospital with heatstroke nearly every year until he'd left at eighteen, so he sat by her desk discussing the story for a few minutes and then went back to his computer to check the South Florida weather. The city of Sebastian was in the grip of a heat wave.

That night he lay awake listening to the dripping shower and wondered if it would be pathetic to call Karen about the landlord's phone number, decided against it and woke at an unspeakably early hour to board a southbound plane.

GAVIN HAD been back to Florida only once in the past five years. He flew into Boca Raton and when he stepped out of the airport the heat made him gasp. He drove a rental car down the freeway to the city of Sebastian and called his sister from his hotel room, which was mostly pink and smelled of synthetic cherries.

"I'm glad you're here," Eilo said. "You're sure you won't stay with me?"

"I don't want to impose. The paper pays for my hotel room."

"Want to meet for dinner?"

"I'm supposed to meet with a park ranger later," he said. "How about tomorrow?"

But their schedules were incompatible, and three days passed before he had a chance to see her. He spent his first day in Sebastian and the day after that interviewing conservationists and herpetologists, knocking on doors of the houses closest to the canals to ask residents about their encounters with giant snakes. He took photographs of blue-green water, of shy iguanas at the edges of backyards.

There was an afternoon spent staggering through swamps under a wide-brimmed hat, listening to a park ranger named William Chandler talk about the new monsters that had been appearing since the early '90s. The creatures in the Florida swamps were terrifying and new, and the canals delivered the swamps to the suburbs. Experts speculated that some of the animals had been blown deep into the swamps by Hurricane Andrew—greenhouses that had held snakes had been found shattered and empty once the storm had passed—but most were abandoned pets. Small glittering lizards who'd seemed manageable enough when they were babies but then outgrew aquarium after aquarium until they'd become seven-foot-long two-hundred-pound Nile monitors with eerily intelligent eyes and extravagantly pebbled skin, perfectly capable of eating a small dog. Or Burmese pythons, purchased when small, abandoned when the owners got tired of having to feed them live rabbits. Capable of swallowing a leopard whole, William Chandler told him, and therefore capable of swallowing a human. All of these creatures multiplying in the brackish far reaches, the suburbs coming out to meet them. All Gavin could think of was the heat pressing down upon him, but he blinked hard against the spots swimming before his eyes and wrote down everything Chandler said. Insects hummed in the trees.

By night the suburbs glimmered anonymously from his window, but even by daylight it was difficult to grasp the terrain. There had been considerable development in the decade since Gavin had lived here, and nothing was quite as he remembered. The present-day Sebastian was like a dream version of his hometown, much larger than it had been, filled with unexpected shopping malls and new condominium complexes, entire new neighborhoods where once there'd been trees or swamp. Once this had been the outer suburbs but now there were suburbs that sprawled out still further, linked up with exurbs by lacework patterns of freeways. The heart of the city was difficult to find. The suburbs circled wetlands, and there were monsters in the swamps. He wrote about the pythons and the Nile monitors, William Chandler and the frightened residents who lived alongside the canals, working deep into the night in the cool light of the hotel room.

"How do you like being back in Sebastian?" his sister asked. Their schedules had finally coincided on his last night in Florida, and they'd met at a seafood restaurant near the hotel. Eilo was only thirty-two but her hair was mostly gray now, and she'd recently cut it very short against her skull. The haircut made her eyes look enormous. She was wearing a suit.

"It's exactly the way I remember it," Gavin said.

"A diplomatic response," Eilo said.

"Except even more sprawling."

"It never ends," she said. "You can drive from here to Miami without leaving the suburbs. How's Karen these days? She couldn't come with you?"

"We broke up a month ago. She moved out."

"You broke up? Even though she's pregnant?"

"She's not pregnant anymore." Gavin remembered, sitting here, that he'd thought seriously about naming the baby after Eilo.

"Gavin, I'm sorry."

"Thanks. Me too." He didn't want to talk about it. "How's the real estate business?" They spoke on the phone every couple of months, but he hadn't seen her in so long that being in her presence was unexpectedly awkward.

"Never better," she said.

"In this economy?"

"Well, I do deal exclusively in foreclosures." Eilo was looking at her plate. She hesitated a moment before she spoke again. "How's your health?"

"Fine," he said. "A bit touch and go in the summertime, but I stay indoors and take taxis when it's hot. Is something bothering you?"

"I don't know if I should tell you now," she said.

"Tell me anyway."

"Part of my job is inspecting homes. I inspected a property on Pauline Street a few weeks ago, a place that had just been foreclosed on that week. The property owner's name was Gloria Jones. Older woman. She was taking care of a little girl."

"Taking care of her?"

"She referred to the girl as 'my ward.' I actually never saw the up-stairs, so I don't know if the girl lived there or not. She was . . . listen, I know this sounds crazy, but the little girl looked exactly like me. It was like seeing myself as a kid."

"So she was half-white, half-Japanese?" Gavin wasn't sure where she was going with the story and was already a little bored by it.

"I was struck by her. I have to take pictures of the home for the real estate listing, and I made sure the kid was in one of the shots." She reached into her handbag and extracted a paperback. She'd placed the photograph in the middle for safekeeping.

"Oh," Gavin said. "I see what you mean." For a disoriented mo-ment he thought he was looking at a photograph of Eilo as a little girl. European and Asian genes in delicate combination, the same straight dark hair and thin lips, the same faint scattering of freckles on her nose. It took him a moment to realize that the eyes were different. His sister's eyes were brown, and this little Eilo's eyes were blue. But the similarity was uncanny. She stood at the edge of the shot, by the win-dow of an almost empty dining room.

"She's ten years old," Eilo said. Gavin was beginning to understand even before Eilo spoke again. "Gavin, I asked the kid her name when Gloria was out of the room. Her name's Chloe Montgomery."

"Montgomery?"

"That was when I knew," Eilo said.

"She looks exactly like you. Where is she now?"

"I have no idea. To be honest, the woman caught me taking the kid's picture and started yelling at me, so I got out of there quickly. I drove by the house two days later, but they'd already moved out. I don't know where they went. I thought you should know."

"Can I keep the picture?"

"Yes. Of course." She was quiet for a moment. "I'm sorry," she said. "I know this can't be easy, especially given . . . I thought you should know."

After dinner Gavin walked out to his car and drove past his hotel on purpose. He wanted to keep driving for a while, alone in the air conditioning. He turned off his cell phone. He was thinking about the girl, the other Eilo. Thinking about trying to find her, trying to imagine what he might say if he did. *My name is Gavin Sasaki. You look exactly like my sister. I had a girlfriend named Anna who disappeared ten years ago and you have her last name. I know this sounds crazy but I think we have the same genes.*

Three

On her last morning in Virginia Anna sipped her coffee and stared up at the sky. It was a clear bright day, clouds passing over blue. She was tired in a way that made the world seem insubstantial. The sun was rising and the park held a dreamlike sheen. No leaves on the trees but the air was bright. She sat on a swing with her first coffee of the morning, scuffing her shoes in the sand. Only when she looked at her daughter did she feel awake.

Chloe lay on her back in the stroller staring up at the clouds.

Anna and Chloe were in the park when Liam Deval came to them. Anna looked up—a man approaching over the lawn, the sunrise behind him so she couldn't see his face—and because she couldn't see who it was she assumed the worst and thought she was finished, she clutched the chains of the swing so tightly that blood began to throb in the palms of her hands, she tried to steel herself but her last thoughts raced together and all she could think of was how sad it was that she'd had so little time with her daughter. She looked at Chloe, trying to memorize the soft flush of her skin and her wide unfocused eyes, her miniature hands clenching and unclenching above the blankets, the heartbreaking smallness of her fingernails, but then Liam called out her name over the grass. Anna let her breath out all at once and blinked away tears.

"It's you," she said, "I'm so glad it's you," but she understood immediately that something was wrong. He held her for a moment and stroked her hair when she stood up from the swing, glanced over his shoulder before he looked at her again.

"Anna, we have to leave again," he said. "I think he knows you're here."

Four

The morning after the dinner with his sister Gavin woke early in his room in the Ramada Inn, troubled, and lay still in the bed for a few minutes before he remembered the photograph. He turned on the bedside light and went to the desk to retrieve it. The girl stared back at him, ten years old and the image of his sister, half-smiling in an unfurnished room.

He showered and packed quickly, checked out of the hotel, and drove toward the airport for five minutes before he remembered that he still had one last interview. A woman in a planned community far out near the swamps, a friend of William Chandler's. He pulled into a parking lot to check the directions and had to read them three times. It took him twice as long to reach his destination as it should have. He kept forgetting street names, making wrong turns, looking for roads he was already driving on. Where had they been all these years, Anna and the girl? They were all he could think of. If the house where the girl had been staying had been foreclosed, what if she was in a homeless shelter? Or what if it was worse than that, what if she was on the street? The thought of his daughter sleeping under an overpass. He found the condominium complex—far from anywhere, almost beyond Sebastian city limits—and sat in his car for a full two minutes staring at the photograph before he went in.

He sat drinking a glass of water in a large bright kitchen, taking notes and trying to concentrate on what the woman was saying. Her name was Ella Thompson and she wanted to tell him about her children.

"When I was out with William Chandler the other day," he said, "he told me you saw a Burmese python in your backyard."

"Oh, I *did*," she said. "Well, not in the backyard exactly, but there's this point where the yard sort of blends into the canal, and—" She was interrupted by the chime of a doorbell. It was her neighbor, a beautiful woman of about fifty with very high cheekbones and silver hair, here to see if she might borrow a stepladder, and yes, she would be delighted to speak with the reporter from New York for a few minutes. She talked about the beauty of Florida, the flowers and the palm trees and the endless summertime, blue pools.

"And how long have you lived out here," Gavin asked, "by the swamps?"

"A few years." The neighbor smiled. "It's funny. We thought we were coming closer to nature," she said, "but all along nature was creeping closer to us."

Gavin said his good-byes and drove to the airport. He found himself staring at children in the terminal lounge. On the flight north out of Florida he tried not to think about anything except the story he was writing, William Chandler in hip waders standing up to his knees in the swamps at the far edge of the suburbs, a radio-tracking device beeping in his hand, "This means there's a python right at our feet, Gavin, right at our feet, you just can't see it because the water's so murky." The nervous residents of the outer suburbs, gazing out their back windows at canals. The conservationist who'd told him that the creatures in the swamps meant they were entering a time when every place would look the same as every other place, the same pythons, the same parrots, the same palm trees from Florida to Indonesia to Argentina, an ecological flattening of experience. He worked steadily until the island of Manhattan appeared below his window, and then he closed his laptop and tried not to think about the girl during the descent.

THE FIRST thing Gavin heard when he opened the door to his apartment was the leaking shower. It seemed to be getting worse, the drips more frequent, but he still didn't know where the landlord's phone number was and now he was too distracted to care. He left his suitcase in the apartment and took the subway to work. The newsroom seemed somehow changed in his absence. There were fewer people here than usual. A sense of dissipation hung in the air. It reminded him of the time when he'd come in late on a Christmas Eve to wrap up a piece and found the newsroom a shadow of itself, a ghost town. But the difference now, he realized with a lurching feeling in his stomach, was that a dozen desks had been cleared. Silas's papers and notebooks and the photograph of his wife had vanished, his computer monitor a dark window reflecting Gavin back at himself and behind him a ghostly version of the newsroom, all shadows and pale smudges of light.

"You missed all the fun," his editor said when he came to her.

"Where's Silas?"

"Sit down." There was a tiredness around her eyes that he hadn't seen before. He sat by her desk. "We were treated to a speech the day after you left," she said. "Declining ad revenue, ever fewer subscribers, the relentless expectation of free online content, et cetera. You've heard it before. It's a boring story."

"Why didn't you tell me?"

"Why didn't I take the time to call you in Florida and explain that twelve of your colleagues had been laid off? Because believe it or not, kiddo, I've been a little busy in their absence." She told him the names and some of them were friends of his.

"Christ," he said. "Can you tell me anything else?"

"You're wondering about your job. I'm wondering about mine too." Julie sighed. "I don't know what to tell you," she said. "You're in a strange position. On the one hand, you're not that senior. On the other hand, that means you're relatively cheap. No offense."

"None taken. I've seen my pay stubs."

She took off her glasses and massaged her temples for a moment before she spoke again. "Listen," she said, "just between us, there's likely to be a second round of layoffs."

"Do you know who . . . ?"

"No. But I know they're looking to make some cuts in the newsroom." She put her glasses back on and blinked at him. He liked her glasses. They were a stylish rectangular shape that he admired. "Gavin, your stories are always good," she said, "but if there was ever a time to make them better, this is it. There's going to be some scrutiny over the coming weeks."

"Whoever writes the best stories gets to stay employed? Are you serious, Julie?"

"Just write the best stories you can, Gavin, and try not to think about it too much. I'm giving you a heads-up because I don't want to lose you."

He settled back at his desk with his notes from Florida and tried to concentrate. He'd reached this morning's interview. Ella Thompson in her house by the canal, her neighbor. *We thought we were coming closer to nature, but all along nature was creeping closer to us.* He'd decided this was the quote that would close the story, but then he glanced again at the page and his breath caught in his throat. He'd written the neighbor's name as Chloe Montgomery.

Gavin swore softly. Whatever the neighbor's name had been, he was certain it wasn't Chloe. He was almost certain it had started with an L. Lara, Lana, Laurie, Louise? He tried to transport himself back to the scene: the kitchen island with the stools and the cup of coffee before him, Ella telling him about her children, the doorbell ringing and the neighbor walking into the room. "Gavin, this is L——!" Ella Thompson says brightly, but the name is a blank.

Gavin flipped through the pages of the notebook. He had been so distracted that morning, all his thoughts taken up by Anna and Chloe, that he'd seemingly neglected to write down the neighbor's telephone number. He called Ella Thompson, but her phone only rang endlessly, and he remembered her telling him that she was about to leave on vacation. He found contact information for the management office and spent some time arguing with a secretary and then her boss, but they refused to reveal names of residents.

He knew that if he went to Julie, she would tell him to cut the quote. The story worked without it but the quote was the grace note, the quote was sublime. It was evening now, lights gleaming softly on the empty desks. He wished Silas were here.

Gavin submitted the story, went home to eat takeout food and stare at his television. He didn't sleep well. In the morning he sat at his desk again, reading the paper, and the last few lines of the piece filled him with dread.

> *But for residents of the houses closest to the canals, the matter has become more pressing. "We thought we were coming closer to nature," said Lemuria Gardens resident Chloe Silas, "but all along nature was creeping closer to us."*

.   .   .

"EILO," GAVIN said, "do you think I should be looking for the girl?" It had been only two weeks since he'd returned from Florida, but it seemed much longer. It was a particularly dark March in New York that year. The rain was unceasing. He hadn't been sleeping well. He had dreams where Anna was in some unspecified trouble and it was entirely his fault but he couldn't find her, and other dreams where he was losing his job. He had taken to staying in the newsroom for twelve hours at a time to escape the emptiness of the apartment and his own racing thoughts, but he couldn't concentrate on his work. Silas's desk remained empty. He hadn't realized how much he'd depended on Silas, his jokes and his freakish grasp of grammar, his company in the cafeteria at lunchtime. They went out drinking twice, but without the shared newsroom there wasn't much to talk about.

"I don't know, Gavin. I'm not sure what I'd do in your place," Eilo said.

"And you've never heard anything about what became of Anna?"

"Nothing," Eilo said. "No rumors, no sightings. I heard her sister Sasha had a gambling problem, but that was years ago already."

The clamor of the newsroom was all around him. Usually this was his favorite place in the world but today the sound jangled his nerves.

HE FELT that he was slipping, but it wasn't just him. The city of New York had gone dark so quickly, and at times Gavin was dazzled by the speed of the fall. Because it hadn't actually been that long since he'd been walking hand in hand with Karen down Columbus Avenue and they'd come upon a newsstand with a *New York Magazine* cover that read "The Second Gilded Age" in gold letters, and the head-line had seemed perfect to him. This is the second gilded age, he'd tell himself, looking around at his fellow diners at expensive restaurants or studying photographs of $1.3 million one-bedroom apartments in the windows of real estate offices. The phrase fit the era. But within months the stock market had plummeted and banks were collapsing, everyone was losing their jobs and there were food shortages in the soup kitchens, and the second gilded age seemed distant.

JULIE PUT him on the team covering the Jonathan Alkaitis story. The investment adviser had cheated unsuspecting investors of billions in an elaborate Ponzi scheme until his daughter had turned him in to the authorities. In that time of collapse and dissipation the stories all but wrote themselves—there were charities that had lost everything overnight, former senior executives who'd taken up employment at Starbucks, entire families living in motel rooms—but the Alkaitis story wasn't coming together. Everyone already knew the bare facts, the staggering sums lost and the collapse of charitable foundations, the ruined retirements, the litigations and blame. Gavin needed a quote, a good one, but none of Alkaitis's victims had anything to say that was worth printing or that hadn't already appeared in another paper. Proud old men in business suits averted their eyes and brushed past him on the sidewalk, which made Gavin feel despised and invisible. A twenty-one-year-old recently deprived of his trust fund gave a quote that made Gavin close his notebook and walk out of the room—"I can't *believe* I have to work for a living now. I mean, who the fuck *works*? It is *so unfair*"—and one or two people all but snarled as they turned away from him. Gavin talked his way into a series of offices and was escorted out of all of them. A woman laughed bitterly and said "Fuck you *think* my reaction to losing my retirement savings is? Go fuck yourself" before she hung up on him. One man who had lost everything, a retired businessman in his eighties, broke down and began to sob when Gavin called him. "It's okay," Gavin kept saying, "listen, it's going to be okay. . . ." but the man kept crying. Gavin listened until he couldn't take it anymore and gently placed the receiver of his desk phone back on the cradle. He thought all evening about the man weeping into the dial tone and couldn't sleep that night.

On the morning of a particular deposition he stood for two hours under low gray skies outside the law office where several of Alkaitis's victims were being interviewed, lying in wait, but he kept seeing the same people who'd refused comment on all his other attempts. Until a man came through the doors whom he recognized from his research— Arnold Lander, former COO of a midtown consulting firm, an investor who'd lost a little under two million dollars—but who was the woman by his side? She looked about twenty, extravagantly blond with red lipstick, and he realized he'd seen her earlier. She'd been waiting on the sidewalk for a while too, before she'd gone inside to wait in the lobby. She hadn't been in the deposition hearing, then. It was beginning to rain, the first fat drops before the cloudburst, and she was holding a newspaper over her head. Her heels clicked sharply on the sidewalk.

"Excuse me, Mr. Lander," Gavin said, "may I have a moment?"

"No comment," Lander said, without looking at him. He was hailing a cab. He was a tall man, imposing in a dark coat.

"Mr. Lander, please, if I could just—"

"You want a comment?" The woman's voice was high-pitched. She sounded like a child. "It's a nightmare that we can't wake up from."

"Don't talk to him," Lander snapped. "What did I tell you about reporters?"

"Wait," Gavin said, "what's your name?" But the rain had turned to a cold downpour and they were gone, half-running toward a cab that had stopped on the corner. "Excuse me!" he shouted, "please, wait—" The door closed and the car pulled away into a river of taillights.

He looked up photographs of Arnold Lander later at his desk. Lander's image was everywhere—charity balls, a corporate website, various industry events—but who was the woman? She'd appeared to be a solid thirty years younger than Lander. She certainly wasn't the wife in the most recent charity ball photo, but that had been a year ago already. A daughter, secretary, mistress, fourth wife? He'd helped her into the cab, Gavin remembered, but perhaps an older man might do that for a secretary? Men of a particular era and class were taught to treat certain women like porcelain. Gavin knew it was the era he himself belonged to—fedoras! Mechanical cameras! Good table manners!—but this thought was a digression. What mattered was that the author of the perfect quote had walked away from him and he had no idea who she was.

"I need the Alkaitis story," Julie said. "You just about done?"

But for Alkaitis's victims, the disaster continues to unfold. Amy Torren and her husband lost their life savings. "I feel like I'm caught up in a bad dream," she said of Alkaitis's deception. "It's just a nightmare that we can't wake up from. I feel like there's maybe less good in the world than I thought there was. It's hard to take in, to be honest with you. I don't know how I'm going to afford my mother's medical expenses now."

"Hell of a quote," Julie said, when he saw her in the staff kitchen the next morning. He was helping himself to his third cup of coffee. He hadn't slept.

"Thank you," Gavin said. He returned to his desk with a strange feeling of floating. No one could prove that no investor had said those words to him but he still felt sick every time he thought about it. Amy Torren was the name of his eleventh grade English teacher.

As days passed without incident it seemed that both this and the

Floridian woman whose name wasn't Chloe had passed under the radar. But the point, Gavin realized, wasn't whether the woman who'd climbed into the cab with Lander was an investor, or even whether he'd gotten away with referring to her as such when he wrote dialogue for her and gave her a name. The point was that Gavin had opened a door, cracked it just slightly, and he could see through to the disgrace and shadows on the other side. If you tell a lie it's easier to tell another. An abyss yawns suddenly at your feet. At night he went home and stared into the flickering blue of the television and felt almost nothing.

THE SECOND round of layoffs came without fanfare. The first time, Julie told him, when he'd been in Florida, there'd been an anguished speech in the middle of the newsroom by the executive editor, who'd stood on a chair to be better seen but hadn't been able to make eye contact with anyone. Two weeks later the second round was well under way before anyone realized what was happening. The executive editor's assistant called the victims one at a time and asked them to drop by the office, and eleven people didn't come to work the next day. The executive editor sent out a regretful memorandum that began with the words "As you may have noticed . . ." and included the phrases "online content" and "a changing media landscape." The word "rightsizing" was used. There was a regrettable possibility, the memo concluded, of future cuts.

Gavin read it twice, put on his fedora and went for a walk. He'd always thought of the newspaper as a ship sailing over a digital sea. Now that it was obvious the ship was sinking he didn't know what to do with himself, he couldn't imagine not being a newspaperman and in Karen's absence the newspaper was all he really had. Everyone he'd liked had been laid off now except Julie. He sometimes caught himself composing letters in his head. Dear Chloe, dear Anna, I wish I knew where you were. I have failed in my responsibilities. The thought of you keeps me up at night. It was raining in his apartment and he kept forgetting to shave in the mornings. The newsroom an ocean of empty desks. He sat in front of his computer, marooned.

"I've been meaning to ask you," Julie said. "I don't remember seeing an Amy Torren on the list of Alkaitis's victims."

"Oh, the investments were under her husband's name."

"Okay," she said, with an air of relief. "What's her husband's name?"

"Jacob Fischer," Gavin said. It was just the first name that came to him. Fischer was the man in his eighties who'd lost everything to Alkaitis and cried on the phone.

G AVIN'S NEXT story was about cuts to funding for playground maintenance in the Bronx. He traveled far north on the subway to reach a desolate neighborhood where wind moaned around the corners of low brick buildings. It was cold and he spent an hour standing by a playground on a street that scared him, trying to get suspicious mothers to talk to him about broken swing sets. That was when the mothers showed up at all—more often it was gangs of half-feral eight- and nine-year-olds who hit the swing set with sticks and threw rocks at the slide, stared blankly at Gavin when he tried to talk to them and snickered as they walked off. They knew about lone men in playgrounds.

He stood at the edge of the playground, alone after forty-five minutes of trying to get people to talk to him, and tears came suddenly to his eyes. The slide was rusted. There were broken bottles in the grass. Was this the sort of place where his lost daughter might play, in whatever transitory postforeclosure hellhole she might have landed in?

Gavin took the train back to the newsroom, where he wrote the story and then stared for a long time at the blinking cursor on the screen. A memory of Karen, lying beside him on the sofa on a Sunday afternoon. One of their last happy Sundays together, late in the third month of her four-month pregnancy. They'd told Eilo and Karen's parents but almost no one else. Sunlight angled through a window and caught in her hair. Had that only been two months ago? *If it's a girl, we'll name her Rose,* she said. *If it's a boy, Thomas.*

> *As local parent Rose Thomas put it, "It's really the children who are suffering. The cuts in playground funding have been a nightmare for us."*

Gavin read the quote over and over again. Seeing the words on the screen made them real, even though he hadn't sent them to anyone yet, even though this could still be undone. There had been two lapses now but turning back was still possible. There could still be an evening years or decades from now when he might look back at a strange period far earlier in his career, a few shadowy months before the Pulitzer but after his fiancée had left him when he'd started to slide but pulled himself back just in time, two stories with small lies in them and then no more after that.

But everyone knew there would be more layoffs at the newspaper and the story as written was a dud, filler, a flightless bird, all facts and budget numbers and no humanity. The Rose Thomas quote was exactly the sort of thing a concerned parent would say. When you came down to it, he thought, it was a question of names again, the same as that shadow across his Florida story had been. It was something *he'd* said, and he was almost certainly a father. Did it matter, did it actually matter that the words on the screen had been said by a parent named Gavin Sasaki, not a parent named Rose Thomas? He hadn't slept well since Florida. He was so tired tonight.

"Go home," Julie had said, two hours earlier. She usually stayed much later but tonight she said she had a headache. She'd walked past his desk with her coat over her arm, going home to cook dinner in a microwave and listen to classical music with her eyes closed. "We're probably about to get laid off anyway." This had put him into a tail-spin. But now a curious calm had come over him, and *nightmare* seemed excessive. He closed his eyes for a moment and then retyped it: *The cuts in playground funding have been awful.* It was eleven p.m. and he was almost alone here, the few night production people quiet at their desks, a janitor emptying trash cans.

Rose Thomas walks the two blocks from her public housing unit to the neighborhood playground every morning. She moves slowly, her four-year-old daughter, Amy, at her side. Ms. Thomas would like to take her daughter to play somewhere else, but there's nowhere else to go.

"I'll never understand why they thought they could cut funding," Ms. Thomas said on a recent morning, pushing her daughter on a swing. *"Is having a safe place for my child to play really too much to ask?"*

Gavin had taken a few photographs of the playground. Not for the story—the paper would send a freelance photographer with a camera made in the current century—but for himself. He had the film developed later that week and he spent some time at his desk looking at the images, the rusted swing sets, paint flaking from the monkey bars. If his daughter was in the care of a stranger in Florida, then what had become of her mother? He was thinking of the last time he'd seen Anna. He'd been playing a concert behind the school with his high school jazz quartet, he remembered. She'd thrown a paper airplane at him through the dark.

Five

The last time Gavin had spoken with Anna, a little over ten years before Karen left him and his shower in New York started dripping, they were sitting together on the back porch of her house in Sebastian and his shirt was soaked to his back with sweat. Gavin was eighteen, in his last month of high school. At the end of summer he was going to New York City to study journalism. Anna still had a year of high school left and the weight of the conversation they hadn't had yet—the *what happens to us now that we'll be in different states?* talk—was opening up longer and longer silences between them.

"Have you ever wanted to live somewhere colder?" Gavin asked, as a means of avoiding the conversation for at least a few more minutes or perhaps, he realized as he spoke, as a way of approaching it indirectly.

"Where would I go? I've never left Florida."

"I don't know," he said, "but I've been fantasizing about cold weather since I was five."

"I love Florida." Anna's voice was languid. "Permanent summer." She was watching the fireflies rise up from the grass.

"Don't you ever want seasons?"

"You're just too pale and heat-sensitive. Summers are easy for every-one else."

"I've heard that," Gavin said.

"Well," she said, "you'll be leaving soon."

Gavin took her hand. He heard voices at that moment somewhere in the house behind them, a shrill escalation and response. Anna's parents were fighting again.

"When I saw you the other day," he said, "you said there was some-thing you needed to tell me."

He'd run into her in a school corridor. She'd seemed nervous and tense. But now she only shook her head, distracted. The tenor of the fight was growing louder and sharper. Anna and Gavin were silent for a moment, listening. Gavin watched the frantic fluttering of moths against the porch light.

"Listen," Anna said, "maybe you should go."

The screen door slammed and Anna's half-sister Sasha was outside. They shared the same volatile mother but had different fathers, and Gavin had always been under the impression that Sasha's father was better than Anna's. Sasha was usually at her father and stepmother's house across town. Tonight she nodded at Gavin and stepped away from them into the shadows of the yard. Her hands shook around the flame of her lighter. Sasha was a friend—they were in the jazz quartet together, Gavin on trumpet and Sasha on drums—but tonight she seemed foreign in the shadows by the porch, a tense stranger with bitten-down fingernails. She exhaled a cloud of cigarette smoke.

"You should probably leave," Sasha said. "Don't go through the house."

"Will you be all right here?"

"We're always fine," Anna said. Gavin leaned in quickly to kiss her.

He walked around the side of the house, the fight still faintly audible through the exterior walls, down the driveway to the street. It was only ten blocks from Anna's house to his, but ten blocks was long for him in the heat. He stopped halfway to look up at the sky. He'd been reading about constellations recently, and had fallen particularly in love with the North Star. It always took him some time to find it in the haze of streetlight but there it was. True north, the direction of his second life, New York. He felt in those days that he was always on the edge of something, always waiting, his life about to begin. He was always impatient and always wanted to be somewhere else and as he walked away from Anna's house that night his desire to escape south Florida was almost a physical ache.

Later he heard sirens passing. Anna was absent from school the next day, and the day after that. They traded a few voice mails, but he could never seem to reach her. Her cell phone was always turned off when he called. He asked if he could come over but she said she wasn't feeling well. He saw her twice at school but only in passing, at a distance—getting into Sasha's car at the far end of the school parking lot, slipping quickly through the door to the girls' restroom at the other end of a long corridor. He loitered near the door for fifteen minutes but she didn't come out.

THE LAST official week of classes at the Sebastian High School for the Performing Arts passed, the drama production and end-of-year concerts and the art show. There were only exams now, running all week, the hallways deserted for long periods in the middle of the day. Gavin ran into Sasha on the day of his English and biology finals. She was smoking a cigarette on a bench by the parking lot.

"Hey," she said. She smiled fleetingly, but her voice was too flat.

There had been rumors about her in the past week. He'd heard she'd lost money in a poker game in some kid's basement, but the number shimmered and expanded with each retelling: she'd lost fifty dollars, no, a hundred. Five hundred, seven, maybe a grand.

"You waiting for someone?"

"I just had my math final," she said. "I've got a half-hour to kill before swim team."

"You okay?"

"Fine. I mean, you know, whatever."

He nodded, but was troubled by this. She was going to Florida State to study English literature and he'd never known her to be so inarticulate.

"I heard about the poker game," he said. He meant this to be sympathetic, but she winced and he immediately regretted mentioning it.

"Really? Where'd you hear about that?" She spoke without looking at him, smoking and gazing out across the faculty parking lot.

"I don't know," he said. "Around."

"That's one thing I won't miss about high school," she said. She exhaled a series of smoke rings. "The fucking small-mindedness of it all."

"Sorry, I didn't mean to stir up—"

"It's like, look, if I lose twenty-seven dollars at poker in some girl's basement, is that really actually the end of the world? Is that *really* worth spreading rumors about? I have a job. It's twenty-seven dollars. We usually play for pennies. Seriously, no one has anything better to talk about than *that*?"

"It's no big deal."

"Right, that's what I think." She drew savagely on her cigarette. "It's no big deal. There's another game next week and I'm going to win it back."

"Right," he said.

"I will miss swim team, though," she said. "That's the one thing about high school I didn't hate, that and the music."

"Have you seen Anna around?" A week had passed since he'd left Anna and Sasha in the haze of their backyard.

"I've seen her around school a couple times, but I haven't talked to her. I've been staying at my dad's place."

"I think she's avoiding me."

"The kid's a screwup," Sasha said. "I'm sorry, you know I love her, but."

Gavin didn't know this, but he said "Sure," and made a conciliatory gesture. Everything in his life seemed awkward and graceless except the school he was entering at the end of summer. In his mind Columbia University was taking on the dimensions of the Emerald City from *The Wizard of Oz*, a hard spired brightness on the horizon. He was going to be a different person there, someone confident and urbane who never got laughed at for wearing a fedora.

"Sasha, is she okay? At home, I mean?"

"Why wouldn't she be?"

"Those bruises she gets. She'll say nothing's wrong, but come on."

"She's anemic," Sasha said. "She forgets to take her iron pills. She bruises if you look at her funny."

"I'm serious," he said.

"Look," Sasha said, "she got the short end of the stick where parents are concerned, no question." Sasha flicked her cigarette butt onto the sidewalk. She drummed her fingers on the cigarette box for a moment and then lit another one. "But seriously, she can look after herself," she said. "She always has. Another year and she's out of the house."

Gavin didn't know what to say to this, so he looked down at the sidewalk and said nothing. The day was too hot and he felt the familiar weight in his limbs, the leaden exhaustion that would turn to dizziness and then heatstroke if he didn't get indoors quickly.

"I have to go," he said. "See you next week at the concert?"

"It'll be the best concert ever," Sasha said.

GAVIN DIDN'T see Anna again until the night of the concert, when he looked up from playing "Bei Mir Bist Du Schön" on his trumpet in time to watch the paper airplane sail toward him through the dusk.

They had attended a school devoted largely to music. None of the quartet aspired to be professional musicians except Jack, but the local public schools were atrocious and the High School for the Performing Arts was the magnet school closest to their houses. If you were in Jazz Orchestra it was possible to earn extra credits by forming your own ensemble under the supervision of the faculty, so four of them had established an outfit they'd called the Lola Quartet after a German film they'd all liked with *Lola* in the title. They'd been playing together for three years and had gradually become good enough to win awards at regional and state high school music competitions, but now it was almost over. Now they were graduating and going to college in different states and it was wrenching, actually, the thought of the quartet being finished. Gavin had been trying not to think about it.

For their farewell performance they'd set up behind the gym in the back of a pickup truck with two battery-powered lights rigged up on the cab, shining over their instruments and casting long shadows on the grass. Daniel on bass and Gavin on trumpet, Sasha on drums and Jack on his saxophone that evening. Jack was going to music school for jazz piano, but he was freakishly talented and could switch instruments as the song required. The two dozen or so kids slow dancing in the sun-scorched grass were mostly drunk members of the Swing

Dance Club and their friends and dates, except that they'd been at this for a couple of hours by now and the music wasn't really swing or even particularly danceable anymore. Everyone was a little strung out from the heat, lapsing into slow motion.

The Lola Quartet was playing "Bei Mir Bist Du Schön" for the second time and a pretty girl named Taylor from Choir was singing in her best dusky lounge voice. They were all in love with the music and also a little in love with Taylor, or at least Gavin was and he imagined that everyone around him was caught up in the same dream. And then he caught a flash of white out of the corner of his eye and that was the paper airplane, arcing down through the air to land at his feet. He knew only one person with aim that perfect. He looked up and saw her, Anna standing just beyond the dancers at the edge of the light, and he half-smiled around the mouthpiece at her but she didn't smile back. There was something urgent in the way she looked at him. They hadn't spoken in two weeks.

Jack was taking a solo. Gavin picked up the airplane, unfolded the wings and read the two words written across the creased page: *I'm sorry.* And the night kept moving, the dancers swaying and the music unceasing, but it seemed to Gavin that something had shifted, an electrical charge passing through the air. When he looked up Anna had disappeared. He jumped down off the back of the truck and made his way through the dancers, his trumpet a long dim gleam in his hand, and Sasha called after him but he didn't look back.

This far out into the suburbs the scrub forest was everywhere, peninsulas of low bushy trees creeping in between subdivisions. He called Anna's name. He thought he saw her once, a flash of white that could have been her dress, but it was only moonlight. He couldn't hear the music anymore. Gavin kept walking until the brush opened into a bulldozed swath of dark earth, a future development of some sort. A 7-Eleven glowed bright on the far side. Beyond the convenience store the outer suburbs continued, glimmering toward the distant black of the swamps. He turned away from the lights and walked back into the trees, back to the high school where the music was over now, the dancers dispersing and Sasha packing up her drum kit, Taylor singing drunkenly in her boyfriend's arms.

"Where'd you go?" Sasha asked.

"I thought I saw Anna."

"She was just here a few minutes ago. After you ran into the trees."

"Where is she now?"

"I don't know, I didn't see where she went," Sasha said. "I was packing up the drum kit."

"Well, if you see her, will you tell her to call me?"

But Anna didn't call, and school was over. Gavin had taken his last exam. He called Anna six times and left messages but she didn't call back, and no one answered when he knocked on her door. He called Sasha, but Sasha was staying at her father's house and hadn't seen her sister since the day of the concert. She was distracted and tired, working two jobs to save up before college. In two of his six messages Gavin had asked Anna to come to the senior prom with him, so he went by himself in the hope that she might be there. He sat for a long time in the gymnasium under streamers hung from the ceiling, watching girls in bright dresses and boys stiff in rented tuxedos dance to music he didn't like. Anna was nowhere. Late in the evening Taylor slid into the chair beside him, hopelessly drunk with fake diamonds in her hair. Her dress was a cloud of pink.

"Hey," she said, "I heard Anna's pregnant."

"What?"

"Is it just a rumor?" Her smile was lopsided. She was sliding off her chair.

"It's just a rumor," Gavin said. "Where did you hear . . . ?" But a knot of her friends had swirled around her, helping her up. She stood, giggling and unsteady, and they swept her away. He saw Jack in a corner, drinking too much from a sloppily concealed flask with a redheaded cellist from the eleventh grade, but Sasha and Daniel were both absent. He remembered that Sasha was working tonight. Out in the parking lot Gavin tried to call a taxi, but half the schools in Sebastian had prom that night and the dispatcher's phone rang unanswered. He looked back at the school, at the light and the music spilling out from the gymnasium and all the girls in long dresses who weren't Anna, and he wanted very much to get away from there so he set off on foot, five miles of heat that brought him to his knees just inside the front door of his house and sent him to the hospital for a night.

"You can't do this kind of thing," Gavin's doctor told him. Gavin had had the same doctor all his life. There was a degree of mutual exasperation. "I've been treating you for heat exhaustion since you were a kid."

"Surely you don't expect him to miss his own prom," Eilo said. She'd driven down from college to be with him and had so far been his only visitor.

"I expect him not to walk five miles in hot weather," the doctor said. "You'd think he'd have figured this out by now. Have your parents arrived yet?"

"They're stuck in traffic," Eilo said, because this was easier than explaining that their father was on a business trip and their mother was most likely at home drinking. She flashed the doctor her most winning smile and left the room to deal with the discharge paperwork.

Florida was caught in a tropical heat wave. The air conditioner in Gavin's bedroom rattled and hummed, and when he stood by the window he felt heat radiating through the glass. Three days passed before he was well enough to go outside again, and Anna still hadn't called. Two months slipped by without her. He was leaving for New York in a matter of weeks. The quartet was a memory. Jack was still around but Daniel had left town already without saying goodbye, which was puzzling. Gavin supposed they weren't best friends, exactly, but they'd spent an enormous amount of time together and he'd thought they were fairly close. He'd known Daniel since the first grade and didn't understand why he'd disappear without saying anything. Daniel had told Jack he was going to Utah. Jack thought he'd maybe gone there to work for his uncle's construction company like he'd done the past two summers. Sasha was working days in a clothing store and nights in an ice-cream parlor.

It was increasingly clear that Anna had left him, that *I'm sorry* meant *I'm sorry but it's over* or *I'm sorry but I can't do this anymore*. As the weeks passed the fact of her absence began to seem like something he could live with. He didn't hear from her again, and in the fall he went to school in New York City.

The journalism track at Columbia. His ideas about his future were vague. But he'd been obsessed with film noir and detective novels from the ninth grade onward and had decided long ago that he was going to be either a newspaperman or a private detective.

TEN YEARS later in the newsroom of the *New York Star* Gavin handed in a piece about cuts to playground funding in the Bronx, went out into the cold air and took a northbound subway to his apartment. The sound from the leaking shower was like rain. He lay on the sofa to listen to it, just for a moment, and woke stiff and disoriented at six a.m. He showered and found a clean shirt, took the subway back to the newsroom. It was a blue-tinged morning, a cold wind in the streets. In the light of day it was obvious that he'd made an unforgivable mistake. He called Eilo from his desk.

"It's just such a strange situation," he said, meaning everything. "I never imagined this could happen."

"I'm sorry," Eilo said. "I thought about not showing you the photograph. Are you okay? You sound a bit . . ."

"I keep thinking, if the kid was staying with that woman whose house was getting foreclosed, what happened to Anna? And I keep thinking that I should have known," he said. "Her sister always said she was fine, but the way she vanished like that. The rumors at the prom."

"Well, if we're to be honest with ourselves, I guess we both always knew it was a possibility," Eilo said. "I keep thinking of that time we ran into Sasha buying baby clothes at the mall, how off she seemed that day."

"What?"

"You don't remember this?"

"No," he said. "What happened?"

"I can't believe you don't remember. We ran into Sasha in the mall, and she had a bag from Babies 'R' Us. You said, 'Who had a baby, Sasha?' and she seemed so jumpy, she just stammered something and walked away without really answering you. It was weird."

"Why were we in the mall together?"

"We were buying a gift for Mom for her birthday."

"I don't remember this." A passing reporter glanced at him, and Gavin realized he was speaking too loudly. He made an apologetic gesture and sank down further into his chair. "I don't remember," he said, quieter now. "What was it we got for Mom?"

"One of those horrible little glass figurines she likes," Eilo said. "I think it was a dog."

"I really don't remember," Gavin said. Eilo's memory was impeccable. He had no reason to doubt her. He wondered, as he hung up the phone, if he'd always known that Anna was pregnant and had managed to block this fact from his mind in order to leave without guilt for New York. This idea was somewhat more than he could live with, and he felt himself slipping deeper into fog.

Six

Some things Gavin remembered:

Her enormous headphones. Anna in the evenings cross-legged on the floor of his bedroom with her homework all around her. She liked constant music but Gavin could study only when the room was quiet so she'd put on her headphones and retreat into sound. She liked electronica, mostly '80s stuff that didn't move him, New Order singing about a thousand islands in the sea. The headphones were a shiny robin's-egg blue, surprisingly heavy when he tried them but the sound was perfect. Sasha had bought them for her, a Christmas present.

A small scar just above her right ankle from a bicycle accident when she was six.

Dark hair falling over her face, blue eyes, a habit of drawing little circles instead of dots over her *i*'s when she did her homework.

Her extravagant charisma. Was charisma the word? He tried to analyze it sometimes. He knew there were obvious reasons why everyone liked her, why half the school was half in love—she was pretty, she was kind, she laughed at everyone's jokes and she knew how to listen—but also she was capable of drawing blood. The tension between her loveliness and her violence was captivating. Once a girl spit her gum at Anna's feet and Anna delivered a swift punch to the girl's jaw, tripped her, tore her clothes. Anna came back in after recess laughing with a bleeding lip. Gavin saw her pass by and trailed behind her, watching the way the crowds parted before her all the way to the girls' room. She was suspended twice in the tenth grade for fighting.

A tattoo of a bass clef on her left shoulder—

The tattoo story: before she transferred to Gavin's high school Anna had run away three times in search of peace and quiet or maybe in search of adventure and change, the story shifted a bit with each telling. She'd fallen in with a dangerous crowd at her old school and a police officer had brought her home at two a.m. She'd been gone for three days but her parents hadn't reported her missing. She was high out of her mind, laughing in the foyer while her parents talked to the cop, a black new tattoo bleeding softly on her shoulder, and the story Sasha told Gavin was that the cop had seen the squalor of the house and called Family Services, and it was the social worker's idea to get Anna transferred to the magnet school. Something about getting her away from her sinking friends, a new environment, the positive influence of her less-screwed-up older half-sister, but Anna never talked about any of that, Anna only smiled and touched the tattoo on her shoulder and said "Even when I'm stoned I have good taste in tattoos."

She showed him the graffiti she'd done in the park before she'd transferred to the magnet school. Pinkish tags faded by rain and sunlight on the wall behind the bleachers. She went quiet looking at them. An earlier version of herself had spray-painted *NO* over and over again in big bubbly letters. She said it wasn't what it looked like. *NO* stood for New Order.

Her favorite joke—

—Knock knock.

—Who's there?

—Interrupting pirate.

—Interrupting pirate wh—

—ARRRRRRR!

The way she went still in the presence of music. You could talk to her while music was playing but she'd only be half-listening to you because she was also half-listening to the music. She didn't play an instrument—she said she didn't want to play at all if she couldn't play perfectly—but she wanted to work with music someday, work beside it somehow. She said maybe she'd be a DJ or a music producer or something.

She listened to the Lola Quartet and liked them but it was the wrong kind of music, not electronica, her heart wasn't really in it. Gavin didn't mind. She leaned back on the sofa in the basement where they used to practice, half-lost in the shadows at the edge of the room, staring up at the ceiling, crossing and uncrossing her legs, and when he raised his trumpet to his lips he often thought *I am playing for you* but he never told her this.

Seven

Gavin's last story was about a fire in Brooklyn. It was a horrible assignment, the worst he'd ever had to do. A nine-year-old girl had died and every time he thought of her he thought of Chloe. He went to the scene and stood across the street from the burned-out apartment. Three windows on the fourth floor were blackened holes in the brick, smoke stains rising toward the sky. Shattered glass glittered on the sidewalk below. He longed at that moment to be anywhere else.

"It's a nightmare we can't wake up from," neighbor Sarah Connelly said. "I keep thinking of her playing hopscotch on the street the way she used to in the summertime, and I just can't believe she's gone."

The day after the story came out Gavin was summoned into a conference room. Julie was there, along with the editor-in-chief and, unnervingly, the directors of the personnel and legal departments. All four stared at him as he sat down. Gavin sat on one side of the conference room table, and the four of them sat on the other. He wasn't sure where to look. For a long moment no one spoke, until Julie cleared her throat.

"Gavin, I spoke with Jacob Fischer this morning," Julie said.

Gavin opened his mouth, but didn't speak.

"The Alkaitis investor who lost his retirement," Julie said, apparently interpreting his silence as confusion. "Turns out he doesn't have a wife."

"You can't be serious," Gavin said. It was difficult to summon the appropriate tones of incredulity and lightness, but he managed. "The woman I quoted, Amy Torren, she said she was Fischer's—"

"Aren't you curious to know why I was speaking with him?"

"I—"

"I called him because the dead girl's mother called the paper last night," Julie said. She was looking at him as if she'd never seen him before. He noticed that she was very pale. "The mother of that girl who died in the fire in Brooklyn. Apparently the dead kid didn't play hopscotch."

"Well, look," Gavin said, "the neighbor said she used to play hopscotch all the time. Maybe she played hopscotch while the mother wasn't home."

"She was in a wheelchair," Julie said.

It was clear from the way she was looking at Gavin that everything was over, absolutely everything, so Gavin stood up from the table and left the room without saying anything else. He went back to his desk, picked up his bag and fedora and walked out of the newsroom without speaking to anyone. Outside the air was very bright, and he pulled his fedora low over his eyes. It was only one in the afternoon. He couldn't face his empty apartment yet, the leaking shower and the piles of paper on the floor, so he turned south and walked all the way down to Battery

Park City, stood looking out at the Statue of Liberty for a while before he turned inland and wandered into the Financial District. He lingered in various bars and small parks all day. In the evening he made his way home through the darkening city, let himself into his apartment and sat for a while on his sofa staring at the opposite wall. The dripping from the shower made a constant, almost musical sound. He was drunk, drifting in and out of sleep. It seemed improbable that he was no longer a newspaperman. It seemed like something that might have happened to somebody else.

Eight

On the day Gavin lost his job in New York, Daniel was sitting alone in a meth dealer's living room in the outer suburbs of Salt Lake City. He hadn't played a musical instrument of any kind in ten years.

Daniel had lived in this house for a time just after high school, a few miserable long months after he'd driven up from Florida when he'd worked every day for his uncle's construction firm and fretted constantly about providing for a baby who had turned out not to be his and gone for long jogs in the deepening evenings with the neighbors casting suspicious glances at him. The jogs were meant to clear his head but they'd only made him uneasy. Moving through the streets toward or away from this house that he didn't particularly want to return to, wondering what he was going to do about the baby and the girl, feeling in those moments like the only black man in the entire washed-out state.

But the house had been subjected to a gut renovation, and the interior was unrecognizable to him now. The room where he sat was a white rectangle where two stiff gray sofas faced one another under track lighting, a wall of windows looking out over an aggressively landscaped backyard. From the tint of the sunlight he could tell that the glass was one-way, that if anyone were outside on the empty white gravel pathways they'd see only a mirror if they tried to look in. The falling-down wooden fence he remembered from all those years ago had been replaced by a high stone wall. He had the disoriented thought that he was perhaps in the wrong house altogether.

He'd come here to negotiate, but the negotiations hadn't even begun and already he was tired and shaken. Two hours earlier in the Salt Lake City airport the call had come through that his grandmother had died in Florida, and the sense of being in the wrong place was overwhelming. He wanted nothing more than to return to the airport and fly home. He'd been shown in by an enormous unsmiling man who'd told him to take a seat, that Paul would be right with him, but Paul hadn't appeared and it had occurred to Daniel that he might be killed here. He wasn't stupid enough to carry his service weapon—the enormous unsmiling man had frisked him just inside the door—and he felt defenseless without it. Through the mirrored glass the sky held a greenish tint, sunlight weak on the carpet.

He had been waiting for an hour and twenty-two minutes now, and the silence of the house was absolute but he knew it wouldn't be possible to leave. Inside this house there were other people, he was certain of it, other people waiting as silently as he was or carrying out their business on the other side of soundproofed walls. He thought it likely that the man who'd frisked him was standing outside the door. It was possible that he was being observed. He looked around for a camera and didn't see one but that of course meant nothing. Daniel closed his eyes and thought of his children.

Nine

New York City was cold. It was early April, but in the world outside the apartment the rain was streaked with snow. When Gavin wasn't looking for jobs online or handing out résumés he was reading the papers—although not *his* paper—and everything was wrong: there were stories about people waiting hours to get into job fairs, increasing strains on the food-stamp program. There were suicides and lost fortunes, hungry children and people who had slipped down into new, previously unimagined dwellings: a van in the parking lot of a grocery store in Queens, a boat on the oil-bright surface of the Gowanus Canal, a relative's garage in Westchester County. He understood, reading these stories, how easy it was to sink.

Gavin had never been very good with money. He had several thousand dollars of credit-card debt that he'd been carrying around for a while, and it was growing at a rate that he wouldn't have thought possible. On the day he lost his job he'd already accidentally fallen a month behind on rent, a matter of forgetting to mail a check to the landlord—Karen had always taken care of this—and when his paychecks stopped coming he began paying credit cards off with other credit cards. His checking account balance was dwindling. He had no savings.

All of his friends had either been associated with the newspaper or he'd met them in journalism school. Gavin didn't try to contact them. He was aware that he was a disgrace to his profession. None of them called him, which was unsurprising but disappointing nonetheless. For the first time in his life he had too much time on his hands and he was afraid of it, the empty hours echoing all around him with nothing to think about but failure, so he went out of his way to establish a routine: he spent the day drinking coffee and searching for jobs online or sitting in the park and circling jobs he wanted to apply for in the classifieds, and then in the evening he boarded a southbound F train and traveled deep into Brooklyn to listen to music at Barbès, a narrow sliver of an establishment between a tanning salon and a sandwich shop.

Step inside and it was just another bar, all chatter and shadows and the faint smell of stale beer, but at the back of the room was a window, a red paper umbrella attached to a wall, a doorway covered by a velvet curtain. The window was almost soundproof. From the dark of the bar he would stand and look through into a brighter world, a small room with a lit-up sign that read Hotel d'Orsay and a few rows of people sitting on uncomfortable chairs. Under the Hotel d'Orsay sign musicians set up their instruments, plugged in their amplifiers, milled about drinking beer while the audience stared at them, tested the mikes at their leisure, eventually got around to settling down behind their instruments, and then played some of the finest music Gavin had ever heard.

At Barbès he was at his best, his calmest and least desperate. He'd been obsessed with jazz in high school and listening to it again was like coming home. He'd had a friend in high school with a touch of synesthesia who saw light when he heard music, and he liked to think of this when he listened. He could lose himself in the music for a while and he sometimes felt that he was a part of something that mattered, a witness to evenings that might be written about later on.

He was there for Deval & Morelli's last performance, for example. They were a guitar duo who played the nine o'clock set on Mondays. Their last performance was on a cool night in May toward the end of things, some time after Gavin had run out of cash and had started paying for everything with credit cards. He didn't know if Arthur Morelli and Liam Deval were famous in any widespread, conventional way— there were so many gradations of fame now, it was hard to tell anymore what kind of fame counted and who stood a chance of being remembered later—but he thought they were brilliant and on the nights when they played the room was packed. Gavin went every week and stood at the back so he could duck out easily before the tip bucket for the musicians was passed around. He felt bad about this, but he had no cash anymore.

Arthur Morelli was older, an unsmiling man in his late thirties or early forties who played with a heavy swing. In his solos he wheeled out into wild tangents, he pushed the music to the edge before he came back to rhythm. Liam Deval looked about Gavin's age, late twenties or early thirties, the star of the show: a perfect counterpoint to Morelli, all shimmering arpeggios and light sharp tones. Gavin had never seen anyone's hands move so quickly. His skill was astonishing. Jazz slipped into gypsy music and back again, a thrilling hybrid form. Gavin knew it wasn't new, what they were doing, but it was the first time he'd encountered it live. There was a bassist and occasionally a drummer, one solo each per set but otherwise strictly backup. Everyone was backup to Liam Deval, including Morelli. It was obvious that they were a duo in name only.

They played the nine o'clock set every Monday, until a particular night in June when it seemed to Gavin that there was tension between Deval and Morelli during the first set. They took a break, during which they murmured inaudibly but furiously in a back corner. They started the second set unevenly. Something was off—Morelli was glaring at his guitar and when he took a solo he went too far out and the beat was lost. Deval's glissandos were ungrounded. The guitars went subtly but maddeningly out of sync. The bass player closed his eyes and struggled to keep the rhythm. When the short set was over they packed up their instruments without looking at one another. Deval slung his guitar case over his back and walked out of the room without a word. Morelli looked up at him when he left, his expression unreadable. The bass player was glowering and wouldn't look at either of them. Morelli left a few minutes later, and after that the nine o'clock set on Mondays was a large beautiful woman with squared-off bangs and red lipstick who played exquisite melodies on a ukulele, a dreamlike wave of strings and horns and soft drumbeats rising up behind her.

J U L I E   S E N T him an email. She wanted to know if there was anything he wanted to tell her. There was, there was, but he sat paralyzed for some time before he managed it. "Some of this you already know," he wrote, but he listed them all anyway: the woman in the Florida story whose name wasn't Chloe, the imaginary concerned parent in the Bronx playground with the child who also didn't exist, the woman who probably wasn't an Alkaitis investor climbing into a taxi in the rain, the day he stood across the street from a burned-out apartment and couldn't bear to speak with any of the neighbors or get any closer to the scene: it seemed a banal downfall when he read it on the screen. He said he was sorry and hit send. He waited days for a response but there was nothing.

. . .

The drip from the showerhead in Gavin's apartment had turned into a steady trickle and now it leaked a stream of hot water day and night. Gavin wasn't paying rent anymore, which made the situation awkward, because once you've stopped paying rent you can't really call the landlord to complain about repairs, and spending his own money on a plumber was out of the question. In a way he didn't mind it. The sound lulled him to sleep. The leaking water was scaldingly hot, which made the room fill permanently with steam. The bathroom grew strange and almost subtropical. Cool drips fell from the ceiling, water slid down the walls, the paint bubbled.

Gavin imagined the damage being done to the paint job was irreparable, but this struck him as a reasonable trade-off for the landlord's failure to do anything about the broken light in the stairwell. He stood barefoot in the bathroom some mornings, rain falling from the ceiling, and wondered what Karen would do in this situation. The obvious answer, of course, was that Karen would never have allowed this to happen in the first place. He was pretty sure the dark spot in the northeast corner of the ceiling was turning into a mushroom. His reflection in the fogged-up mirror stared back at him with a fixed, somewhat shell-shocked expression. He wondered how much more he could lose.

Ten

S ome weeks earlier, in a suburb of Salt Lake City, Daniel had
been waiting for an audience in a meth dealer's living room.

He sat alone for two hours before the door finally opened.

"Daniel," Paul said. He'd changed very little since Daniel had seen
him last, although Daniel had forgotten about his tattoo, a large bright
goldfish on the side of his neck. It was obvious that if he was still dealing meth, he hadn't indulged in his product. His teeth when he smiled
were even and white, and he had none of the hollow-eyed blankness
Daniel saw in his drug arrests. His handshake was firm. "I'm surprised
to see you again. What's it been, ten years?"

"About that. How's business?"

Paul shrugged. "Honestly?" he said, and for just a moment Daniel saw a flash of the man Paul had been when they'd first met, when
they were working construction together during the summer before
Daniel's last year of high school. They'd been friends once. "It's all
cartels now," he said. "It's not like it was. I don't even work for myself
no more."

"They pay you a salary?"

"Something like that."

"I see you renovated the house," Daniel said.

"A few years back. I like it like this. Clean, that's the word the decorator kept using. Clean lines." Paul sat on the hard gray sofa across from him. Except for the carpet, which was deep enough to silence every step, nothing in this room was soft. "Now," he said, "why don't you tell me what you're doing here?"

"Paul," Daniel said, "my grandmother died this morning in Florida."

"My condolences."

"Thank you. I don't like to think of her death in these terms, but the fact of it is, she told me a while back that I'd be getting some money."

"And this is, what, a business proposition?"

"Paul, I'd like to pay back Anna Montgomery's debt. The hundred and twenty-one thousand." His gaze kept drifting to Paul's hands. He had watched Paul beat a man almost to death once and he wished he could forget what it had sounded like, Paul's fists against the man's limp body. He wished he could forget that he hadn't intervened.

"Awfully generous of you, Daniel, settling someone else's debt."

"Well, I feel a certain responsibility. I brought her here."

Paul smiled. "Your conscience troubling you?"

"It always has," Daniel said.

"You've got the money with you?"

"I don't. I wanted to come here quickly and work something out, but it's likely the estate won't be settled for a few weeks."

"What do you mean, you wanted to come here quickly? Quickly after what?"

"I think we both know," Daniel said.

Paul was impassive.

"The *photograph*," Daniel said, "the photograph of Chloe," but even as the words were leaving his mouth he understood that he had made a colossal mistake, because before Paul's face returned to impassiveness and he leaned forward to begin negotiating the repayment there was a brief light in his eyes, the faintest flicker of confusion, and Daniel saw that Paul had had no idea what Daniel was talking about.

"Has she been in Florida all this time?" Paul asked, when their negotiations were nearly at an end. He had insisted upon a substantial amount of interest. Daniel tried to console himself with the thought that he was doing the right thing after all these years, but he was sick with remorse. He had thought that the photograph of Chloe meant Paul had found them, but it seemed obvious now that Paul had no longer been looking. It wasn't that Paul had found the woman who'd stolen a hundred and twenty-one thousand dollars from him, then— it was that Daniel had brought her whereabouts to Paul's attention.

"No," Daniel said.

"I went to a lot of trouble to find her, back then. I even hired a private detective, but it was just a dead end once I got to Virginia."

Daniel wasn't sure what to say to this, so he said nothing.

"You're a police officer," Paul said, switching tracks.

"A detective," Daniel said.

"What kind of detective?"

Daniel was silent for a moment, but he was too afraid of Paul to lie. "Major Crimes division," he said. "I'm in the Vice and Intelligence unit."

"Vice and Intelligence? What's that translate to in English?"

It occurred to Daniel that no one in the world knew where he was today. If he disappeared in Utah he might never be found. "Gaming," he said. "Prostitution, prescription fraud, narcotics."

"Narcotics." Paul seemed amused by this. "Well, you keep up the good work," he said. "America's children depend on you, man. Daniel, there's one last thing. Did you know my mother was in the insurance business?"

"No," Daniel said, "I don't believe you've ever mentioned it."

"Well, she was. My mom and I, we didn't see eye to eye on most things, but one thing she always used to say was, a person's got to have insurance. And you know, I think she was right about that."

"I'm not sure what you're getting at," Daniel said.

"When I come down to Florida," he said, "for the payment, I want the girl there when I'm counting the money. Just in case the count's off."

Daniel held his gaze.

"Come on," Paul said, "don't look at me that way. If you're in narcotics, you know how it works these days. You pay with money, or you pay with your family."

Eleven

avin made a list of things he didn't need anymore. Number one: electricity. He bought candles in a dollar store and set them up in old beer bottles, which he half-filled with water to counterbalance the weight, and thus he was serenely prepared when the lights blinked out. Number two: the home phone, but this was redundant, because his phone was the kind with a digital call display that plugs into the wall and therefore hadn't worked since the electricity ended. Number three: gas. This one was obvious. He wasn't cooking anymore, and anyway he hadn't opened the fridge since the day the light switches had stopped working. At first he'd thought about emptying it out and cleaning it, taking the dead food out to the curb, but lately he'd been thinking about taping it shut.

There was a night when Gavin stood in the apartment with candlelight flickering all around him and thought, *Someday soon this will all be gone.* He was listening to classical music on an old battery-operated radio that he'd pulled out of the closet, part of the emergency preparedness kit he'd assembled with Karen a few years back. The Brandenburg Concertos sounded staticky and far away and he had a disoriented feeling that nothing in the room was real. His papers, his clothes, his books, this detritus he'd accumulated all around him, these shadows in these darkened rooms. He could live without most of it, but not all, so he began carrying an overnight bag when he left the apartment. A spare set of toiletries purchased on a credit card—why not?—and a change of clothing, the only clothes he owned that he absolutely couldn't stand to give up: a pair of particularly excellent pin-striped pants, a crisp white shirt that he loved, his best corduroy jacket. The bag also held his camera—the 1973 Yashica with a perfect lens—and a couple pairs each of underwear and socks, his passport, an umbrella, a broken gold pocket watch he'd found at a stoop sale, his laptop, power adapters for the computer and the cell phone. He felt overburdened and weighted when he went out in the mornings.

There were several unopened envelopes from his landlord on his kitchen table. He hadn't paid the rent in some time. He knew that someday soon he'd come home and his belongings would be scattered on the street or closed away behind a lock for which he didn't have the key, and he had salvaged the best of them. He never left the apartment without his favorite fedora.

Gavin had always taken pictures, but now it was different. He took as many pictures as he always had—of angles of light, of interesting graffiti, of street corners—but he no longer bothered to get the film developed. That had always been the expensive part.

S OMEWHERE ALONG the way, perhaps in high school, Gavin had fallen into the habit of mentally framing himself in an imaginary photograph and murmuring the caption aloud, mostly to avoid taking his life too seriously. *Noted journalist Gavin Sasaki stands in line at the super-market.* Or later, *Former reporter Gavin Sasaki ducks out of Barbès before the arrival of the tip bucket.* Or later still, *Disgraced newspaperman Gavin Sasaki debates whether to put one sugar or two into his Venti latte and simultaneously ponders the ruins of his life.* Gavin was spending all his time at a Starbucks near his apartment. His bank account was empty and he'd maxed out two credit cards, but there were one hundred and forty-one dollars left on a third. In the absence of any better ideas, he thought he might as well spend it all on sandwiches and coffee. In one last heroic effort he had fifty résumés printed at a Kinko's, and he walked the streets for two days distributing them at any place he thought he could possibly work, restaurants and coffee shops and bookstores, places that sold cell phones, clothing shops. When the résumés were gone he went back to sitting at Starbucks with his cell phone and his laptop plugged into the wall beside him, but none of the fifty businesses called him back. When the phone finally rang it was his sister.

"I tried to call you at home," Eilo said. "The message said your phone number's out of service."

"Yeah," he said, "it got cut off a few weeks ago."

"Gavin, what the hell's going on?"

"It's a long story, but my job's gone and I'm practically living at Starbucks."

"Jesus, Gavin. When I saw you four months ago you seemed fine."

"Four months ago I *was* fine," he said. This wasn't entirely true, when he thought about it, but at least four months ago he hadn't known that Chloe existed, and four months ago he hadn't been consumed by guilt. He was increasingly certain that he'd known Anna was pregnant.

"Did you read the paper this morning?"

"Which paper?"

"*Your* paper," she said.

"Why? Should I?"

"Well," she said, "maybe not, if you haven't seen it yet. I'm not going to ask why you did it—"

"Wait," he said, "there's a story about me?"

"—But Gavin, if you want to come home—"

"*Home?* Eilo, you know how I feel about Florida—"

"I'm saying if you need a job," Eilo said, "my business is expanding."

"Real estate? But I have no experience—"

"What I'm saying is that if you want to cut your losses, Gavin, if you want to leave New York for a while, if it's all come unglued and you don't really have a reason to be there at all anymore and it happens that your phone's been cut off, I can offer you a place to stay and a job."

"In Florida," he said.

"Gavin," she said, "why don't you go buy a copy of the paper and then call me back when you've had a chance to think about it."

He went out and bought the paper. He was on the front page. It was a brief story, three short columns below the fold, but there was his face, the photo from his employee ID card, and the headline was "Star Journalist Committed Fraud." For a moment he was flattered that they'd called him a star journalist, then he realized they just meant he'd been a journalist for the *Star*. He read the first few lines, about a promising young reporter who'd invented characters and written dialogue for them for his stories, and let his gaze slide over the paragraphs that followed—there they all were, Amy Torren and the others, a congregation of ghosts—and then he came upon a sentence that stopped him cold: "This episode is deeply regretted by everyone here at the *New York Star*, and marks a low in the 82-year history of the paper."

He was almost in tears when he called Eilo back. "They plagiarized the *New York Times*'s Jayson Blair apology," he said, before she could say anything.

"The what apology?"

Gavin was pacing back and forth by the newsstand. The sidewalk blurred and quivered before him. "That bit about marking a low in the history of the paper? Eilo, they lifted that from the *Times*."

"Gavin," she said, "what difference does it make?"

"Plagiarism matters," he said. "They teach you that on the first day of journalism school. Actually, you know what? Before journalism school. I think they covered that in maybe the ninth grade. It makes a difference, Eilo, believe me. I would never, I would *never*—"

"Gavin."

"I would never do it, Eilo. Yeah, I lied. I made up people who gave me quotes because real people are so goddamn disappointing, Eilo, real people have nothing good to say when something happens, you ask them for a reaction and they just stare at you like 'uh . . .' and they can't string a sentence together, they're pitiful—"

"Gavin, I'm worried about you."

"Yeah, well." He meant for this to sound tough, but there was a lump in his throat. "It's all gone to hell," he said, and he forced a laugh but it sounded wrong. "I'm an unemployed guy with a bad reputation and no electricity."

"Gavin, I want to buy you a ticket to Florida," she said. "Will you come back down here for a while and stay with me?"

"Eilo," he said, "I can't let you—"

"You'd do the same for me," she said. "Go home and pack and I'll call you with your flight information, okay?"

G AVIN ARRIVED home just as the locksmith was leaving. There was a notice of eviction on his apartment door and his first thought was that now Karen wouldn't be able to find him, but he'd been avoiding her since he'd lost his job and she hadn't called once. It occurred to him

that she'd very likely seen the story in the *Star* by now. He stood looking at his apartment door for a moment, thought about tearing down
the eviction notice, calling a different locksmith and pretending to be
locked out, but he knew that locksmiths in Manhattan ran in the two-
hundred-dollar range for lockouts and if he was going to lose his apartment anyway, why not today? He had the important things with him,
the camera, the computer, his favorite hat.

Back out on the street he wandered aimlessly for a while. The city
was pressing down upon him. He thought at that moment that he
might've done anything to escape the gray of the city, his static life, and
that thought—*anything*—made him stop in his tracks. It was the worst
thought he'd had in a while, because what was left to lose? His hands
were shaking. He sat on a bench on a traffic island in the middle of
Broadway until his cell phone rang.

"Eilo, I want to get out of the city today," he said. "Can we do that?
I don't recognize myself."

"Well, I was going to ask if you wanted to come next week," she
said, "but I suppose there's no reason why you couldn't fly down this
afternoon. Does that give you enough time to pack your things?"

"I don't have things," he said, "so yes. Thank you."

"Hold on a moment." He heard the clatter of her typing and then
she was quiet, reading a screen. "It looks like there's a flight departing
LaGuardia in five hours," she said. "I'll book you a ticket."

She gave him the flight information and he wrote it on his hand,
hailed a taxi and watched the city slip away from him. It was late spring
but a cloud hung low over the streets and Manhattan had already
turned into a ghost of itself, gray with tower lights shining high in the
fog. At LaGuardia he paid for the taxi with a credit card. He bought
an extra pair of socks and two cheap paperbacks in the terminal. He

refused to look directly at the *New York Star* in the newsstand. He'd checked in hours early. He paced the length of the terminal and read both paperbacks cover to cover. It occurred to him in the airplane that he might never live in New York City again, and he was surprised to discover that the thought came as a relief. Night had fallen by the time the plane began the descent. The lights of Florida glimmered to the horizon, one suburb bleeding into another along the blackness of the Everglades.

Eilo met him at the baggage claim.

"Gavin, where's your luggage? Don't you have a suitcase?"

He shook his head. A crease of worry appeared on her forehead, but she was kind enough not to make further inquiries. The heat struck him when they stepped out of the terminal. The old dread came over him, childhood memories of dizziness and heatstroke, but in the cool of Eilo's air-conditioned car it was possible to forget all this for a moment. Eilo flicked between stations on the radio, her hand lit pale by the console lights. The interior of the car smelled faintly of lavender. The outskirts of Boca Raton bled into the outskirts of Sebastian and the streets became gradually familiar, except it seemed to him that Eilo was making all the wrong turns.

"Where are we going?"

"I've moved," Eilo said. He saw in the passing streetlight that she no longer wore a wedding ring.

"You and Mike . . . ?"

"He met someone."

"I'm sorry. How long has it been?"

"Three months. We're not legally divorced yet." Eilo took an off-ramp that spiraled down into a dim wide street, made a sharp right turn and pulled up into the driveway of a low-slung brick house. The house looked large and Gavin supposed it was relatively nice, as houses went—he vastly preferred apartments—but when he got out of the car the air was filled with sound. After a moment he realized that the freeway was almost overhead, massive pylons rising up just beyond the backyard.

"Eilo," he said, "you're living under the freeway?"

"We're not *under* the freeway," she said. "It's behind the house. And you can't hear it from inside. The place is completely soundproofed." She punched a code into a console by the garage door and went back to the car, got in and drove into the garage, and Gavin found himself alone on a suburban driveway. He was thinking about how he'd frame the image if he were taking a photograph. The bright square of the garage door opening at the lower left corner of the frame, darkness all around it and above.

Twelve

After the negotiations were complete Daniel left Paul's house in the suburbs and drove his rental car back to the Salt Lake City airport. When he showed his boarding pass to the security agent he found that his hands were shaking. The visit with Paul had taken longer than anticipated; once he'd cleared security he had to half-run through the terminal, jostling people and apologizing, a gasping nightmare of bright lights and slow-moving people and distant elevator music. Daniel arrived at his gate at the last possible moment and as the plane rose out of Salt Lake City he stared down at Utah's sci-fi landscape, abandoned planet. Unearthly forms of brown and white, high plateaus and long ridges with violet shadows lengthening alongside. He was having some difficulty catching his breath. Daniel was a large man and the run hadn't been easy.

He'd admired the landscape that morning when he'd flown in. He'd never seen this part of the country from the air before and he liked the austerity of it, the opposite of Florida's feverish greenery and lakes, but now on the return flight he was distracted by his calculations. The debts of his life were as follows: his rent, which was minimal, as his

house was small and in a bad school district. His cellular telephone—
Daniel considered landlines an extravagance—and his television. He
watched only sports and the news, and had canceled the cable some
time ago. Groceries and takeout food. He had pared all of these expenses down as far as possible, because on top of them he paid alimony
and child support to two ex-wives and four children. He didn't take
vacations and worked considerable overtime. There was no extra
money and there never had been. He expected that the inheritance
would cover the debt, but it had occurred to him that coming up with
the extra money for the interest would likely require a second job.

Still, though, did it matter? The plane ascended into a cloud and
Utah was lost beneath him. What was a second job in the face of a
chance to erase a long-ago mistake, to make amends? He'd walked for
ten years with terrible guilt and the thought of being free of this was
exhilarating. Money is opportunity. He'd known this all his life. But he
realized then why he was having such trouble catching his breath, well
over a half-hour since his dash through the terminal: if you pay with
money or you pay with your family, then what would happen to his
children if he couldn't come up with the interest? His memories of
Paul suggested that there were very few things that Paul was unwilling
to do. He stared unseeing out the window into white.

Thirteen

The strangest thing about waking up in Eilo's house was the silence. In Gavin's apartment in New York he'd heard birdsong in the mornings from the tree outside his bedroom window, soft sounds of traffic from the streets. But now he woke in the mornings in a soundproofed house as closed as a space station, cool air humming through a vent in the wall. The carpets silenced his footsteps. He usually opened his bedroom window a crack to admit the outside world, just to be sure that it was there, and the noise of the freeway behind the house flooded in. The sound reminded him of the ocean.

In the mornings he showered, dressed, made himself breakfast in Eilo's vast kitchen, walked down the length of the house to the rec room that Eilo had turned into an office. She had bought four desks and a wall of filing cabinets in anticipation of future expansion, but the transition from rec room to office was incomplete. There was still a pool table in the center of the room, left behind by the house's previous owners, half-hidden under files and neat stacks of paperwork. Gavin and Eilo's desks were fifteen feet apart but she was miles away. By the time he reached the office she was usually on the telephone, and there was always a stack of folders waiting on his desk. Each one labeled with the address of a house slipping rapidly from its owner's hands.

E ILO CAME into people's lives in the last few weeks before they left their foreclosed houses. Her business card identified her as an R.E.O. broker—she and Gavin had a halfhearted debate over whether she should change it to O.R.E.O., since R.E.O. somehow indicated "other real estate owned" and Gavin was troubled by the missing letter. Banks retained her to sell foreclosed properties. The first task of the R.E.O. broker, she told him, is to determine whether anyone's living at the property, and if so, Gavin, you offer them cash for keys. This means settling on a sum, a few thousand, for them to clean the place and leave. The goal is to sell the home as quickly as possible.

He shadowed Eilo for a week and observed the rituals of the trans-action, and on the following Monday he went out on his own. Eilo and her husband had had three cars, for reasons that Gavin could never re-member because the explanation was so tedious, and Eilo had some-how ended up with two of them. She gave him the keys to a little blue Kia that reminded him of a toy. Another task of the R.E.O. broker was to take photographs for the real estate listing. She gave him a digital camera and insisted he use it.

"It's the twenty-first century," she said, when she gave it to him. "In case you hadn't noticed."

"Yes," he said, "I'm painfully aware."

He drove out to Emory Street, where a couple had been slipping into financial perdition for some months. The property was far from Eilo's house, almost beyond the outer suburbs. The suburbs broke apart and subsided into disconnected gated communities strung along the wide road, each block a mile long, and then there were gaps between the walled villages with straggly trees and enormous signs advertising future developments, the occasional enormous church or synagogue, a sprawl of outlet stores. The outlets had been far out of town when Gavin was a kid, but now the city of Sebastian had come out to meet them.

The house on Emory Street was small and neat, the lawn an impeccable rectangle. He took a photograph of the house from the street— the camera had a maddening way of beeping when the picture was taken—and another of the freshly painted front steps with pots of roses on either side. He took unnecessary pictures of the neighborhood from his position on the front step until a woman answered the doorbell.

"I'm Gavin Sasaki from the real estate company," he said. "I believe you spoke with my colleague Eileen earlier in the day."

"Oh," she said. "Please, come in."

She was polite and embarrassed, a straightforward cash for keys transaction—they settled on two thousand dollars for her and her husband to clean and vacate the premises within thirty days—and he was gone in a half-hour with a camera full of photographs. There were two more stops to make but he suddenly couldn't stand it. He pulled off the freeway and drove into a mall parking lot, turned off the ignition and sat still for a moment. Missing New York and Barbès and Karen. With the air conditioning off the heat crept in quickly, so he got out of the car and crossed the white light of the parking lot to the mall.

There was something familiar about the place. He wandered through the Cinnabon-scented air, looking for anything that might trigger a memory, but he wasn't sure if he'd been here before or if it was just that all malls looked the same to him. He went down to the food court, bought a blueberry smoothie that tasted mostly of sugar, and found a secluded bench beside a pillar. His forehead was damp with sweat beneath his summer fedora. Halfway through the blue smoothie, his cell phone began to ring. *Washed-up ex-journalist and reluctant digital photographer Gavin Sasaki contemplates the number on his cell-phone screen for just a moment before he answers.*

"How did it go?" Eilo asked.

"Fine. I gave her two thousand dollars."

"Good. That's perfect. You could've gone higher."

"I know," he said. "I started at one."

"Good work. You're going on to the other two houses?"

"I just stopped at a mall for a minute."

"Take your time," she said. "It's a hundred and five degrees today."

The next two houses were easy, although the woman at the second house was crying a little. "We just didn't think it would come to this," she kept saying, and he wanted to tell her about his apartment in New York, the rain dripping silently from the bathroom ceiling and the gaping abyss of his credit-card debt, he wanted to commiserate about ruinous financial decisions and lost homes, but instead he just said "I'm sorry about all this," which was against Eilo's rules. She'd warned that apologies weakened his bargaining position.

He reached an agreement with the tearful woman, and the drive back to Eilo's house was long and still. The heat made everything unreal. Palm trees in the distance separated from the earth and floated upward. There was something dreamlike about the movement of cars on the expressway, false lakes shimmering on the pavement ahead. He liked the solitude of driving, all these cars traveling around him with one passenger each. He wondered where Karen was at that moment. Living her life in New York or in some other city, waking each morning and putting on clothes that were unfamiliar to him, perhaps even spending time with someone else by now, a life that he'd slipped out of.

Unsettling to think of himself as someone else's memory. He found himself wondering how Anna remembered him.

Aside from the music, the robin's-egg-blue headphones, the spray-painted *NOs* in the park in Sebastian, the scar and the tattoo and the way her hair fell across her face when she leaned over her homework, what he remembered about Anna was that he'd loved her. He couldn't remember her ever being unkind to him, from the day they met in a corridor outside one of the band rooms, Sasha's pretty little sister, until she threw a paper airplane at him through the still night air.

On long drives through the suburbs he found himself thinking of Anna constantly. He'd let her slip away so easily. He assumed it was too late to make anything right, for Anna or her daughter, but it had occurred to him that the least he could do was find them.

Fourteen

███████████████████████████████████

Night had fallen by the time Daniel's airplane descended into Florida. He picked up his Jeep and drove the long straight road from Boca Raton to the city of Sebastian, a haze of insects in the air around every streetlight. Impossible not to dwell on the ragged decade that stood between today and the last time he'd gone to Utah, the marriages and divorces, his children, the guilt and the disappointments. He was calmer now that he was home. The blessed familiarity of these streets. Terrible to have to give the inheritance to Paul, but it seemed to him that paying off Anna's debt was honorable, and the idea of honor brought him peace. He drove home to the rented house where he'd been living in the long blank year since his second divorce, showered and drove to his mother's house. His grandmother had been ill for years now, a long slow fade into confusion and morphine, but the fact of her death was still somehow startling to him. His mother's eyes sparkled with tears.

"I'm sorry I wasn't here," he said.

. . .

Daniel went to the funeral two days later, watched as his grandmother's pitifully small coffin was lowered into the earth. Later in the week he came home from a long day of work and three messages blinked on his answering machine. One was from his mother, terse and businesslike—"Call me when you can"—and the other two were hang-ups, the second hang-up preceded by a sigh. He called his mother and listened to her in a state of increasing agitation.

"Wait," he said finally, "I don't understand. How is this possible?"

"As best we can figure out," his mother said, "she decided to invest in a real estate development. The money's gone."

"How could it be gone?"

"It just is," she said tightly. "She made a mistake."

"But she told me . . ." Daniel was sitting in the shadows of his living room. He hadn't turned on the lights and the light from the street shone blue through the blinds. He felt he might be dreaming. "I just came back from Utah," he said.

"Utah? Were you visiting my sister?"

"I needed the money," he said. "I thought I had it, I thought the will was being settled this week, she *told* me—"

"What did your grandmother tell you, Daniel?" Her voice was thin. Daniel flinched. She'd just lost her mother and now her son was whining about money.

"I'm sorry," he said.

"She lived a long, full life," his mother said. "If there's no money, Daniel, is it the end of the world? Don't we all have everything we need?"

"You're right," he said. He closed his eyes. "She invested all of it?"

"There wasn't much to start out with," his mother said. "She always talked about how frugal she'd been, all the careful investing she and my dad did, but once we took a look at the accounts, there just wasn't much there. Maybe she thought the real estate development would make her wealthy. Let me put it this way, sweetheart. After the bills for the nursing home and the hospital are settled, after we pay the accountant and the lawyer, I estimate we'll be left with about twelve hundred dollars. I'll split it with you if you want."

Fifteen

In his lost career at the *New York Star* Gavin had begun all his stories with a new page in his notebook, names and ideas and associations scrawled out into the margins. At the beginning of his second week in Sebastian he drove to an office-supply store and bought notebooks—he couldn't find the kind he liked best, but close enough—and wrote *Anna* across the top of a page. But where to begin? He had already spent some time trying to find Sasha, but had gotten nowhere. She wasn't in the telephone directory and seemed to be among the disconcerting population of people who don't exist on the Internet. He wrote *Sasha buying baby clothes at mall?* beneath Anna's name and *The Lola Quartet* below that. It was evening, the lights of the freeway streaming across the top of his window behind the reflection of the room. He considered for a moment but could think of no other leads, and he was distracted by the distant sounds of Eilo hitting her heavy bag.

Eilo had a heavy bag rigged up in a spare bedroom. She'd had it professionally mounted. The room was otherwise unfurnished. There was only the punching bag hanging still in a corner, Eilo's boxing gloves lined up on the gray carpet below. At five in the morning she was in the punching room and at six she was at her desk. Eilo disappeared occasionally during the day and during these absences Gavin heard the muted sounds of her gloved fists hitting the bag wherever he went in the house, a distant percussion. Afterward she was calmer, more focused, and she returned to work until at least seven or eight in the evening, long past the point when Gavin had stopped even pretending to upload new home listings to the website and was reading the news on his laptop instead. Eventually one of them would say something about pizza or Chinese takeout, and a while later they would be sitting in the living room watching TV and eating off the coffee table. It seemed to Gavin that she liked having him there. She never went out in the evenings.

"At a certain point all your friends are couples," she said, when he asked about this. "You move through the world in pairs. They had to pick one of us."

"So they picked the guy who left their friend?"

"Apparently his girlfriend's lovely." She smiled as if she'd told a joke, and he realized how rarely he saw her smile. In all of his memories she was serious and efficient: Eilo sitting by his hospital bed after the time he'd walked home from his miserable senior prom and gotten heatstroke, Eilo putting a Band-Aid on his knee when he'd fallen off his skateboard at age seven, Eilo buying him a jacket at the mall when he was ten. What all these memories had in common was the absence of his parents, but he'd always known where they were: his father was at the office or on a business trip, his mother at home watching television. Neither of them had ever displayed the slightest interest in his or Eilo's activities. He'd never understood why they'd bothered to have children.

"When did you last see Mom and Dad?" he asked, sitting with Eilo on the living room floor that night. Eilo didn't own a table.

She finished her slice of pizza, considering the question.

"I don't know," she said. "Maybe a couple years ago?"

"I'm thinking about visiting them tomorrow."

"Why would you want to do a thing like that?" Eilo stood swiftly and carried the empty pizza box to the kitchen.

"I don't know," he said to her receding back. He did know. He was beginning an investigation and it had to start somewhere, but he didn't want to tell Eilo about it. He wanted something of his own. "It just seems like a kind thing to do."

Their parents lived in a development called Palm Venice, no more than a half-hour away by car. The neighborhood had been imagined in the late '50s as Florida's answer to its namesake, a tropical paradise where you might travel by boat to your neighbor's house for a barbecue, but the canals that ran behind everyone's back lawns connected eventually with the swamps and therefore now harbored a glittery-eyed population of giant lizards and snakes. Residents saw pythons swimming in the canals sometimes, undulating ribbons with teeth. The lizards, the Nile monitors, watched the human world from the edges of backyards. A local woman swore she'd seen an anaconda but no one believed her. Still, Gavin thought as he was parking the car, there was no reason why not. As he walked up the concrete path to the front door he was remembering walking with William Chandler, murky water up around their knees and his legs soaked with sweat beneath the hip waders, a thermos of ice water in his backpack. The cool of the thermos against his spine the only thing preventing him from fainting in the heat. These are ideal conditions for an anaconda, Chandler had said, you can quote me on that.

His parents had purchased their house after Gavin and Eilo had left home. He'd been here twice before, and he sometimes thought of it as a mausoleum. It was cool and almost silent, five thousand square feet of pale walls and white carpets. He hadn't seen his mother in some time. She was somewhat wider than he remembered when she opened the door.

"Oh!" she said. "Gavin! *Sweetheart.* It's nice to see you again."

"You too," he said. He wasn't sure what to do next, so he hugged her. It was awkward. She exuded a complicated medley of scents: expensive face creams, perfumed lotions and cleansers and fabric softeners, a note of lemon in her hair. But mostly wine, a barely perceptible sweet staleness on her skin.

"Are you just passing through on business?"

"I'm not passing through. I'm living with Eilo."

"You live with Eilo and Mike?"

It wasn't his story to tell, but it seemed impossible not to now. "They've broken up. Eilo and Mike aren't together anymore."

"Close the door," she said. "You're letting in the heat."

They stood for a moment looking at one other. He tried, as he always had, to read the expression on her face. She had the warm but oddly blank half-smile she wore in most of his memories.

"Well, come in!" she said, too loudly. "Come in! How long have you been back in Florida?"

"A few weeks." He was following her into the kitchen.

"Would you like a Coke?"

"Just water, thanks. Or orange soda if you have it." But she wasn't listening, she was setting a Coca-Cola and a glass of ice before him, turning back to the fridge for a half-empty pitcher of sangria. He watched her in silence.

"It's the most refreshing thing this time of year," she said. She was pouring herself a glass.

"You drink that stuff all year."

"Are we going to get nasty about drinking again? It's *natural*," she said. "It's fermented grapes and fruit pieces. Vitamin C. You need to loosen up a little. Well, cheers," she said.

"Cheers." Gavin picked an ice cube out of his Coke, let it melt on his tongue while he watched her. "How have you been?" he asked, around the ice.

"Oh, just fine," she said. "Just fine indeed. Enjoying life in the sunshine state."

"But what've you been doing?" He knew what his mother did—she watched television, she shopped, she drank too much, she went for manicures and got her hair done and ate dinner either alone in front of the television or at expensive restaurants with her friends, she passed out on the sofa—and he wasn't sure why he was pressing the point, except that the house made him somehow claustrophobic despite its vastness and being with her always made him desperate for substance. Tell me something real, he wanted to scream at her sometimes, tell me anything at all, but as always she managed to deflect him.

"Why would I be doing anything out of the ordinary?" she asked.

"I don't know what the ordinary is," he said. "I haven't seen you in a while."

"Two or three years," she said agreeably. "You came down for that one Christmas."

"I think that was five years ago," Gavin said.

"Five," she said. A flicker of uncertainty crossed her face. "Really?"

"Is Dad home?"

"He's on a business trip."

"Where did he go this time?"

"New York," she said.

This hit Gavin harder than he would have expected. How often in these past ten years had his father come to New York City without telling him? How many times had they passed within blocks of one another, how frequently had his plane passed over Gavin's apartment? When Gavin had stood by the window in the *New York Star* newsroom in the mornings, sipping his coffee and looking down at the teeming masses of humanity forty-three stories below, how many times had his father been among those dark specks on the sidewalk?

"Excuse me a moment," Gavin said. He left her sipping sangria in the kitchen and set off down the hall in the direction of the closest bathroom, where he splashed cold water on his face and contemplated climbing out the window. It wouldn't be difficult. He was on the first floor. The frosted-glass window was open just a crack and the outside world with its grass and leaves and flowers looked like freedom to him. On his way back he veered into the dining room. It had an underused emptiness that reminded him of unpopular museum halls and pristine Park Avenue lobbies. There were stiff-backed upholstered chairs that no one ever sat in, a glass table with space for fourteen.

His mother's collection of glass and crystal figurines occupied most of an oak cabinet along one wall. He opened the cabinet door and let his eyes play over the cherubs and the tilt-headed cats until he found a glass dog of indeterminate breed with very large eyes and a tiny stick at its feet. He extracted it carefully and carried it back to her.

"Mom," he said, "where did you get this one?"

"Oh," she said, "you and Eilo gave me that for my birthday one year. It was the summer after you graduated high school, right before you went north."

He looked at the dog in his hand, but there was no spark of recognition. He'd hoped the glass dog might jump-start his memory, but he couldn't remember buying it, and he certainly couldn't remember Sasha in a shopping mall with a bag full of baby clothes. His mother's birthday was in late August. He would have been days or at most a week or two from departure. She was pouring herself another glass of sangria. She looked up at him and they both knew what he was going to say. He delayed for a moment but his next line was inevitable. He knew his part in the script.

"I thought you were going to cut down a bit," he said, as gently as possible. "That last time I saw you."

"Christmas. That was the last time I saw you, wasn't it?" She sipped the sangria and then set it down on the countertop with exaggerated care. "Christmas is a very stressful time. You would be a better person if you were a little more compassionate, I think." She had never been a kind drunk.

"I thought we'd agreed not to talk about that Christmas," Gavin said. He had come down with Karen against his strenuous objections. Karen had insisted, she thought it was strange that they'd lived together for two years and she'd never met his parents, she didn't seem to believe him when he told her what his parents were like. He'd tried to explain what ghosts they were, how uninterested they were in their children. But Karen's parents loved her, she had only ever had good holidays, she didn't understand. They'd come down to Florida and stayed at a hotel—an extravagance, Karen thought, because she couldn't imagine visiting family for Christmas and not staying with them, but Gavin had to draw the line somewhere—and Gavin's mother had lapsed into incoherence and finally passed out at the table near the end of Christmas dinner.

"Well," Gavin's mother said, "you brought it up, darling, didn't you?"

"I should go," Gavin said.

"So soon," she said. She was looking past him at the screened glass doors to the flower garden. He turned, but no one was there. His reflection imposed over a chaos of leaves and flowers. "You won't stay for dinner?" She was trying, it seemed to him, but her heart wasn't in it, and when he thought about it neither was his.

"It was nice to see you," he said. "Give Dad my regards."

He left her there in the living room and let himself out into the sunlight. The glass dog was in his pocket. He drove past the turn for Eilo's house and continued on to the police station.

"I DON'T UNDERSTAND," the desk clerk at the 33rd Precinct said. "You're saying your kid's missing?"

"I'm saying I have no idea where she is and I'm afraid she's in trouble," Gavin had been having some difficulty explaining the situation. "We've been over this twice. I don't know how to explain it differently."

"I don't know either," the desk clerk said, "but please, help me out here. The kid's missing, but you said you've never met her before?"

"She might be fine," he said. "I told you, she might be with her mother."

"But you've never met the kid?"

"Gavin?" The voice was familiar. A passing detective, an overweight man in an enormous gray suit, had stopped by the counter. He was entirely bald, his shaved head shiny under the fluorescent lights, and he was intensely familiar but it took Gavin a moment to place him. "Gavin Sasaki," the detective said.

"Daniel?" The sight was disorienting. The Daniel Smith he remembered was a skinny kid with an Afro and wire-framed glasses, high-top sneakers in Day-Glo colors, t-shirts for bands no one had ever heard of and retro ties. It was impossible to reconcile him with this large slump-shouldered figure standing by the counter in the 33rd Precinct. "You're with the police?"

"I am." Daniel glanced at the desk clerk, who gave him a meaning-ful look. "Come back to my office," he said, and Gavin followed him back into the depths of the police station, to a small gray room with no windows, a plastic chair on either side of a table that seemed to be bolted to the floor.

"Your office?"

"I don't have an office. I use the interrogation room when I want a little privacy." Daniel closed the door and settled into the chair across from him. "So I'm walking by the front desk," he said, "on my way out to get a sandwich, and I'm thinking to myself, *Isn't that Gavin Sasaki? The trumpet player?* So I come a bit closer, and I swear I hear something about a missing kid. We got a missing kid on our hands here, Gavin?"

"No, it's not—look, she wasn't abducted, it's nothing like that. I just don't know where she is and I'm worried about her. Like I was saying to your colleague, I think she might be in trouble and I don't know how to find her. She could be with her mother."

"With her mother? But you've got, what, joint custody? Visitation rights?"

"It's not that. I've never met the kid."

Daniel held up his hand. "Back up," he said. "You've never met your daughter?"

"Okay, look, let me start at the beginning."

"Please do."

"You remember my high school girlfriend, Anna? Used to hang out with us when we were in the quartet together?" A faint sense of absur-dity: he couldn't shake the notion that he was being interrogated by a bass player. Difficult to think of Daniel as a cop. "She just dropped out and vanished at the end of the eleventh grade. I heard some rumor about how she'd gone to Georgia to live with an aunt. But then recently

I found out that there's a kid in Sebastian, a ten-year-old girl with Anna's last name. She looks like me."

Daniel had gone still.

"And I just—I don't know if going to the police is the right way to do this." Gavin paused but Daniel only stared at him, a hard unreadable gaze, so he continued, foundering now, "As I was saying to your colleague, I have no idea how to go about finding her. She could be with her mother. I'm just afraid she's—"

"You went to New York," Daniel said. An unpleasant smile was pulling at his mouth. "Right after we graduated high school."

"Yeah, I did. I got into Columbia."

"My most recent ex-wife's from New York," Daniel said. "She introduced me to the *New York Star* a while back. I still read it online sometimes when I can't sleep. It's no *Times*, as I'm sure you were painfully aware for the duration of your career there, but it's actually not a bad publication, all in all. Bit of a fabulist, aren't you?"

"Daniel, I—"

"Look, Gavin, it's nice to see you again. But seeing as how you lost your last job because you invent people, I'm having a little trouble with this phantom-kid story."

"She exists," Gavin said. He had realized, too late, that Daniel didn't like him, but he couldn't think of a reason. It made no sense—hadn't they always been friendly? He was trying to recall if they'd had a falling-out all those years ago. He couldn't remember one. "Don't you remember when Anna left town? This was just after we graduated high school, right before I went to New York. I think she was pregnant with my kid."

"You lose your job, life's not going so good, you get a little confused. It's a stress response. Look, I see it pretty often. I'm not entirely unsympathetic, but the thing is, I don't have a whole lot of time for this kind of thing. You know how fucked up this place is now? Nothing like when we were kids. We grew up in paradise, Gavin, comparatively speaking."

"It never felt like paradise to me."

"That's just because you got heatstroke every ten minutes. Place was pretty nice for everyone else. Look, I got this case on my desk now, I shouldn't be telling you this—" he folded his hands together on the table—"a thirteen-year-old trades her baby brother for a bag of Oxycontin and then runs away from home. Unbelievable, right? And yes, we got the baby back, but this is what we're dealing with down here. So listen, great to see you, and I hope you've been keeping up the trumpet—" he was standing now—"but all I ask, Gavin, is that you not waste my time with your invisible people."

"Daniel, she's not some figment—"

"You know, there's something my dad used to say to me, Gavin. He said, 'You start telling lies, son, no one ever believes you after that. It's like diving into a lake, and your clothes are never dry again.' So you're telling me this story about a phantom kid, but the thing is, Gavin, your clothes are all wet." He opened the door to the room. Gavin was at a loss for words, a little shaky, still trying to reconcile this man with the scrawny kid who'd played bass beside him in high school, trying to understand. "You've already done a swan dive, as far as I'm concerned."

HE CROSSED out the question mark after *Sasha buying baby clothes at the mall* in his notebook, and set the stolen glass dog on the windowsill. It was the only adornment in the square white room. He liked the way the light struck it. Under *The Lola Quartet* he wrote the names of the members besides him—*Daniel Smith (bass), Sasha Lyon (drums), Jack*

Baranovsky (piano/saxophone)—considered a moment, and went to the kitchen to search for a phone book.

There were ten Baranovskys in the city of Sebastian and none of them were Jack, but he remembered Jack's childhood address and found it in the directory, the third Baranovsky from the top. He called Jack's mother. Jack still lived in Sebastian, she told him. She gave him an address on Mortimer Street.

"Perhaps it'll be good for him to see you," she said.

It took him some time to find Jack's house. It was in one of the oldest parts of the suburbs, a run-down district near Sebastian's empty downtown core. The streets here were set in a grid, small houses crowded together behind unmown lawns. The end-of-afternoon light cast the street in a beautiful glow but the disintegration was obvious. There were rooftops with tarps over them, camping trailers parked in driveways with children sitting on their steps. Gavin slowed the car, counting off numbers.

The house at 1196 Mortimer was set back from the street on a weed-choked lot, the front lawn half–taken over by exuberant palm fronds. There were broken bottles in the weeds by the driveway. The cement steps and the walkway were cracked. He rang the doorbell and waited for what seemed like a long time. The neighborhood was quiet. He heard cicadas and crickets and frogs, distant voices, a car. The smell of a barbecue in someone's yard. There was a flutter of movement in a curtained window across the street.

The girl who opened the door was young, perhaps thirteen years old. There was something unkempt about her, neglected, glassy eyes and unbrushed hair. She needed a bath. She was very pretty, but she had the look of a girl for whom beauty had been a mixed blessing.

"Hello," he said. "Is Jack Baranovsky here?"

It seemed to take a moment for the question to travel through the air between them. When it reached her she blinked and nodded slowly.

"Can I come in? He's a friend of mine."

The delay was shorter this time. "Okay," she said. She stepped aside, and when he walked in he almost gagged. The smell of the house was mold, mostly, but also someone had spilled beer on a carpet. The air was still and hot.

"Do you know where Jack is?"

"There," she said. She made a vague motion toward the back of the house.

The room he found at the end of the hallway was a kitchen, but it also seemed to be serving as a living room and a library. An overstuffed sofa took up half the room, books stacked precariously on the grimy linoleum all around it. The countertop by the stove was a mess of take-out containers, flies moving lazily above them. But here at least was a little more air, a sliding glass door open to an overgrown backyard.

The man reading on the sofa looked up, and for a moment Gavin didn't recognize him. He was unshaven and his eyes were red. He badly needed a haircut. His clothes hung off him, and Gavin understood why his mother had sounded so sad on the phone.

"Jack."

"Hello," Jack said. He put his book down. There was no recognition in his eyes, but the sight of a man he didn't recognize in his kitchen didn't seem to trouble him.

"Gavin Sasaki. High school. The Lola Quartet."

"Oh, wow. Gavin." His face lit up like a child's. "Hey, sit down. I don't get that many visitors. It's so nice of you to come."

"Hey, of course." There was a shifting movement of cockroaches along the edges of the room. "I'm back in Florida for a while, thought I'd look you up. How've you been?"

"Oh, I'm *good*," Jack said. He was beaming. "I'm good, you know, just staying with a friend for a while."

"So you don't live here?"

Jack gestured through the sliding glass door, and for the first time Gavin noticed the tent out back. It was on a raised cement platform under an orange tree.

"Nah, it's my friend Laila's house. I'm just camping here for a while," Jack said. "I always really liked camping, you know?"

"I didn't know that. Jack, who's that girl who answered the door?"

"Oh, that's Grace," Jack said. "She's Laila's little sister or her step-sister or something. I think she's just here for the summer." He blinked very slowly. "How are you doing? You doing okay?"

"No," Gavin said. "Not really." The Jack he remembered, the Jack who'd leaned on the band-room door frame and flirted with every girl passing by in the hallway, seemed very far from here.

"Well, I'm sorry to hear that." Jack really did sound sorry. "Things get bad sometimes."

"Are all these books yours?"

"All of them," Jack said. Gavin knelt to examine the stacks. Mostly jazz history, a few musicians' memoirs, a lot of Whitney Balliett. *American Singers, New York Jazz Notes, Django Reinhardt: A Life in Music.*

"It's a good collection." Jack was beaming when Gavin looked up. "Do you still have that synesthesia thing you used to talk about in high school? You still see music?"

"Still the brightest thing in the room," Jack said.

"I always wished I could see it too." Gavin stood, but standing over Jack was a little awkward, so he sat on an arm of the sofa. "Jack, can I ask you something?"

"Sure, sure. Ask me about anything except college. I don't like talking about college very much."

"Do you remember that night when we played the concert behind the school?"

Jack blinked, concentrating. "Why? What concert?"

"I was just thinking about it the other day. It was the last performance we did. We played 'Bei Mir Bist Du Schön' twice and Taylor was singing."

"'Bei Mir Bist Du Schön.'" Jack sounded doubtful. "I think I remember that one."

"We used to win competitions with that song," Gavin said. "But this concert, we were playing on the back of Taylor's dad's pickup truck. We drove it onto school grounds and parked behind the gym, used it as a stage."

"But how would we all fit in the bed of a pickup truck? Me, you, Sasha, Daniel, the double bass, the drum kit?"

Gavin was silent. He couldn't remember how they'd all fit. It seemed improbable in retrospect.

"I mean, the drums alone," Jack said. "Drum kits are kind of big."

"Okay, so maybe it wasn't in the back of a pickup truck," Gavin said, "maybe I'm remembering wrong, but it was definitely behind the school in the unbelievable heat. And then Anna came up to the edge of where the swing kids were dancing and threw a paper airplane, and—"

"A paper airplane?"

"My point is, Anna came to the concert that night," Gavin said. "You remember her? My high school girlfriend?"

"Sure. Short blond hair, real pretty."

"Well, she was pretty, but her hair was long and dark. That was the last time I saw her. Do you know what happened to her? Back then, or after high school?"

Jack shrugged and looked away. His smile was gone. He was fumbling in his pocket. "Hey," he said, "you don't mind, do you? I've got this back problem." He held up an unlabeled bottle of pills.

"Go ahead," Gavin said. Jack swallowed three without water. "Sorry about your back."

"Yeah, well. The pills help."

"I need to know," Gavin said. "I really need to know where she is. I know you and her were friendly, I mean, we were *all* friendly, I just thought maybe you'd kept in touch. I wondered if you ever saw her again after that concert."

Jack leaned back against the sofa cushions. He stared up at the ceiling for a moment before he spoke. "You should ask Daniel about all this, Gavin."

"Daniel as in Daniel Smith? The bass player who turned into an asshole cop?"

"He helps me out sometimes," Jack said. "You shouldn't call him that. He's nice." His eyes were drifting shut.

"Jack! Jack, wake up."

Jack's eyelids fluttered open.

"Sorry," he said. "Nodding off when there's company. Way to be a bad host, right?"

"It's okay," Gavin said. "When was the last time you saw Anna?"

"I dunno. While back." Jack's eyes were closing again. "Few years ago."

"How about Chloe?"

"Sweet kid," Jack murmured.

"Jack," Gavin said, but it was hopeless. Jack was snoring softly. Gavin stood and checked his clothing for cockroaches. Out in the dark-ened hallway the girl was standing where he'd left her. Her eyes were closed and she was leaning against the wall, her forehead pressed to the edge of the door frame. He remembered a fairy tale he'd read as a kid, or perhaps Eilo had read it to him—a story about a castle in the middle of a labyrinth of thorns, everyone sleeping for a century inside. There was something eerie about the drugged silence of the house, a spellbound stillness that made him want to run. Gavin held his cell phone near the girl's face and took her picture. She startled awake at the digital click of the shutter and stared at him, blinking. He closed the door, went back to his car and drove as quickly as possible away from there.

In his room at Eilo's house he sat on his mattress with the notebook on his lap. He wrote *Has met Chloe* and *Pills* under Jack's name.

Gavin put the notebook down and went to the window. The squalor of the house and the tent in the backyard weren't things he wanted to think about. He'd always liked Sasha and Daniel but Jack was the one he'd felt closest to. Gavin wore fedoras and read noir and watched *Chinatown* over and over again and Jack understood, Jack was in the wrong decade too, Jack was going to be a jazzman. There had been long stoned hours in Jack's basement after school, listening to jazz and talking about how things used to be, how things were going to be, talking about anywhere other than the stultifying present.

Gavin's room was at the back of the house, facing the freeway. On the far side of the yard pylons rose up with dark shadows beneath them, cars passing in a blur of light high above. How could he have let Jack slip away so completely? The traffic was no more than two hundred yards from him, but with the windows closed the room was silent. There were evenings when he didn't understand the world at all.

"You're certain you don't know where they went?" he asked Eilo that night. "Chloe and that woman she was with?" They were eating Thai food out of takeout containers.

"I drove by the house two days after I took the photograph," Eilo said. "They were gone already."

"No forwarding address?"

"These people don't always leave forwarding addresses," Eilo said. "They used to, before the economy tanked, but sometimes now they just disappear."

"I've been thinking about trying to find them," Gavin said.

"Good luck," Eilo said. "I wouldn't know where to begin. Have you thought of hiring a private investigator?"

I want to be the private investigator. He couldn't bring himself to tell her this. "I'll look into it," he said.

In the morning Gavin returned to the police station.

"I'm surprised to see you again," Daniel said. He had kept Gavin waiting for an hour. His fingers tapped almost silently on the side of his coffee cup, a nervous flicker. "Aren't you hot? Wearing a fedora in this heat?"

"It's a summer fedora," Gavin said.

"And here some of us make do with baseball caps."

"I went to visit our multitalented piano and saxophone player yesterday," Gavin said. "You remember Jack? He speaks highly of you."

Daniel sighed and his face softened a little. "Sure," he said, "I try to keep an eye on him. He's been arrested a couple times."

"I asked him about Anna," Gavin said, "and he said to ask you."

"Me? Why would I know anything about your high school girlfriend?"

"Well, she hung out with us at school, with the quartet. We were all friends."

"I don't know that you were much of a friend to her. Was there some reason you wanted to see me, Gavin, or is this strictly a social call?"

"What do you mean by that comment? How was I not a friend to her?"

"I'm pretty busy," Daniel said. "You know, doing police work and stuff. I'm going to get back to work now."

"Okay, look, the main reason I came is, Jack's staying in this house on Mortimer Street—"

"Eleven ninety-six Mortimer," Daniel said. "I've been there. Lovely home, isn't it?"

"A girl answered the door when I knocked. No older than thirteen or fourteen, maybe twelve, stoned out of her mind. Jack said she was his roommate's sister or her stepsister or something, just staying there for a while. I came to see you because I thought maybe she was a runaway."

Daniel took a slow sip of coffee. "I'm getting the strangest sense of déjà vu," he said. "Have you talked to a shrink about these phantom girls you've been seeing?"

"I knew you wouldn't believe me. I took her picture." He passed Daniel his cell phone and Daniel studied the image for a moment. The phone looked very small in his hand. "Her name's Grace."

"Wait here," Daniel said. He pushed himself up on the edge of the table and left the room. Gavin waited alone in the interrogation room for twenty minutes, listening to the hum of central air conditioning and staring at the fine cracks in the paint on the opposite wall until Daniel returned.

"Thanks for the photo," Daniel said. He was awkward now, looking away. "The tip might be useful to us."

"A runaway's got to be worth a couple of questions, right?"

"Gavin—"

"Two minutes of your time."

"Fine," Daniel said. "A couple of questions."

"Do you know what happened to Anna after high school?"

"She left town after the eleventh grade and went to live with her aunt in Georgia. I thought everyone knew that."

"You know what's funny? She was my girlfriend for two years and we spent half our waking hours together, and she never so much as mentioned that aunt in Georgia."

"I've really got an awful lot of work to do," Daniel said. He opened the door.

"You said two questions."

"Thanks for stopping by, Gavin."

"My cell phone?"

"See, now there's your second question. It's at the front desk."

Gavin walked back out into the heat with his fedora in his hands.

Part Two

Sixteen

Jack was good but not good enough for Juilliard. He auditioned after high school and didn't get in, but what he found strange—and in retrospect this should have been a warning sign, he thought—was that he was almost relieved. In the September after high school he packed up his car and drove north to South Carolina. His roommate at Holloway College *was* good enough for Juilliard, but he saw New York City as an inevitability and wanted to stay in the South a little longer. Jack's roommate was from the suburbs of Miami. He was going to play every major city on the continent no matter where he studied, because he actually was that impressive. Jack liked him, though he was prone to grandeur in his drunker moments.

"My name is Liam Deval," he would say, raising a glass of beer or introducing himself to someone in a bar, or sometimes, when he didn't know anyone else was around, quietly to his reflection in the men's-room mirror, "and I am going to be famous."

When he did this at bars everyone would laugh and buy him another drink because his delivery was hilarious. Everyone knew he wasn't really kidding, but it didn't matter because he was the best

guitarist any of them had ever heard. "The only real difference between me and Django Reinhardt," he said once when very drunk, "is
that Django did it first."

"Well, yes," Jack said. "Exactly."

Deval only laughed. Just as they both understood that Deval was
going to be a star, they understood that Jack's days were numbered.

Jack had been on his way out almost from the moment of arrival.
He couldn't have said how he knew this. He couldn't even have
explained what exactly was wrong. He had been touched lightly by
synesthesia; mostly it was a small matter of sounds being attached
to colors—the impression of red left by car horns, for example, the
dandelion-yellow sounds of his parents' doorbell—but music was brilliance, music was light moving through the air every time he heard it.

Playing with the quartet, switching back and forth between piano
and saxophone, practicing for endless hours with Gavin and Sasha and
Daniel, traveling to competitions—in short, all the things he loved—
none of these things seemed to relate in any way to the sudden grind of
Holloway College, the evenings when he played piano alone in a small
white practice room and got lonelier and lonelier by the hour, the clin-
ics, the harshness of teachers. Music had always been bright and now it
was dimming. He knew his teachers only wanted him to be the best
pianist he could possibly be but they all knew he was missing something, whatever it is that carries a musician over the gap from merely
proficient to outright spectacular, and sometimes he wanted to pack up
his car and drive back to Florida when he thought about the things
they'd said to him.

The pills helped. He could float a little. In the weeks leading up to
the winter break he started to take them more frequently. His skill
was unlessened but nothing seemed quite real.

"You seem more relaxed these days," Deval said. They were in their room at the end of another day. Deval was on the edge of his bed, listening to music. Jack had been toiling in a theory workbook earlier, but now he was staring into space.

"It doesn't have to be stressful," Jack said.

"I envy you. I'm more stressed than I thought I would be." They'd been here a few months and Deval's bravado was becoming a little threadbare. Holloway College wasn't Juilliard, but it also wasn't easy.

"You're good," Jack said. "You don't need to . . ." he was thinking "take Vicodin" but said "worry" instead.

"We're *all* good," Deval said. "Otherwise we wouldn't be here."

Jack wasn't sure anymore if he was good or not. He'd been confident of his talent in high school, but lately he was certain of nothing. The winter break arrived and on the long drive back to Sebastian he toyed with the idea of not returning to Holloway after the break, of perhaps enrolling in community college in January and getting a degree in something practical. Business management? Economics? Accounting? He wasn't really sure what the practical degrees were. He'd never wanted to do anything but music and now he didn't even want to do that.

It was disorienting, being back in Sebastian. Now that he'd left and seen another place it looked less familiar somehow, as if the town were forgetting him. That was the year when the streetlights turned from amber to blue. The blue ones apparently used less electricity and would save the city some money, but they cast the suburbs in a cold and foreign light. On his third or fourth day back Daniel and Sasha came over and passed an hour or two in Jack's parents' basement, where they'd brought their instruments and practiced sometimes in the days of the jazz quartet. Gavin hadn't come home. He was in a communications program at Columbia, full scholarship. No one was surprised that he'd cracked the Ivy League—his grades had always been better than anyone else's—but they *were* surprised that he'd stayed in New York for Christmas. They sat together in the basement, Jack and Sasha and Daniel with Gavin ostentatiously absent, and it seemed to Jack that their missing instruments were like ghosts. He'd been thinking a lot about ghosts lately, after a movie he'd seen, and the thought of a translucent ghost saxophone sitting next to him was oddly appealing.

The silence was awkward. He thought of these people as his closest friends, but it seemed that without music there wasn't much to talk about. He was seized by a mad desire to confide in them—I miss everything about high school and I'm not the musician I thought I was, I don't know what I'm doing anymore, jazz has always been my life but now it's slipping away from me and my talent isn't going to be enough—but he couldn't imagine how to begin.

"Do you still play?" he asked Daniel, to fill the silence.

"Haven't touched the bass since that last concert," Daniel said. Jack smiled at this. The last concert, on the back of the truck behind the school, was one of his favorite memories. The heat and the music, a final perfect evening, dancers trampling the grass. He missed the quartet with an unexpected force. It had been a nice thing, all of them playing together.

"I wish Gavin were around," he said.

Daniel made a dismissive noise. "Convenient that he's not here."

"What do you mean?"

"You know what?" Daniel said. "I wouldn't come back here and show my face either. His girlfriend disappears, and he runs off to New York?"

"Disappears? I heard she moved to Georgia to live with her aunt." Jack looked at Sasha. "That's what you told me."

Daniel muttered something inaudible. Sasha shot him a look.

"Anyway," Sasha said, in a let's-change-the-subject way.

Daniel didn't say anything. There was something altered about him. He seemed more pensive than he had been, his voice strained.

"Let's face it," Sasha said, "I don't think Gavin's parents would notice if he came home for Christmas or not."

"Are they really that bad?" Jack was interested. He'd heard rumors.

"I heard that when Gavin was in the hospital last spring with heat exhaustion, the night after the prom, his sister Eileen was the only one by his bedside. And she goes to school like three hours away. Eileen drove out as soon as she heard and their parents weren't even at the hospital."

"It could be worse," Daniel said. "People have families that are worse than that." Daniel was taking a year off before college. He said he'd mostly been in Salt Lake City since the end of high school, working construction with his uncle and staying with friends, but when pressed for details about his time in Utah he said he didn't want to talk about it.

"What's with you?" Jack asked.

"Nothing," Daniel said. "I just think maybe people shouldn't run off to New York when their girlfriends are . . . look, never mind. Whatever."

"But she wasn't even in Florida anymore. She'd left. She'd gone to live with her—"

"Can we drop it?" Daniel said.

Sasha looked away. They knew something, and Jack was excluded. He went out that night without them, drove alone through the wide streets until he reached the Lemon Club, a run-down jazz bar in a strip mall on the edge of town. The bartender—an older man with a permanent sneer who usually glared at Jack like he was daring him to order a drink, just daring him—barely glanced up when Jack entered.

Jack had gone to the club one or two nights a week in high school, but he'd never come in alone before. He listened to a fairly decent trio from Denver and then—because neither Sasha nor Daniel had called him—went back again the next night with his little sister Bridget. It had dawned on him that he didn't know Bridget very well anymore, she'd somehow slipped away and eluded him, and he thought maybe music would help. It did. She was enraptured by the fifteen-year-old jazz violin prodigy they'd gone to hear and seemed happy to be out with him.

"Jack." He looked up and the Band teacher who'd supervised the Lola Quartet was standing by their table. Jack hadn't seen him come in.

"Hello, Mr. Winters," he said. He was unsure of the etiquette, post-graduation. Should he have called him Steven? Mr. Winters was talking about Holloway College, the excellence of the program in which Jack was enrolled, how he hoped Jack was taking full advantage of the opportunities before him. A note of wistfulness in his voice.

"I'm proud of you," Mr. Winters said, and Jack managed a smile. His midyear review hadn't gone well. His teachers had noted a spaciness, an inattentiveness in general, an overall lack of improvement. It hadn't occurred to him that flunking out of music school would mean disappointing Mr. Winters, but he saw now that of course it would. Jack called Sasha and Daniel the next night and left messages, but neither of them called back. He returned to Holloway a few days early.

THE DRIVE from Sebastian to Holloway College took him a little more than ten hours. Jack drove slowly, in no particular rush, stopping every so often to stretch his legs. A part of him wanted to remain suspended between school and home forever. He hadn't played piano at all over the break, and the thought of the hours he needed to spend in the practice rooms made him tired.

The sense of limbo was increased by the landscape he traveled through. He pulled off the interstate into towns that all looked the same to him. He tried to find things to differentiate them, some kind of proof that he was passing through parts of three different states, but there was almost nothing. Only the names of the towns varied, and the towns were like envelopes with all the contents the same. The same gas stations, the same restaurants, the same chain stores with the same logos shining out into the deepening twilight. It was a relief to him at the end of the day to make the last exit off the interstate, to drive along the narrow roads that led up to the college, to turn the corner on the sweeping drive and see the white buildings and lights of Holloway rising up at the top of the hill. At least, he thought, this wasn't a place that could easily be mistaken for somewhere else.

He parked the car and walked up the long pathway to the hall where he lived. The security guard nodded at him when he flashed his identity card. He saw no one else. It was still only the day after Christmas, the building deserted, almost everyone home with their families.

There was a baby crying when Jack stepped off the elevator on the fourth floor. He stood still in the hall for a moment, listening. The presence of a baby in Lewins Hall seemed so impossible that he wondered fleetingly if he might be listening to a ghost: could a baby have died here? Maybe a hundred years ago? The idea of a baby ghost was interesting. The building seemed like the kind of place that would lend itself to hauntings. The crying subsided. Silence descended over the halls. The corridor was so quiet now that it was possible to entertain notions of being the last man on earth as he walked past closed doors, but when he opened the door to their room Deval was there, sitting on Jack's bed with a baby in his arms. He'd forgotten that Deval was staying at school through the holidays. The child, who had a wisp of dark hair and a face red from screaming, was drifting off into a fitful sleep.

"Congratulations?" Jack said.

"Thank you. It's a girl."

"Whose is it?"

"A friend of yours came by," Deval said. "She brought a baby."

"I don't think I have any friends with babies."

"Oh," Deval said, "I think you do. Unless she's some kind of con artist and she's just using us for our shower facilities."

Jack dropped his bag on the floor and sank into an armchair they'd rescued from a dumpster together a month or two earlier. "What's my friend's name?"

"Anna. She's in the shower."

"Anna?" The only Anna he knew was Gavin's lost girlfriend. He was having a hard time imagining the chain of events that would result in her appearing in his dorm room in South Carolina with a baby. "Anna Montgomery?"

"I think so," Deval said. "I can't remember her last name, but it was something like that." He was smiling at the sleeping baby. "I got the baby to stop crying," he said. "I think I should get a medal or something."

"She just came today?"

"An hour ago. You mind if she spends the night? I already told her it was okay."

"I don't mind," Jack said. The door opened just then. It was Anna, but an Anna greatly changed. She looked older, far more tired, and she'd cut off all her hair; it was dark with water but he could see that she'd dyed it blond.

"Jack," she said. She still sounded the same.

"Anna. What are you doing here?"

She smiled instead of answering him. "Is it okay if I stay the night?"

"It's fine with me," he said. Anna reached for the baby. Jack didn't know much about babies, but it seemed to him that this one was very small. "How old is it?" he asked.

"She," Anna said softly. "Not 'it.'" She was gazing at the baby's closed eyes. "Her name's Chloe. She's three weeks old."

"That's young," Jack said. "Where are you going with it? I mean her. Sorry. I didn't know you had a baby."

"I'm on my way to Virginia," she said. "My sister has a friend there who I can stay with for a while."

"But I just saw your sister over the break," Jack said. "She didn't say anything about . . . weren't you with an aunt? I heard you'd gone to live with your aunt in Georgia." He'd also heard a crazy rumor that she'd had a baby and it had been stillborn, but he decided not to bring this up.

"I've been in Utah," Anna said.

"Utah? Why Utah?"

"Long story," Anna said, in a tone that made it clear she didn't want to tell it.

She slept that night in Jack's bed. Jack slept on the floor. The baby slept on the floor too, lying on her back on the seat cushion from the armchair. The baby kept waking up crying. Toward morning Jack drifted off to the sounds of Anna singing the baby to sleep, a lullaby about a night bus out of Salt Lake City, and when he woke he was alone and the room was filled with sunlight. It was almost noon. He showered and set off in search of breakfast. In the dining hall he sat alone with a sandwich in a sea of plastic chairs and then wandered the campus looking for someone to talk to, anyone, but the only people he saw were security guards and the maintenance crew and they all seemed busy. Later he ran into three other students whom he knew— two violinists and a singer, from places too far away or from families too poor to travel home for the winter break—and he sat with them for a while in the cafeteria. The singer, Bernadette, was talking about George Gershwin's "Summertime." She thought it was about death. Her argument seemed solid to him and the conversation was interesting but all his thoughts were of Anna. Sixteen or seventeen years old with her impossibly young infant, traveling by means unknown up the coast to Virginia. The dorm room was still empty when he returned there in the late afternoon. Could Deval have gone with her to Virginia? It was the only explanation he could think of.

DEVAL WAS still gone when Jack woke in the morning. He ate alone in the cafeteria again and wandered the campus without finding anyone to talk to, but Bernadette called him in the late afternoon. "It's me," she said, as if they'd ever spoken on the phone before, and then added, "Bernadette."

"The Summertime girl," he said, and caught himself wondering how she'd obtained his number.

She giggled. "You must think I'm incredibly morbid," she said. "But listen, I'm having a party tonight."

"A party? Seriously? Is there anyone left on campus?"

"That's why I'm having it," she said. "We should all stick together. It's cold."

It was nice to think of not being alone for another long evening, so when night fell he put on a clean shirt and left the dorm. It was an unusually cold night, the coldest he'd ever seen. There was a light frost and the grass sparkled underfoot. Jack wasn't sure that he'd encountered frost outside a freezer before. He knew what it was but couldn't stop staring at it, stooped down once to touch it. The sparkling turned to cold water on his fingertips. Jack stood for a moment in the middle of the Commons, looking up at the stars. He'd meant to practice today but hadn't. It had been two weeks since he'd played the piano and nothing about the thought of sitting down at a keyboard was appealing to him. He closed his eyes for a moment. He had a feeling of slippage, of pieces coming apart around him. He opened his eyes quickly and he was still on the Commons, the air cold on his face. There was movement around one of the girls' dormitory buildings at the far end of campus, an impression of voices, he hurried on and in a few minutes he was safely among other people, fifteen or twenty students in the suite where Bernadette and her roommates lived. He hadn't thought there were this many people on campus.

"You came!" Bernadette said. She was flushed and lovely, already a little drunk, wearing a miniskirt that he couldn't help but notice was short even by miniskirt standards. "I'm so glad you're here."

"I'm glad I'm here too," he said. "What's this we're listening to?" She was pressing a plastic cup of beer into his hands.

"The Klezmatics," she said. "I don't love them, except this one song. Can you hear it? It's klezmer, but it's also jazz."

"I don't know that much about klezmer," he said. It was nice to be in a conversation with someone instead of alone in the dorm room, and he didn't want the moment to end. She had hair that caught the light, dark curls falling over her shoulders.

"Then stay a while and keep listening," Bernadette said. "Another drink?"

She floated away from him. He didn't know anyone else here but they all seemed to know each other. Jack stayed as long as possible in the warmth and the brightness, trying to find a conversation, until sometime near midnight he glanced across the room and Bernadette was kissing someone else, a cellist whose name he could never remember. He drifted outside and over the sparkling grass to Lewins Hall, drunk, the stars wheeling. He hoped Deval might be back from wherever he'd gone, but the room was dark and still. He slept with his bedside lamp on, a t-shirt thrown over it to blunt the light, and woke hungover to the smell of scorched fabric.

FOUR DAYS later Deval came into the room one morning while Jack was getting dressed, waved instead of saying hello, lay down on top of his bed, and closed his eyes.

"Where were you?"

"I drove her to Virginia," Deval said. "Then I hung around for a few days."

"Where in Virginia?"

"Somewhere in the middle. Place called Carrollsburg." He kicked off his shoes. "Have you ever seen her tattoo?" He gestured vaguely at his shoulder without sitting up.

"I could've taken her."

"It was a spur-of-the-moment thing. You were asleep."

"So you saw where she's living?"

"It's an okay place," Deval said. "Quiet little house in a small town. Nowhere anyone would look for her. She's got the whole basement to herself. I think it'll be okay."

"You know what's weird? The last time I saw her, she had all this long dark hair, and now it's short and blond. It's like she was in disguise."

"Yeah, about that." Deval sat up. "She's got a complicated life," he said. "She asked me to tell you—well, to ask you, I guess—look, she doesn't want you to tell anyone you saw her. Seriously, no one. It's really important, okay?"

"Okay."

"When I say important, I mean this is like the most important thing anyone's ever going to ask of you."

"Okay, I get it. I won't tell anyone."

"Thanks." Deval lay back down on his bed.

DJANGO REINHARDT was a prodigy at thirteen playing the cafés of Paris. A burn victim at eighteen when he came home from a gig and knocked over a candle in the caravan where he lived with his young wife. The materials for the celluloid-and-paper flowers she made to supplement their income were highly flammable, and the caravan flashed quickly into flame. A small miracle at twenty, when he emerged from a long convalescence after the fire that ruined half his left hand and revealed an improbable new technique: he worked the frets with two fingers and made his own substitutions for the standard major and minor chords. The miracle was that he played better after the fire than before. He carried the fire with him through all the days of his life, in his two curled fingers and in the way he used a match to hold the bridge of his battered guitar up to the proper height.

"A *match*," Deval said. "Of all the things he could have used."

Deval's mother had given him a biography of Django Reinhardt as a high school graduation present, and he liked to read his favorite sections aloud in the dorm room at night. Jack appreciated the distraction.

Django Reinhardt was always good, but he was at his best with Stéphane Grappelli. They met as members of a fourteen-piece orchestra that played uninspired music for tea dances, Grappelli on violin and Reinhardt on guitar, until one day Grappelli broke a string. He played a few notes of a jazz melody, trying to get his violin in tune, and

Reinhardt echoed him on guitar. A bass player and a rhythm guitarist jumped in, and this was the beginning of the Quintette du Hot Club de France. They played together with enormous success. Reinhardt hadn't spent much time in school as a child; Grappelli taught him how to read. Reinhardt went on a shaky American tour without him, dabbling in electric, traveling unsteadily with unfamiliar guitars, but only when he returned to Grappelli did he sound like himself again.

"Why are you telling me so much about Grappelli?" Jack asked. "I thought you wanted to be Reinhardt."

"Because this is what I keep wondering." Deval was sitting up on his bed, bright-eyed in the lamplight. The Quintette du Hot Club de France playing on his stereo, the underwater sound of old recordings. "I can play the guitar and maybe I'll be really good someday, Jack, but who will be there with me? Who will be my Grappelli?"

DECEMBER SHIFTED into a colorless January. Jack didn't want to be at music school, he knew he was taking too many pills, he knew the little baby with the wisp of dark hair was probably Gavin's and he couldn't imagine why he wasn't supposed to tell anyone about it, but Deval had repeated three or four times that Jack should tell no one he'd seen Anna or the child. He hinted that Anna was in some kind of trouble. He made it sound as though lives were at stake, but still he managed to appear perfectly serene as he moved through his days. Skipping half his classes, spending hours in the practice rooms, reading about gypsy jazz and listening to scratchy recordings of the Quintette du Hot Club de France in the evenings. He was making long phone calls to Virginia at night.

"I can't tell you how much I envy you," Jack told him once, near the end, when they'd walked down the hill into town to get drunk. It was almost two a.m. Anna had been gone for three or four weeks. Jack and Liam were slumped in a booth in the back corner of a half-deserted Irish bar they'd discovered where the beer was cheap and no one cared what they put on the jukebox, and Jack had been happy earlier but now he was sinking into the morose kind of drunk that lends itself to regrettable statements.

"Yeah, I can see why," Deval said. "I'm in love with an underage girl who lives in hiding in a different state with a fucking baby, school bores me half to death but my mother will kill me if I don't get a degree, and I've got a class in six hours. What's not to envy?"

"You've got the music," Jack said. The idea of having the music or not having the music was something he'd never had an easy time explaining but Deval smiled, Deval seemed to understand, and Jack felt such gratitude at being understood in that moment that he let Deval choose the next three songs on the jukebox.

AT THE beginning of February, Jack left Lewins Hall en route to the practice rooms and a man he didn't recognize fell into step beside him.

"Jack, right?"

"Yes?"

The man was in his twenties, blond, with pale eyes and a ring through his eyebrow. He was dressed in a way that seemed calculatedly forgettable—a gray sweatshirt, black shoes, jeans—but any chance of anonymity was ruined by his tattoo: an extravagantly detailed goldfish on the side of his neck, brilliant orange. Jack found it hard to look away. He hated needles. Tattoos made him queasy. His hand drifted to his own neck in sympathy.

"You seen Anna around?"

Jack stopped walking, so the man stopped walking too. "Anna . . . ?"

"Anna Montgomery, Jack. Anna from Florida. The girl with the baby." He was standing a little too close. Jack could smell his aftershave. There was nothing friendly in the man's blue-eyed stare. "The girl who visited you last month," he said.

"I heard she was in Utah."

"Oh, she *was*," the man said brightly. "She *was* in Utah, Jack, but that was before she came here. Do you mind telling me where she is? I really need to talk to her about something important."

"How do you know my name?"

"Where's Anna?"

"Look, I haven't seen her in almost a year. I knew her back in high school," Jack said.

"Right," the man said. "Back in Florida. You're both from Sebastian, aren't you?"

"Yes."

"And your family still lives there, right?"

Jack felt as if he'd brushed up against the edge of something cold, or as if a curtain had been pulled back for an instant and he'd glimpsed a flash of darkness and moving gears. He'd never been threatened before. He didn't know what to do. He stood blinking in the sunlight with the life of the campus continuing all around him, voices and laughter, the man's calm gaze, and his voice was unsteady when he could finally bring himself to speak. "What do you want?"

"I want Anna Montgomery," the man said. "But if you don't know where she is, I could go ask your family. You've got a little sister still in high school in Florida, right?"

"What? I . . ." There was no way to finish this sentence, so Jack didn't.

"Bridget," he said. "That's your little sister's name, isn't it?"

Jack was frozen.

"Maybe I'll go down there and talk to her," the man said. "I mean, who knows, maybe she'd know where Anna is. You know how these high school girls all talk about each other."

"I don't—"

"I can't say I'll be in a great mood when I get down there," the man said. "Do you know, I was just there? Trying to track down Anna's dropout sister, for almost a week. And it's not like it's all that easy for me to leave town for long periods, in my line of work."

Jack was afraid to ask what this line of work might be.

"So I think by the time I find Bridget," the man said, "I'll probably already be angry. Just for having to go back to Florida again."

"Anna went to Virginia." Jack heard his own voice and wanted to pull the words back through the air.

"Where in Virginia?"

"I don't know," Jack said, "she just said she was going to Virginia and that was it. I heard it was a small town but I don't know which one. That's all I know."

"The problem is, Jack," the man said, "Virginia's such a big place. Last thing I want to do is drive back down to Florida but it'd almost be worth my time to go back down there, talk to your sister, see if maybe she knows more than you do. Who knows, Jack, maybe Anna and Bridget talk to each other sometimes."

"They don't talk to each other. They don't know each other at all."

"I'll ask Bridget myself. Thanks anyway, Jack, I'll be seeing you."

"Carrollsburg," Jack said.

"Carrollsburg?" The man was smiling. "Now we're getting somewhere, Jack. You have an address for me?"

"I don't. I really don't. That's all I know."

"You sure, now? You don't think maybe I should ask Bridget, just in case?"

"I don't know more than that. Bridget doesn't know anything. She doesn't know anything."

"Well, thank you very much, Jack," the man said pleasantly. "You just saved me another trip to Florida."

He turned away. Jack's heart was pounding and he wanted to throw up on the grass. On his way to the building with the practice rooms it occurred to him that he should alert campus security, but when he looked back the man was nowhere to be seen, and what would he say anyway? *A few weeks ago my roommate and I snuck a girl into our room and let her stay overnight in violation of the rules, and, oh yeah, she also had a baby with her, and now some guy wants to know* . . . He needed to talk to Deval. He stepped through the doors into the cool shadows of Armstrong Hall and scanned the last few pages of the practice room sign-in book. *L. Deval, room 17.* He glanced over his shoulder, but through the glass doors behind him he saw only green grass and benignly milling students. The blond man was long gone.

Deval didn't look up when Jack opened the door to 17. He was playing in a style that he'd begun to adopt recently. It was jazz, but glissando shivers of gypsy melodies kept coming through. The effect was uneven.

"Deval," Jack said.

"There's no piano in this one," Deval said, without looking up.

"Please," Jack said. Deval stopped playing. "Some guy just asked me where Anna is."

"What?" Deval set his guitar on the chair beside him, which left nowhere for Jack to sit, so he stood uncomfortably by the door like a kid in the principal's office.

"He came up to me while I was walking, said he knew she'd been here. He knew she'd gone to Virginia—"

"Did you tell him she'd gone to Virginia?"

"Of course not," Jack said. "I told him to get lost." He was shivering. "He was menacing, Liam. He threatened my sister. He had this look about him, this—"

"Yeah, some people aren't nice," Deval said. "Don't get hysterical. What exactly did he say?"

"He said he knew she'd been here after she was in Utah. He asked me where she was. What did she do in Utah, Liam?"

"She stole money from a meth dealer," Deval said. He was putting his guitar back in its case. "Listen, I'm going to go get her."

"You're leaving now? In the middle of the semester?"

"She doesn't drive. I'll call the dean's office from the road and tell them I've got a family emergency or something. Don't tell anything to anyone."

Deval didn't go back to the residence hall. He left the practice room and walked quickly to his car, threw his guitar in the backseat and drove away.

JACK WAS thinking about a movie he'd seen once. He couldn't remember what it had been called, but it was set in the eighteenth century and there was a boat, and a sailor who'd been a disappointment to everyone had jumped overboard with a cannonball in his arms. When he closed his eyes Jack saw the sailor descending, pale in dark water with a cloud of bubbles rising silver around him, the weight of the cannonball carrying him down to some other place. "The truth is," the captain had said at the sailor's funeral, "we don't all turn into the men we had hoped to become." Or words to that effect. Jack wasn't sure he was remembering it exactly.

"It's true," Jack said to his reflection in a darkened window, in reply to the captain of the movie ship. "It's just the way it is." He had taken too many pills. It was four a.m. and Deval had been gone for a week. With every passing day he became more certain that Deval and Anna and the baby were dead. He knew he should call the police, but every day and every hour made the call less possible. The first question would be *Why didn't you call sooner?* and with each passing hour the question would be more pointed, and then what would he say? The truth is, Officer, I'm not the man I wanted to be. The truth is, I gave up a girl at the slightest threat and now everyone's in trouble and I think both Deval and the girl are probably dead by now and the fault's entirely mine and I've been thinking it might be better for everyone if I take this cannonball in my arms and leap into the ocean.

Jack waited a week, then two, but Deval didn't return. At the beginning of the third week a postcard arrived.

All's well. Not coming back. Got rid of phone.—LD

The card was postmarked Detroit. The relief that all was well—Deval must have arrived in Virginia in time—was supplanted almost immediately by a colossal loneliness. It seemed impossible that Deval wasn't coming back. His belongings waited untouched in their room, his books, his sheet music, his clothes strewn around the bed. Jack kept expecting someone to come and collect them, but no one did.

The pills weren't working the way they had before. Jack still floated but the blurred contours of the world made everything seem unreal in the manner of a bad dream. He spent a lot of time lying on his bed listening to music on headphones, Nina Simone, Django Reinhardt, Coltrane and Parker, all the emissaries of a kingdom that was slipping away from him. There was no pleasure in playing the music himself. Sometime during the fifth or sixth week he stopped going to classes.

After seven weeks he packed up his things in the middle of the day while everyone else was in class, loaded up his car and drove south.

JACK DROVE to the Lemon Club nearly a year after his return from South Carolina. The bartender glared at him the way he always had when Jack was in high school, and Jack laughed out loud. It seemed inconceivable that high school had been less than two years ago. He'd just turned twenty and felt vastly old. The fact that he was still under-age was a joke.

He'd recently come out of rehab for the second time and he felt skinless, his bones exposed to the open air. His hands shook. Every light was too bright. He knew he could repair this awful fragility with a pill or two but that was the *point*, he'd promised his parents, he was wracked with guilt for how expensive he imagined rehab must be al-though they kept the numbers from him. "You don't want to drift through life all *addled*, Jack," his mother's voice as she served him din-ner his first night home, breadcrumb-covered casserole in a blue dish from childhood, these impossibly moving small details that kept him perpetually tripped-up and on the edge of tears. In rehab he'd spent a lot of time watching videos and now his thoughts were a fog of old movies.

"You're sure you're good to go out?" his father had asked. Jack had been home for three weeks and tonight was the first time he'd been out by himself. His parents had taken him to dinner and a movie a few times but since he'd been back he'd mostly spent his evenings watching TV with them. *Law & Order* episodes with their soothingly formal two-act structures, a glass of warm milk delivered by his mother and then the same routine since childhood, washing his face and brushing his teeth and closing his eyes under a constellation of glow-in-the-dark stars and planets shining down from the ceiling of his childhood room. Bridget called sometimes. She was going to college in Colorado and had a cautious way of talking to him that he didn't like very much. By day he was working in a coffee shop in a mall, making lattes and cappuccinos behind a shining silver machine. A boring life on paper but he liked it, actually, the quiet of it, the peace. He played his saxophone in the backyard after work in the afternoons. He'd come home from music school and there it was in his room where he'd left it, a gleaming brass miracle leaning up against the bookcase. He hadn't played the piano in a year.

A jazz pianist from Des Moines was headlining. He'd heard of her back when he was in music school and it seemed a good reason to go out so he'd dressed carefully and combed his hair. He chose a table at the front in the hope that if the music was beautiful it might sweep him up, but the pianist didn't appear when he thought she would. Instead a man came onstage with a guitar and started fiddling with amplifiers.

"Excuse me," Jack said, to the fiftyish couple at the next table. He would've preferred not to bother them, but they seemed to have programs and he needed information. "Is there a warm-up act?"

"There is," the woman said. She was black, and he found the brilliance of her blue eye shadow mesmerizing against the dark of her skin. All the girls he'd dated had worn such subdued makeup. It would be nice, he thought, to be able to paint blue shimmering powder on yourself, and he realized that she was holding out the program for him, so he took it quickly and said, "Thanks very much."

"You're welcome." She was looking at him strangely. He had moments throughout the day when he thought everyone in the room was staring at him, and this was one of them. The program said the opening act was *Deval & Morelli/Guitar (with Joe Stevenson/Bass, Arnie Jacobson/Percussion)*. He must have smiled, because the woman said,

"Well, that seemed to make you happy," and he said, "Yes, it does," although he of course couldn't be certain that this was the same Deval. He was in the habit of looking for Deval's name in the news every morning. No day passed without Jack wondering if the man with the goldfish tattoo had found them.

But then the other guitarist came up on the stage and it was Liam Deval, it was actually him. At first he just introduced himself and Arthur Morelli without really looking into the audience, started in on the set with his eyes on the guitar. Halfway through the third piece Deval looked up and saw Jack, and for a moment he faltered. Morelli gave him a questioning glance. Deval recovered quickly, slipped back into "Minor Swing." His year hadn't been wasted. In music school he'd been good but now he was remarkable, his talent hardened and sharpened, a knife. He played with a heavy swing and made Django Reinhardt's chord substitutions. For the first time in a while Jack felt perfectly at peace. The music was radiant.

"Let me buy you a drink" was the first thing he said to Jack when the set was over. At the bar Jack ordered a ginger ale and sipped at it in silence while Deval settled up with the bartender.

"Hey now," Deval said, "are you okay?"

"I've been like this since I got out of rehab," Jack said. "I'm sorry. It's embarrassing. Nothing's wrong. I can't help it." He held a cocktail napkin to his eyes but the tears wouldn't stop coming.

"Rehab," Deval said. "Christ, I'm sorry, and here I am offering to buy you drinks."

"It's okay. It was only ever pills." Jack stared at the bar and with tremendous concentration forced his eyes to stop watering. "I'm fine."

"Pills." Deval seemed at a loss. "I should have realized, I should have noticed . . ."

"You left your things in the dorm room," Jack said.

"I didn't want *things* anymore," Deval said. "It was easier just to leave them. It's hard to explain."

"Why did you get rid of your phone?"

"We were so paranoid. We didn't know what he'd do, we thought maybe there might be some way to trace our calls." Deval sounded embarrassed. "We thought there might be a private detective involved, the way he found you in South Carolina so easily."

"Anna and the baby, are they . . . ?"

"I think I got to Virginia just in time," Deval said.

Seventeen

Anna had thought that being on the run would be more exciting. The night she left Utah with the baby and the money she'd been terrified, but also she had gazed at her wide-eyed reflection in the bus-terminal bathroom and thought about how tragic she was, how pretty and how doomed and how alone in the world, thoughts that embarrassed her later when she remembered them. She'd run away before but this was something infinitely more dangerous. She had wept for hours on the bus, silently with her child in her arms, because she was perfectly adrift now and she was afraid, so afraid, knowing almost nothing of the man from whom she'd stolen a hundred and twenty-one thousand dollars or of what he might do when he discovered the theft. She put on her headphones and listened to electronica—an epiphany from childhood: when all lies in disarray there's still order in music—and this was how she missed Daniel's call. She listened to the voice mail a few hours later, shaking. Apologies, recriminations, a plea to go anywhere but Florida because Florida was where Paul thought she was going. She changed her ticket at the next stop and spent a long time waiting in a dusty waiting room for a bus that pulled up glinting in the sunlight, continued on to South Carolina, where she convinced Jack's roommate to hold the baby while she took her first shower in three days.

"Did you name her after someone?" Liam Deval asked on the first night. It was three in the morning. Anna was feeding the baby in the common area and Liam had come out to sit with her. Jack was asleep on the floor of the dorm room.

"A friend," Anna said.

The one true friend she'd ever had, when she thought about it. Chloe LaFleur, hair dyed bright pink and loops of steel through her ears and eyebrows and nostrils, Chloe who was trying to make herself as hard and spiked and dangerous-looking as possible, Chloe who skipped school with Anna and showed her how to use a can of spray paint and told her about punk music and death metal. They were inseparable in junior high until Anna transferred away. Anna told her about the Chemical Brothers and New Order, but they wanted different things out of music. Anna wanted steadiness and predictability, music with rules. Chloe wanted noise, Chloe wanted music she could listen to while she threw bottles against the underpass at the back of the park, Chloe wanted a soundtrack for destruction.

But Chloe was the one Anna could call crying from a pay phone because she'd run away from home again—because someone had thrown all her things out the window in a drunken rage, because her sister was at her father's house and Anna was alone with wolves, because someone had given her another bruise she'd have to lie about at school on Monday, all the countless reasons for leaving that could come up in a given evening—and Chloe was the one who'd tell her to come over no matter what time it was, Chloe would meet her in the park, Chloe would go with her to the tattoo parlor when she was high and wild, when everything was moving too quickly and she was desperate to mark this moment on her skin.

A month after Anna switched to the new school Chloe LaFleur moved to Indiana to live with her grandparents, and Anna didn't see her again. Still, she knew immediately what to name her baby when the nurse told her it was a girl. In the darkness of the residence hall at Holloway College she prepared a new bottle and leaned down to kiss her daughter's beautiful new skin.

LATER THERE was Virginia in all its calm and its peace, before Liam came to her in the park and spirited her away again.

"Where are we going?" she asked, on the way out of town.

"You're under no obligation," Liam said. Driving five miles over the speed limit, glancing every so often in his rearview mirror. They were passing through fields dusted with snow, black skeletons of winter trees. "I'll drive you anywhere. But I want to go to Detroit, and I'd love for you to come along."

"What's in Detroit?"

"A gypsy guitarist," he said. "Someone I've been wanting to study with for a while."

Three or four blurred days of travel, then, but when they reached Detroit she found herself unprepared for the stasis of hiding. After a few cramped days in a motel they found a cheap one-bedroom apartment, and then the sensation of flight dissipated and days began to slide past without incident. She stared out the window at the winter snow, played with Chloe and sang to her, changed her diapers and prepared endless bottles, watched music videos, thought about enrolling in a GED program but didn't do anything about it, cleaned the apartment to techno music.

The small peculiarities of living with someone. When Liam shaved he left a fine dusting of hair in the sink. When she woke in the night she found herself staring at him in the darkness. The lines of his shoulder, his neck, the stillness of his sleeping face. *I am someone who sleeps next to someone else in a queen-sized bed every night.* She wondered if this was what being married was like. She didn't recognize her life and felt vastly old.

"Will your parents look for you?" he asked. He didn't think she was vastly old. He fretted about her age.

"No," she said. Even if anyone reported her missing, she told him, she'd run away three times before so the Florida police would have listed her as a runaway.

Liam found a job as a waiter. He hated it but was qualified for almost nothing else except teaching guitar lessons, which he said he couldn't stand the thought of. He came home exhausted and played his guitar alone in the living room, until at the beginning of their second week in Detroit he went from work to a housing project far from their apartment and returned home late in a state of elation. He lay on the bed, his clothes still smelling of the restaurant. Anna lay beside him with her head on his chest.

"Tell me what it was like," she said. Chloe was sleeping in the crib by the bed. She didn't like leaving the apartment but she did like hearing about the outside world.

"What part of it?"

"All of it. You leave the restaurant, you take the bus to the housing project, you walk up to the door . . ."

"I walk up to the door," he said, "the door of the tower, and I'm thinking, what the hell am I doing here? The place is desolate. A whole block of brick towers with small windows, leafless trees. There are all these dangerous-looking kids loitering out front in their huge puffy jackets. When I get close to the door they're staring at me and laughing, the girls sucking their teeth at me. So I have to go in then because if I turn around now I'm scared they'll jump me, maybe steal my guitar.

"So I go into this terrible dark hallway, it smells like urine and there's garbage lying around, step into the elevator and then up to the seventh floor. It's better up there, not as dirty. There's music playing somewhere, television voices behind the doors and it seems less dangerous, just another place where people live their lives, and I'm feeling awfully judgmental all of a sudden for being afraid of the building. So I find the apartment, 7M, and a woman answers the door—"

"How old is she?"

"Maybe fifty? I'm bad with ages. She opens the door with the chain still on and asks me who I am through the crack, so I tell her who I am and that I have an appointment. And she says, 'Oh, Stanislaus is so looking forward to meeting you,' with a very faint Eastern European accent, like this isn't her first language but she's been here a long time. She opens the door and I'm face-to-face with this really elegant woman, her hair and makeup all done, nice clothes. I'm standing here in t-shirt and jeans, filthy from the restaurant, and it's embarrassing all of a sudden, like I should have dressed up to meet them.

"And then Stanislaus comes in and he's a wreck, maybe sixty, he drags his leg and he winces like he's in pain, you can tell his nose got broken once or twice, but his wife brings him his guitar and he starts playing, Anna, and I can't tell you . . . he can do things I can't, and it made me think of Jack, actually, this thing he used to say—"

Anna shifted in the bed. She was afraid she might have put Jack in danger. She didn't regret coming to Holloway College because if she hadn't gone there she wouldn't have met Liam, but the mention of Jack's name always filled her with guilt. Chloe whimpered in her sleep in the crib by the bed.

"This thing he used to say," Liam said, "when we were in school together." He said this as if the time when he'd been in school with Jack were much more distant than three weeks ago, as if Liam's belongings weren't still scattered in the dorm room in South Carolina where Jack still slept every night. "We'd be listening to a musician, someone really good, and Jack would go, 'Damn, he has the music,' or 'She has the music'—"

"He used to say that in high school too, but I don't think I really understood what he meant."

"The way I think of it," Liam said, "it means the musician's a conduit. It means music's something that moves through him, like religion or electricity. I'm up there in a tower in the scariest neighborhood I've ever set foot in, all these kids waiting to rob me out front, and here's this man who comes into the room half-crippled, he's a bit gruff and he doesn't really have much to say to me, just asks for the money for the lesson up front and I'm wondering if coming to Detroit to study with him was a terrible idea, but then he sits down and starts playing and it's like nothing I've heard. This man, he's broken-down and poor and he lives in a hellhole, but he has the music."

The idea of having the music—something you could hold inside yourself, a library of notes, a collection—made her happy. "Do you have the music?"

"I'm so close," Liam said. "I think I'm getting closer."

"To the music?"

"To the music," he said. "I can't really explain."

Anna fell asleep beside him and when she woke two hours later— Chloe was whimpering—he was gone from the bed. She found him in the living room, playing softly and haltingly in a style she'd never heard before. He smiled when he saw her but didn't stop.

Chloe liked the music. She flapped her arms and made excited small

noises, she grinned toothlessly at Liam and kicked her feet, and after
some time had passed Anna and Chloe fell asleep on the sofa. When
they woke together Liam had gone to work. Anna redyed her hair and
trimmed it while Chloe was napping. The sting of bleach on her head,
the familiar ritual of turning herself blond, soft pieces falling around
her ears. She sometimes didn't remember what she'd looked like in her
old life. She sometimes didn't remember who she'd been. A distant
version of herself had run away from home and gotten high in the park
and skipped school to smoke cigarettes under an overpass, but there
were days when these seemed like someone else's memories.

SHE COULD have gone outside but she didn't. She thought of Paul
constantly and her memories of him made her heart beat faster, a panicked blackness at the edges of her vision. Their neighborhood was
half-empty, every third or fourth building boarded up. There were
cracks in all the sidewalks, and no one ever threatened her but she didn't
feel safe. She felt watched when she walked down the street with Chloe,
all the windows of all the buildings filled with malevolent eyes. There
was nowhere to go but the park down the street and that was a broken-
down place, swings hanging lopsided and rust on the slide. There was one
swing meant for a small child that still hung the way it was supposed
to, but that swing made a ghastly shrieking sound when she pushed
Chloe on it—rust on the chain—and Chloe didn't like the noise.

When Liam came home at night he was tired and exhilarated. After
his shift in the restaurant he would board a bus to the projects, where he
rode an elevator to the seventh floor of a brick tower and spent two hours
with Stanislaus. Later Anna sat on the floor of the living room and listened to him practice. She'd liked listening to the jazz quartet back in
high school but this was different, this was something she didn't have

words for. Chloe loved it too. When she was big enough to sit up, she sat on the carpet and stared at Liam while he played. There were moments of unbearable beauty when Anna closed her eyes in the living room while Liam played his guitar and everything rushed away from her until it was just the music, just Liam, just her daughter and the softness of the carpet where she lay on her back to listen to him, scents of cleaning products lingering in the air. The perfection of their lives together.

"I love your music," Anna said. He put down his guitar and kissed her. There were moments when everything was easy and bright.

Anna knew that Liam worried about her, the way she stayed indoors almost all the time. He pressed her sometimes to think about the future. "What are you going to do with your life?" he asked, near the beginning, when they'd just arrived in Detroit.

"I'm going to look after Chloe."

"What were you going to do before Chloe?"

"I wanted to be Brian Eno," she said.

"What?"

"I was going to be in the music industry in some way. I used to think I'd maybe be a producer or a DJ or something."

"You still can."

"I know," she said, "maybe I'll still do it." But the future was abstract and none of it mattered as much as Chloe did. The idea of leaving Chloe with a stranger was unthinkable. She was going to be a better parent than her parents had been. She was going to save Chloe from everything bad.

In the spring Liam asked if she'd mind moving to New York. He'd learned all he could from Stanislaus, he said. There was someone else, an old man in Queens who Stanislaus said was among the very best.

"My name is Liam Deval," he said quietly to himself in the mirror when he didn't know she could hear him, "and I am going to be famous." He said it sardonically now, as if he were only kidding, but his ambition was a winged and burning thing.

In early April they packed up the car, strapped the baby in the car seat, and drove southeast with cups of coffee in the cup holders and a map to New York City on the dashboard.

Brighton Beach was on the far edge of Brooklyn, close against the sea. Blue sky and white sand, the edge of the city, a boardwalk running along the beach. The advertisements and signs on the street were in Russian. The grocery store was filled with inscrutable labels. The trains rattled and cast fleeting shadows from the elevated tracks. She was aware at all times that Gavin was somewhere in this city. She felt such guilt when she thought of him. *If it's spring*, she thought, *he's just finished his first year of college*. There were moments when she imagined getting on the subway with Chloe, taking her on the endless train from Brighton Beach to Columbia University, waiting for Gavin by the university gates. But then what? The conversation was impossible to imagine—*I gave birth to your child but I never told you I was pregnant because I decided instead to run away with someone else*—and she didn't need child support. Could he possibly take Chloe away from her? She wasn't sure. It seemed possible. His family had more money than hers did. Did Chloe actually need a father? Anna certainly hadn't needed hers, and anyway Chloe had Deval.

They had a small apartment a few blocks from the ocean. Liam took a job as a waiter in Manhattan and came home demoralized. He had been told that the first week would be training, which meant he wouldn't be paid.

"Isn't that illegal?" Anna asked.

"Of course," he said. He had worked for thirteen hours. He was sitting at the table with his guitar, picking out chords while she made pancakes. An exhausted sheen to his face. "Now ask me if there's anything I can do about it."

"You could quit," she said. They'd had this conversation before.

"I need the job."

"You don't. We have money."

"Anna," he said. "I don't want to use the . . ." The cautious voice he used when they skirted around the edges of the theft. The money was divided between several plastic bags here and there in the apartment—behind the towels, under the bed, at the back of a closet—and she was aware of it constantly.

"You could be playing music all day," she said. "You could rent studio space."

"I'm not—"

"Let me do this for you, Liam. It's not like we can return it."

He laid his hand flat over the strings of his guitar, watching her.

"Did you like working today?"

"No," he said.

"Then don't go back tomorrow," she said.

The money went so quickly after that, but in an odd way it was a relief to watch it trickling away. It was like destroying the evidence of a crime.

LIAM SPENT his days in a rented studio near their apartment. In the evenings he took a train to Queens to work with the man who Stanislaus had said might be the world's greatest living gypsy-guitar teacher, a secret legend. Liam paid him in money and cigars and in return the man showed him everything he could, subtleties of rhythm and technique. He had only one other student, a man named Arthur Morelli who made a decent living as a session musician and played gypsy jazz whenever he could.

Liam brought Arthur Morelli back to Brighton Beach one night a few months after their arrival in the city. The baby was sleeping and Anna was cooking when they came in. She always tried to have something ready for Liam when he arrived home around eleven.

"Sausages," Morelli said. "What a nice surprise."

He was older than Liam, and Anna saw him register her age as they smiled at one another and said hello.

"Would you like some eggs?" she asked.

"I would love some eggs." Morelli sat at the kitchen table and crossed his legs. "So this is what you come home to," he said to Liam. "Lucky man."

"The luckiest," Liam said. He kissed Anna. "Is Chloe sleeping?"

Anna nodded.

"Your daughter?" Morelli asked.

"Eight months old," Liam said, and Anna understood how little he'd told Morelli about his life.

"What's this music we're listening to?" Morelli asked.

"They're called Baltica," Anna said. "I think they're from Canada." The CD played on the stereo on top of the fridge, quietly so it wouldn't wake Chloe. Baltica's sound made her think of snow. A high clear beat with electronic strings in the background sometimes and gentle static, repetitive echoing lyrics if there were any lyrics at all, *I always come to you, come to you, come to you* in the background while she beat eggs in a bowl with a fork.

"Anna, any chance of a hot-lemon-and-honey?" Liam asked.

"What exotic concoction is that?" Morelli's voice had a languor that she liked, as if he had all the time in the world. She realized how rarely she spoke with anyone besides Liam.

"Hot water," she said. She was filling the kettle. "You boil water and then squeeze a lemon into it and then you add some honey."

"It's an addiction," Liam said. "We're thinking about playing together, Anna. A guitar duo."

"Morelli and Deval," Morelli said.

"Deval and Morelli."

"With a bass, maybe," Morelli said. "Drums."

"It sounds like a nice idea," Anna said. "I used to spend a lot of time with a jazz quartet in high school."

"Did you play?"

"No," she said. "My friends and my sister did." Were they her friends? She'd slept with two of them and managed to betray both, put the third in danger by showing up at his dorm room, left the state without telling her sister. The pan blurred before her eyes. She blinked hard and flipped the omelet.

"It's the best idea ever," Liam said, "but I need to study a little more."

"By next spring," Morelli said. Liam had poured him a glass of wine, and he raised it. "To music."

"To next spring," Liam said, and the glasses clinked behind her.

She set their plates on the table and sat with them. This is part of my disguise. Not just dyed-blond hair but plates of eggs too. A part of her wanted to put her fork down and tell Morelli who she really was— Listen, I ran away three times before the tenth grade. Family Services in Florida has a file on me that's probably two inches thick. I stood before a wall with a can of pink spray paint and slept for three nights in the park. I have a tattoo but I was so out of my mind that night that I barely remember the needle. I stole a hundred and twenty-one thousand dollars from a drug dealer in Utah. I am not someone who has always stood in front of stoves cooking eggs for her boyfriend—but of course she didn't.

MONTHS LATER at Puppets Jazz Bar in Brooklyn Anna closed her eyes while they were playing and abruptly found herself disoriented, lost in the sound and unsure of where she was. She opened her eyes in alarm and clutched the seat of her chair. The darkness of the club was like the darknesses of all the other clubs where she'd gone to listen to gypsy jazz since Liam and Morelli had started playing regular gigs together. Where was Gavin tonight? She thought she'd die of shame every time she thought of him. She knew he was somewhere in this sharp and endless city, she knew he could walk in at any moment—did he still love music? And then perhaps she'd tell Liam she had a headache and find a way to leave with her face turned away, perhaps Gavin wouldn't recognize her at once with the short blond hair and that would buy her a few minutes. She was afraid to look toward the door.

Liam found her smoking on the sidewalk after the set.

"I don't know what I'm doing here," she said. "Coming out here like this with Chloe at home. Paying a fortune for a babysitter when you play for me and Chloe almost every night."

"That's just practicing," he said. "It isn't a performance. There's no Morelli, no bass, no drums."

"I like it better," she said. "I like it better when it's just us."

"Well," he said, "you don't have to come to these places if you don't want to." He turned to go back inside and the motion reminded her of another day months earlier in a hospital in Utah, lying on her back in the maternity ward, the look in Daniel's eyes when he saw the baby for the first time and turned away from her. I am always disappointing the ones I love.

. . .

LIAM CALLED Anna from a van between Miami and Sebastian on the morning of Chloe's first birthday. He'd gone to Florida to visit his mother and play a few gigs with Morelli—the Lemon Club in Sebastian, two places in Miami, stops in Celebration and Sarasota. She'd almost gone with him but it still seemed too soon. The thought of traveling with Chloe again was exhausting and her nerves overcame her at the last moment. She imagined Paul lying in wait for her among the palm trees. In Liam's absence the city was vast and gray and empty, an unformed mass pressed up against the neighborhood. She stayed close to the sea.

"I wish you'd come with me," he said.

"It isn't safe."

"I think if Paul were still looking," Liam said, "he would have found us by now."

"You don't think he's looking anymore?"

"I don't," Liam said. "I don't think it's that much money for a guy like him. Anna, you'll never guess who I ran into down here. Jack came to my gig in Sebastian."

"Jack's back in Florida?"

"He dropped out of school," Liam said. "A few weeks after I picked you up in Virginia. He came to see me at the Lemon Club."

"How is he?"

"He seems a little shaky, actually. How's everything over there, love?"

"Fine, completely fine. We're heading out to the beach."

"Give her a happy-birthday kiss for me," he said. She did, while she was bundling Chloe into the stroller.

Anna took Chloe down to the boardwalk. They walked for a while alongside the sea. It was November but the day was unseasonably warm. Anna eased the stroller off the boards and pushed it with great difficulty toward the water, until they were halfway between the boardwalk and the waves. The sand rising over the wheels, impossible to go farther. She knelt to free Chloe from the buckles and straps.

"Want to walk on the sand?" she asked Chloe, who was staring mesmerized over her shoulder. Chloe pointed and cried out "Wucks!" which meant ducks, which was her go-to word for birds of any kind. There were seagulls on the beach today, congregating around a dropped sandwich. Anna pulled Chloe's hat down over her ears, maneuvered her chubby hands into her mittens. "Happy birthday," she said. "I am so glad you're here."

Chloe looked at her and for an instant Anna was certain she understood.

"I would do anything for you," Anna whispered, but the moment had passed and Chloe was squirming now, kicking to be let out of the stroller. Anna lifted her free. They walked on the sand together, Chloe shrieking and laughing at the movement of seagulls and Anna holding Chloe's hand.

Eighteen

woman called Gavin a vulture once. She'd signed a bad
mortgage and she was coming undone. He sensed her de-
rangement as he came into her house, a tension in the air as
in the hour before an electrical storm. She was pinch-faced and furious,
sweating in her kitchen in a dress with an enormous flower pattern
that reminded him of the curtains in his first apartment. He'd been
working for Eilo for some weeks now and had decided that the people
who'd done this to themselves were the angriest. The ones who were
losing their houses because they'd already lost their jobs were despair-
ing. The ones who were losing their houses because they hadn't understood their mortgages wanted to kill him.

". . . Just a bloodsucking leech," the woman said, at the end of an
extended tirade.

"A leech." Gavin was trying to keep his voice mild. "A moment ago
you said I was a vulture."

"I'm going to be homeless," she said, "and you're making money
off me."

He couldn't argue with this. The arguments Eilo had given him— *You're performing a necessary service for a legitimate financial institution, if we don't do this someone else will, it was their responsibility to pay their mortgages and they didn't,* etc.—seemed weak as he stood in this peach-and-blue kitchen on a cul-de-sac near his old high school. He looked down at the papers in his hands.

"Perhaps," he said, "you were given bad advice when you signed the loan."

"Perhaps," she said, "you should get the fuck out of my kitchen."

"The next person after me will be a sheriff's deputy," he said. "I'm authorized to offer you—"

"I don't want your cash-for-keys deal. I want the people who are doing this to me to go to prison for the rest of their unnatural lives." Her voice had risen. He saw movement in the doorway. A small child was staring at him. The child's eyes were very large and there seemed to be applesauce on his face.

"I see," he said.

"Including you," she said, although she was losing steam now. There were tears in her eyes. "People like you should probably just die in prison."

"No one did this to you," Gavin said. "You did this to yourself." She was sputtering at him when he left. He drove four blocks, pulled over on a side street and spent some time staring at nothing, at pale stucco houses and close-cut lawns, each house its own kingdom with souls passing through. There were moments when he thought there might be something hidden in his job, some as-yet-ungrasped larger meaning amid all these people, their fear and their sadness and their disappearing homes, but mostly his work just made him dislike houses. These enormous anchors that people tied to their lives.

. . .

A few weeks after his arrival Gavin moved to Sebastian's empty downtown core. It was unclear to him how these streets had become so vacant, why everyone had decided that their fortunes lay on the perimeter, in an ever-expanding sprawl of split-level houses with screened-in back decks and kidney-shaped swimming pools and azaleas and snakes.

"Snakes?" Eilo repeated, in the car on the way to his new apartment with all his worldly belongings in the backseat. She wanted to see his new place. She didn't understand why he was moving.

"Pythons," Gavin said. "They just really bother me, ever since I did that story for the *Star.*"

"That makes no sense, Gavin. It's not like they're slithering all over the backyard."

Pythons weren't the reason. He wanted to be back on concrete, in the company of neon lights. He'd found a one-bedroom apartment above a Laundromat. It was small, but it would be his, and the rent was cheap. The neighborhood was a lost section of grid in between a handful of squat glass office complexes and a mall. His street was barely two blocks long and all but deserted, a parallel row of low run-down buildings that ended in the mall's parking lot, but he felt no menace. This street was only empty, not dangerous. There was an open-all-night Chinese restaurant across from his apartment.

They unloaded the car in the twilight. His worldly belongings didn't amount to much. Two boxes of new clothes, bedding that Eilo was giving him, the carry-on bag that he'd brought from New York.

"You could stay with me for longer, you know," Eilo said.

"I need my own place," he said. "I've been staying with you for weeks."

"You're making good money. You could rent a perfectly nice house somewhere."

"But I don't like houses," Gavin said. "I don't need that much space."

It wasn't just that. It was all the obvious things, of course—he thought he'd feel better about his life if he were living less obviously off the charity of his sister—but it was also that he needed a private base of operations from which to conduct his investigation. All his thoughts were of Anna and the little girl.

THE MORNING sunlight was brilliant in the new apartment. What was strange was that he felt less alone here than he had in New York. He thought it was perhaps because Karen had never occupied these rooms, therefore her absence didn't fill them. He purchased some cheap furniture, a bed and a mattress, a desk. He filled the second page of his notebook with questions. *Why does Daniel Smith dislike me? Where are Chloe and Anna? What does Sasha know? Who were Anna's friends in high school?*

It was almost like being a reporter again. He woke every morning thinking of his secret investigation, and it was the last thing he thought of before he went to sleep.

WHO HAD Anna been close to in high school? No one, it seemed, when he examined his memories. Almost everyone had liked her but she had had no close friends. Why hadn't he realized this at the time? He was trying to take notes on the people in her life one evening in the apartment, but his pen was stalled after her half-sister's name. Her friends had been a shifty, druggy crowd whom she'd mostly abandoned by the time he had known her, derelicts from her old school. He didn't know any of their names. She'd been nominally involved in the Drama program after she'd transferred to his school, but only to the extent that she was a stagehand in their productions and helped out with costumes and sets. If she'd had Drama friends, he didn't remember them. She'd been on the outskirts of the music scene, but only because she'd been dating him. She wasn't really interested in the kind of music that was being played at the school. She'd spent time with the quartet and with their occasional singer, Taylor.

He found himself reaching for the phone almost without meaning to. His fingertips still retained the memory of Karen's cell number, the pattern on the keypad.

"It's me," he said.

"It's you." Karen's voice was neutral. "How are you, Gavin?"

"I moved back to Florida," he said. "I lost my job."

"Yeah, I saw that story about you." Her voice softened then, as if she'd seen him wince. "I'm sorry. That's probably the last thing you want to talk about."

"It's okay," he said. "I don't even know why I did it." There was a moment of silence.

"You blew up your career," she said, "and you don't know why?"

"It was difficult after you left," he said. "You know it wasn't what I wanted." She was silent. "And then something happened, I found out I had a—" But children were a terrible topic—"I got some news," he said, floundering. "I was horribly distracted. I think I lost my mind a little bit."

She had nothing to say to this.

"But anyway," he said, "how have you been?"

"I'm okay." She was quiet for a moment. "Florida," she said. "I thought you hated hot weather."

"I didn't have anywhere else to go."

"You always said you'd move to Chicago," she said, "if you ever got tired of New York."

"Maybe I'll go there someday. I've been saving money. You remember that weekend we spent there?" The memory had ambushed him that morning in the shower. It had been spring and the trees were blooming. They'd bought pretzels from a street vendor and looked at the animals in Lincoln Park Zoo. They'd had a picnic and Karen had fallen asleep on the grass in Hyde Park.

"It was a nice weekend," she said. "Listen, Gavin, I have to get back to work. I'd love to talk longer, but . . ."

"You got a new job? Congratulations." She'd been an administrative assistant at Lehman Brothers until the day the firm collapsed.

"I'm a temporary night-shift proofreader," she said. "It barely qualifies as employment. Goodnight, Gavin."

"Goodnight," he said. He disconnected and held the phone in his hands for a moment. The apartment was silent except for the air conditioner, the soft hum of the fridge.

Gavin went downstairs to the quiet street. The Laundromat below his apartment was alight, dryers spinning, a woman folding laundry. He drove to the house where Anna and Sasha's mother had lived, but now the name on the mailbox was Sabharwal and there were small unfamiliar children playing in the front yard, throwing a Frisbee that shone white in the gathering darkness.

GAVIN LET a few days slide past in the heat. The temperature was soaring and he found it difficult to be outside. It was almost a pleasure to lose himself in work. The foreclosures were endless. He had as many houses to inspect as he could handle. But he couldn't stop thinking about Anna or the child, an obsessive worry that tugged him out of sleep at night, so the investigation continued. He found Taylor after a half-hour of online stalking, called her and drove at her invitation to a gated community in a section of town that he thought might not have existed when he'd lived here before. He waited ten minutes in his car for his turn with the security guard, who was taking his time interrogating a contractor in a pickup truck.

Inside the gates of the subdivision the streets curved around a park, and Taylor's house was on one of the outer loops. It was pink with gardens all around it, a fountain out front. When he cut the engine the quiet was almost complete. He got out of the car and stood for a moment listening to the falling water. The windows of the house reflected the sky and dark palm fronds.

"I'm sorry I'm late," he said, when she opened the door. "The gates—" he made a vague gesture back toward the entrance, but she only smiled at him blankly. "I had to wait forever to get through," he said. "The security guard."

"I don't understand," she said, although not unkindly, so he started from the beginning again and said, "Sorry I'm late," which seemed to reset the conversation. In her immaculate blue-and-white kitchen she poured lemonade over ice and talked about her life. A year in a music program at a school he'd never heard of, a shift in priorities that led to a BA in finance and then to a job at a bank, a marriage—"Todd's at a conference in Miami, otherwise he'd be here"—unrealized dreams of traveling the world—"I always thought I'd see everything, but then I had kids, so, you know"—and the kids, yes, Amy and Jaden, twins, at their summer day camp this afternoon. Gavin had never gone to camp as a kid—his pediatrician had suggested that a boy who made repeated visits to the ER with heat exhaustion was perhaps not ideally suited to outdoor summer activities in Florida—and he found himself imagining what it might be like. Lakes and sunlight, bright water. It would be nice to get out of the suburbs, he thought. There was so much green here, such riotous growth, but nothing close to true wilderness. When was the last time he'd been away from a city, from a suburb, from clipped lawns and cement? He was thinking about the time he'd gone camping with Karen in upstate New York, the perfect quiet in the morning, a bird gliding over a lake, the smell of tent fabric in sunlight. He realized that Taylor was still talking. He had been looking at her and smiling and nodding as his thoughts wandered. She was still beautiful. The same blue eyes and cascading blond hair, the same smile. He found himself wondering idly if she might want to sleep with him. She was talking about her garden now, and had been for a while. His gaze drifted to the microwave clock. She'd been talking about herself for a little under an hour.

"Well," she said finally, "it's just so great to catch up with you. How's *your* life been?"

This was a competition, he realized. She'd presented him with a gorgeous life and now she wanted to hold his life up to the light and compare. He thought about the photograph of himself on the front page of the *New York Star* and briefly considered spinning something halfway plausible, I am a famous reporter taking some time off to write a book on Florida's exotic wildlife problem, but he didn't want to lie anymore and he knew he wasn't famous so much as disgraced.

"Well," he said, "I went to Columbia. I was a reporter at the *New York Star*. I met a girl and we were going to get married, but then she had a miscarriage in the second trimester and she didn't want to be with me anymore after that. I lost my job and moved back to Florida. I'm selling real estate with my sister."

"Oh," Taylor said. She was looking at him a little desperately, her half-smile slipping. She wanted lightness, he realized. She wanted to

be saved by a self-deprecating one-liner that might keep things moving. She'd told him nothing very serious about herself. If her life had
held the slightest trace of sorrow or any disappointments deeper than
her postponed ambition to travel the world, she'd kept it out of the nar-
rative. He was acutely aware of the soft hum of central air conditioning, the far-off drone of a lawnmower.

"But anyway," he said, "do you still keep up with anyone from high
school?"

"Oh, I do." She smiled to thank him for the conversational rescue
and then launched a twenty-minute monologue concerning people
whom Gavin hadn't thought of in a decade, trips she'd taken with
her high school girlfriends, gossip about people he barely remembered,
the last reunion she'd been to. Kind of a sad affair actually, just
fifty or so people standing around under streamers in the high school
gymnasium—

"Was Anna Montgomery there?" Gavin asked. "You two were in
the same grade, weren't you?"

"Anna? Your high school girlfriend? No. I mean yes, we were in
the same year, but she wasn't there at the reunion. You know, I haven't
seen her in so long," she said.

"Do you remember the last time you saw her?"

"Hoping to rekindle the flame?" Taylor widened her eyes as she
said this, and Gavin understood for the first time that she was killingly
bored.

"We were close," he said, "and I just wanted to find out what'd
become of her. It's like she disappeared from the face of the earth."

"You should maybe ask Daniel about her," Taylor said.

"Really. Why Daniel?"

"It's probably nothing. But do you remember the Lola Quartet's
last concert?"

"Behind the school," Gavin said. "We were playing on the back of your father's pickup truck."

"Yes," she said. "Exactly. I have such vivid memories of that concert, I guess because it was the last one. Do you know, I haven't sung 'Bei Mir Bist Du Schön' since that night? And it was one of my favorite songs. But anyway, that was the last time I saw her. We were playing that song and I remember you took off in the middle of it, just ran into the woods like you were going to be sick or something. We didn't know what the matter was but we were winding down anyway, that was our last song of the night. It was something like two o'clock in the morning, and I remember I saw Anna there. I noticed because she hadn't been there before, it was like she'd just stepped out of the woods, and I thought it was weird for her to come so late in the evening when everything was done, but I was talking to my boyfriend at the time— you remember Brian? That guy who did the penguin imitations?"

Gavin didn't remember Brian or his penguin imitations. He nodded anyway.

"I was talking to him, so I didn't talk to Anna when I saw her. But I remember I looked up a while later," she said, "and she was walking around the side of the school with Daniel, and he was carrying his instrument and she was carrying a duffel bag. I thought it was strange for them to be going off together. I mean she was your girlfriend, not his. But there'd been all this talk about her and I thought, you know, we're all friends anyway so it's probably nothing. But then I remembered it later because when school started up again in September she wasn't there, and it occurred to me that that had been the last time I'd seen her, disappearing with Daniel that night. I never saw her again."

"What kind of talk?" Gavin asked.

"What?"

"You said there'd been all this talk about her. What kind of talk had there been?"

Taylor looked away from him and stood up. "Oh, you know how high school was," she said. "We were all just bored suburban kids telling vicious rumors about each other."

Did he know how high school was? He knew he should, but his memories of those years were for the most part hazy. He remembered small details. The clean waxed-floor scent of the corridors, a band teacher named Mr. Winters raising his baton with pure joy in his eyes, the way sunlight angled through the windows of a particular classroom in the afternoons, Daniel and Sasha and Jack all around him with their instruments and Anna listening somewhere off to the side, long hours in the van driving to music competitions, the pine-scented-disinfectant smell of the locker rooms, a red pencil case with a zipper. "Like what?" he asked. "What were the rumors you remember?"

She was refilling their glasses.

"Just, you know, unkind things . . ."

"Come on, Taylor, I can take it. What were they saying about her?"

"They said—you know, it's *stupid*, just stupid rumors—they said she was . . . well, they said she was *seeing* people. They said it was a bit of a crowded field there right before she left school, toward the end." She returned the lemonade pitcher to the fridge. "I'm sorry. It's nasty. I know it's not true."

"How would you know that?"

"Well, it's just—I guess I should say I hope it's not true. I don't like that kind of thing. They said she was sleeping around, and then the story was that she'd gone to live with her aunt in Georgia, but there was this crazy rumor that she'd left school because she was pregnant and had a miscarriage, or sometimes the rumor was that she'd had a baby and was still living in Florida, just one or two towns over. You know, just rumors. Crazy stuff."

"What about Anna's sister?" Gavin asked. "You ever see Sasha around?"

"Never," Taylor said. "I don't know what happened to her."

He left her house soon after that—"We should do this again," they told one another without conviction—and drove out of the closed streets of the subdivision, past the security guard and out into the larger world. It was five o'clock. He drove to the police station and parked his car within view of the front door—the station shared parking with a mall and an auto-body shop, so he felt reasonably inconspicuous—and waited until Daniel appeared in the station doorway around six.

Daniel didn't move quickly. He was slow, distracted, jingling the change in his pockets and staring at the pavement. He looked up when Gavin said his name.

"You're so persistent," Daniel said. "I admire that about you."

"Daniel, I need to talk to you."

"I don't really have a lot to say to you, Gavin. I don't think we know each other very well." Daniel had resumed his slow progress across the parking lot. "High school was a very long time ago."

"Daniel—" He was almost dancing at Daniel's side, so agitated that he couldn't be still. "Daniel, every time I ask anyone about Anna, they tell me to talk to you."

"Really."

"Daniel, I know she had a baby. I think the baby was mine."

"That's none of my business," Daniel said, "and again, that was really quite a while ago, wasn't it?" He swatted at a drip of sweat on his forehead. "Why don't you drop it, Gavin?"

"Because I think she's my kid," Gavin said. "I want to find her and make sure she's okay."

"And make sure she's okay?" They'd reached Daniel's car, a gray Jeep with a dented fender and rust on the side. "If you'd been paying more attention ten years ago—"

"I want to do the right thing. I'm trying to do something good here."

Daniel looked at him for a moment.

"This is just a shot at redemption for you," he said. "You don't even know the kid. You fucked up your life in New York and you feel like a failure, so now you want to do something good."

"So the kid exists," Gavin said. "Thank you for confirming that."

"Now that we've established your superb interrogative skills, I'd appreciate it tremendously if you'd step away from my car."

"Can you please just tell me where Anna is? That's all I want to know."

"This isn't something you want to be involved in." Daniel was getting into the Jeep. "I don't want to see you again. Are we clear?"

Gavin stepped back, stung, and Daniel closed the Jeep door.

"I've known you since the first grade," Gavin said. "All I want is to talk to you for a minute."

"If you knew more, you'd thank me," Daniel said. "Can you just forget about this? All of it? I'm giving you a gift here."

He left Gavin standing alone in the heat of the parking lot. Gavin thought for a moment about whether he could forget about it, but found that he couldn't.

THE NEXT afternoon at five o'clock Gavin was waiting in the parking lot outside the police station again, but this time he stayed in his car. He had bought pizza and orange soda, and the pizza had given the car a stale pepperoni smell that he knew was going to linger. He had to keep the engine running, because without the air conditioner the car heated quickly and he was afraid he'd black out if it got too hot. He'd run out of orange soda and was debating whether to make a run for another bottle when Daniel emerged from the police station. Daniel crossed the parking lot to his Jeep, and Gavin eased his car out of the lot behind him.

H E H A D two jobs after that. There was the job he did for Eilo, the eight or nine hours he spent at her service. Driving to visit and photograph houses, negotiating with the residents of foreclosed homes, writing up property descriptions at his desk. Eilo liked his work. He neither enjoyed nor particularly disliked the occupation. He wanted only to reach the evening, when the real work began. His secret investigation, the story he was tracking, the focused hours spent waiting for Daniel to appear in the doorway of the police station.

Gavin recognized himself in the evenings—a newspaperman, a private investigator, a man who chased stories and sought out clues—but he didn't recognize Daniel. It was almost inconceivable that this was the same Daniel he'd known all his life until he'd left for New York. He wouldn't have imagined that a person could change so completely, but then, he didn't recognize Jack either.

Daniel always came out of the police station with slumped shoulders, walking slowly with his hands in his pockets. He had an air of perpetual distraction, lost to the world, which made it easy to trail him undetected. He seemed to work six days a week. On two of those days he went to the elementary school, where he picked up his four children. They swarmed all around him, a very small set of twins and two a little bigger. They showed him drawings they'd made and ribbons for accomplishments, papers with stars on them that caught the light from a distance, and in those moments Daniel was a changed man. He smiled, he touched their hair and said things that made them giggle, he inspected every ribbon and drawing. He drove them to his home—a house that looked from the outside to be too small for four children—in a new part of the suburbs that at first Gavin didn't know very well, a section that seemed to have radiated outward from the blank epicenter of a golf course.

Divorced, Gavin decided. Because on the other days Daniel took a different route and drove home alone, avoided the vicinity of the elementary school even though driving near the school would have been faster, parked his car in the driveway and walked to the front door without looking up from his feet. A light went on in one room on the ground floor. All the other windows stayed dark. Some time later dinner arrived, usually in a pizza delivery car. Gavin always parked down the street behind another vehicle, cut his engine and opened the window. He sat alone in his car, watching and waiting, sometimes falling asleep.

He was frightening himself.

THE PROBLEM was that Gavin wasn't really sure what he was looking for, or whether he'd recognize it if he saw it. Daniel's routine was absolute. It wasn't that Gavin was necessarily expecting Anna or the child to simply appear at Daniel's house, if Anna was even in Florida, if Anna was still alive, if the child hadn't vanished into the hell of a homeless shelter. He was looking for something more subtle, a sign of some kind, but he couldn't imagine what it would look like or if he might have missed it a dozen times already. He brought his beloved 1973 Yashica and took photographs of Daniel leaving the police station, photographs of Daniel's house and of the pizza-delivery guy, but he didn't know what he was documenting aside from Daniel's apparently unremarkable life. He was tired from the late nights, and frustrated. In the office with Eilo he drank cup after cup of coffee until his heart raced.

There was more work than they could handle, a new foreclosure or two every day. She was talking about hiring more people. She had a gardener working for her now, a quiet man named Carlos who mowed lawns and planted flowers in front of the houses they were trying to sell. Sometimes instead of going to the police station to follow Daniel home he stayed at Eilo's house and they ate dinner together picnic-style on the living room floor, the way they had when he'd first come down reeling from New York.

"What do you do with yourself in the evenings?" she asked.

"Not much," he said. "Read, watch TV, do crossword puzzles. Drive around." He'd considered telling her about the search for Anna and the little girl, but there was something he liked about having one part of his life that was only his. He'd lost so much in New York and had been left with so little.

On a Friday afternoon he drove back to Mortimer Street. It was one of those golden-light afternoons when the suburbs are at their most beautiful. The air dense with humidity and the heat like a diving bell, sound muffled within. Gavin rang the doorbell. No one came to the door. He stood for a while on the cracked front step before he remembered Jack's tent in the backyard.

He walked around the side of the house, pushing through overgrown bushes that he couldn't identify, dark waxy leaves and bright flowers. An airplane droned in the sky overhead. He stepped out into the yard, grass up to his knees.

Gavin heard his name, but it was a moment before he saw Jack. He was sitting alone under an orange tree in a white plastic lawn chair, a bottle of Gatorade in his hand. There was a book open on his lap.

"You came back," Jack said.

"Of course I did." There were two other plastic chairs in the shade of the orange tree. He sat in the one closest to Jack. "Were you working today?"

Jack was wearing what looked like a uniform, a red polo shirt and black trousers. He was covered in dust. "My friend's got a company," he said. "I help rip carpets out."

"That sounds difficult."

"It's okay. It pays enough to get by." Jack didn't seem to want to talk about it.

"What are you reading?"

Jack passed him the book. *Django Reinhardt: A Life.* It was dog-eared and battered, small tears along the bottom of the dust jacket. Gavin opened the front cover and read the inscription: *To my beloved son Liam on the occasion of his high school graduation with love and congratulations.—G.*

"I wonder who Liam was," Gavin said. He'd found similar inscriptions in books he'd bought used.

"Liam? My roommate from college. You just missed him, actually." Jack took the book back from Gavin and set it on the grass by his lawn chair. "He used to do this thing," Jack said, "back in music school. It was pretty funny, he'd be drunk or whatever, and he'd say—" Jack raised his Gatorade bottle and dropped his voice—"'My name is Liam Deval, and I am going to be famous.'"

"Wait," Gavin said, "Liam Deval? The guitarist? I used to listen to him play in New York."

"Yeah, he was up there for a long time. Always meant to visit him there." Jack's gaze was distant. Aside from his disastrous foray into South Carolina, Jack had never left the state of Florida.

"But he's here now?"

"Yeah, he's visiting Anna," Jack said.

"What?"

"I didn't—I'm sorry," Jack said, "I'm sorry, I always screw up." He was reaching into his pocket. Gavin looked away while he measured three pills into his hand.

"Did you just say Liam Deval's in Florida because of Anna?"

"I can't talk about it," Jack said. "I can't talk about Anna. I promised I wouldn't."

"Promised who?"

"Deval," Jack said. He looked like he wanted to cry. "Forget I said anything."

"It's okay," Gavin said. "It's okay. We won't talk about Anna."

Jack nodded. He was looking at his feet.

"But maybe you could tell me about Deval," Gavin said. "I really love his music."

"Yeah, he's good. Really good. I mean, I was sort of good. I maybe had something. But Deval, he had the music." Jack smiled. "He was trying to be Django Reinhardt. And you know what? He might be as good as Reinhardt was."

"Where's he staying? I'd love to meet him."

"I don't know," Jack said. "A hotel somewhere, I guess. Oh wait, wait, he told me." Jack rested his head on the back of the chair and stared into space. He was still for so long that Gavin glanced up to see what he was looking at. The leaves of the orange tree were brilliant green against the hazy sky. "The Decker," Jack said.

"The Decker?"

"It was something like that. The Dracker, or the Decker, or something."

"He say if he was coming back?" The heat was making Gavin's head swim. He wanted to lie down.

"No," Jack said, "but I hope he comes back. He said he was going to go visit Daniel."

"Of course he was."

"Did you just say something?"

"Nothing. Hey, is he playing anywhere while he's here?"

"Sure," Jack said. "He's got a gig at the Lemon Club."

THE LEMON Club had been open for thirty years and in high school Gavin had gone there a few times, trying to be sophisticated, trying to grasp hold of something that he might use to pull himself up toward adulthood, but he could never find it and as a teenager he'd felt uneasy there, pitifully young, out of his depth and unable to swim. The Lemon Club was a stop on the way to Miami and he'd seen a few big names there. The one he remembered best was a trumpet player, Bert Johnston. He'd brought Anna there in his last year of high school. They'd sat together at a round table just big enough for his Pepsi and her ginger ale—he wished he could order wine for both of them but didn't want to risk being laughed at by the bartender in front of her—and they listened to Bert Johnston's trumpet wail and sing. When Anna reached for his hand he didn't notice, only realized later that her hand was in his and he couldn't remember how it had ended up there. It was too warm in the club, the air conditioner laboring and spitting water over the door, and normally this would have bothered him but that night he was transfixed, that night things were becoming clearer. He was watching Bert Johnston and realizing that he wasn't going to be a musician. It wasn't an unpleasant revelation, just an understanding that his life was going to go in one direction and not another.

"I'll never be that good," he told Anna later, not upset, just stating the fact, but she mistook his tone and tried to console him. The thought of the practice it would take to be a professional musician made him weary. He was reading a lot of noir and wearing a fedora, and he'd already developed backup plans. If he couldn't be a jazz musician he was going to be a newspaperman. If he couldn't be a newspaperman he was going to be a private detective.

The Lemon Club was already a little decrepit in his memories, but it had declined further since then and now the strip-mall parking lot was cracked and had a small palm tree growing out of the middle of it. Most of the other tenants were gone, sections of the mall boarded up. The only other tenants were an off-track betting parlor, an evangelical church and a pizza place with a torn awning.

In his memories the interior was glamorous, but all night places are cheaper-looking in daylight and with the curtains opened the light picked up the grit in the upholstery, the swimming galaxies of dust motes in the air.

"Help you?" the bartender asked, and Gavin realized he was the only customer. The bartender wasn't the sullen-looking old man Gavin remembered. He was young and blond and looked somehow like a lifeguard.

"I was hoping to see the listings for the next couple months," Gavin said. "I heard a jazz guitarist I like might be coming through town." He realized that it was stupid to say "jazz" in that sentence—it was after all a club devoted to this and no other kind of music—but the new bartender was more forgiving than the old bartender had been and didn't even smirk or tell him to get lost, just produced a photocopy of a calendar from behind the bar and scanned it for a moment before he passed it to Gavin.

"I think you maybe mean Deval?" he said. "Only guitarist I see here."

The calendar read *Deval & Morelli*, but Morelli's name had been crossed out.

"Can I keep this?" Gavin asked. The bartender nodded. Deval was scheduled to play in three nights. Gavin went to Jack's house every day after work and sat with him in the backyard under the orange tree, but Liam Deval didn't appear and Jack revealed nothing except his interest in jazz history and the extent of his pill addiction.

On Friday Gavin bought a dark red shirt with gray pinstripes, drove to the Lemon Club an hour before the set and established himself at a small table in the darkest corner, farthest from the stage. He wanted to be invisible. Only a few other people were here at this hour—a couple sitting at a table by the stage, a man at the end of the bar with a tattoo of a goldfish on his neck. Gavin ordered a pint of Guinness. He'd brought his notebook with him, as if he really were either a newspaperman or a detective. His new shirt had cufflinks and he caught himself fiddling with them as he waited.

The club filled slowly. A bass player made his way between the tables and began tuning his instrument. He was followed a few minutes later by a drummer, but there was no sign of Deval. A saxophonist had appeared—a saxophonist? With Deval, who so far as Gavin knew only ever played with Morelli, a bassist, sometimes a drummer?—and he was talking to the bass player while the drummer assembled his kit. At nine twenty the bartender came to the stage and tapped lightly on a microphone. There'd been a substitution, he said. Liam Deval had had to remain in New York at the last minute, a family emergency, but fortunately the great Chicago saxophonist Pedro Lang—who looked too young to be called the great anything, in Gavin's opinion—was in town a day early for his show tomorrow night and had graciously agreed to bless them with his presence two nights in a row and so without further ado, etc., and applause filled the room while Gavin finished his beer.

He thought about leaving but it was nice to be out in the evening for once, away from the quiet of his apartment with the television and the recorded music and his notes, not waiting in his car outside Daniel's house like a stalker. The saxophone player really was great, mesmerizing actually. Everyone who'd arrived to hear Deval stayed to watch him except for the man at the end of the bar whom Gavin had noticed when he came in, who settled up with the bartender and left just before the music began.

In the morning Gavin sat at his desk in Eilo's rec room looking at yellow-pages listings of local motels with names similar to Decker or Dracker, run-down places by highways—*Cable TV! Jacuzzi in Penthouse Suite!*—and trying to ignore his headache. The saxophonist had been good and it was a pleasure to lose himself in music, to sit alone without having to talk to anyone. There was a span of time when he'd thought of nothing but the sound.

The Draker Motel had purchased a square ad with a minuscule photograph in the middle of it, so small that it could have been almost any motel anywhere. He looked it up on the Internet and was momentarily dazzled by the website's flashing red text—*Cable TV!!! Convenient Location!!!*—and a picture of a small white dog that he supposed must belong to the owner. Convenient to what? He looked it up on a map. It was, he supposed, convenient to the interstate.

He drove to a part of the suburbs that was close up against the edge of the wilderness, although it had occurred to Gavin that what he thought of as wilderness might just be a band of wildly lush greenery with another suburb approaching undetected from the other side, like two teams of miners tunneling toward one another under the earth. The streets out here were wide and industrial, self-storage facilities, a junkyard. The Draker Motel stood at the end of an almost-deserted cul-de-sac, two stories of stucco with a balcony running along the second floor.

Gavin stayed in his car for a moment looking out at the heat waves shimmering over the parking lot, put on his fedora and ventured out. The motel office was a small wood-paneled room with tiny palm trees running up and down the wallpaper, an air conditioner rattling in the window. The girl behind the counter looked no older than fifteen.

"You have a nice website," he said. "I liked the picture of the dog."

"Thanks," the girl said warily.

"I'm looking for a guest, a friend of mine. Do you have a Liam Deval staying here?"

"I'm not supposed to say the names of guests," she said.

He opened his wallet and laid three twenties on the counter. "If you're not allowed to say," he said, "maybe I could just take a quick glance at your computer?"

She glanced over her shoulder, slipped the money into her pocket.

"I might get in trouble," she said.

He laid another twenty on the counter. "But do you think anyone would notice? It'd only take me a minute."

She bit her lip.

"Maybe you were in the back," he said. "You didn't hear me come in."

She swiveled the computer monitor so he could see it and pushed the keyboard and mouse toward him, took the money and vanished behind a beaded curtain. He wasn't familiar with the software, but it didn't seem complicated. It was possible to bring up a list of guests' names with a few keystrokes. Liam Deval's name wasn't in the registry.

He went through the list again. There was a D. Reinhardt in room 18. Gavin left the tiny chilled office with its palm-tree-print curtains and laboring air conditioner, followed the numbers down a line of closed doors. The heat was staggering. This side of the hotel was exposed to the full glare of sunlight, the stucco hot to the touch.

He knocked on the door of room 18 and the curtains in the window flickered, but too briefly and too slightly to make out a face.

"Who is it?" The voice came through the window, which he saw now was open just a crack.

"My name's Gavin Sasaki," he said to the curtains. "I'm looking for Liam Deval."

"I don't know you, Gavin," the man said. "Why are you here?"

The heat was making Gavin dizzy. "It's about Anna Montgomery," he said. "May I come in?"

"I have to make a phone call first," the man said. Was this Liam Deval's voice? He couldn't tell. Deval hadn't talked much at Barbès and everyone sounds different behind a microphone. "Could you wait out there for a moment?"

"Of course," Gavin said.

He had been waiting outside for no more than a few minutes when the old fear began to come over him. It was a hundred degrees, heat radiating from the cement and from the building's exterior wall. He was already sweating. Cars shimmered in the parking lot. The angle of the sun was such that the second-floor balcony cast no shade. He glanced at his watch, turned his back on the sun and closed his eyes. Thinking of ice cubes, of orange sherbet, of snow. When he opened his eyes again it seemed to him that a long time had passed so he called out toward the window, "Hello, could I possibly come in?" but there was no answer. He wondered if he was being watched, if Deval—if that voice was Deval, if his instinct that the D. Reinhardt in the hotel log and Deval were the same person was correct and the man in the room wasn't just some malevolent stranger—was still on the phone.

Gavin was too hot for his fedora, so he took it off. He leaned forward, let his forehead rest on the stucco between the window and the door. He was going to get sick from staying out in the sun like this but the least he could do was wait, wasn't it, with Anna and Chloe perhaps so close? The thought of being a father. It seemed possible that they might be in the motel room, mere feet from him on the other side of the wall. It seemed to him that he'd been waiting for a very long time. He wanted to look at his watch again, but it seemed like too much effort to raise his arm. His thoughts drifted. He could help them in some way, do the right thing. He had a job, he could contribute, maybe even go to Chloe's school plays. Maybe they'd all eat dinner together sometimes, a sort of provisional family. He'd wanted his own family for as long as he could remember. He was having some trouble staying upright. His fedora, he realized, had fallen from his hand.

"Please!" he called again, toward the window.

"You're going to have to wait," the voice said. A note of panic. "I can't reach anyone."

"Who are you calling? Daniel?"

"How do you know Daniel?"

"How do I know him? I don't know." Gavin was aware that he was mumbling. He couldn't think of how to explain how he knew Daniel; the whole mundane history of elementary school and high school, first grade field trips to museums and seventh grade parties in basements and the jazz quartet seemed like too much to explain all of a sudden. "It's been a long time." He was having trouble concentrating. "Listen," he said, louder now, "I'm not going to give up. I'll stay here all night. I'm going to keep chasing Anna and Chloe forever if I have to."

"Forever?" the man's voice was almost squeaky now. "Are there others with you?"

"What? No, I'm alone," Gavin said. "I'm alone." It wouldn't be so bad to take a short nap, would it, just to drift off for a moment or two? He felt too sick to open his eyes. How long had he been out here? He was seized by a sudden chill. What was strange was that the wall of the motel was softening. He was sinking into it.

There was a sound as if from a long way off, and he realized that the door had opened beside him. Gavin stood upright with tremendous difficulty. His legs were like water.

The man's voice was nervous. "Why did you come here?"

Gavin was so dizzy now that he could no longer see. A blinding wash of swimming dots over his vision, a haze.

"I'm here for Anna," he said. The open doorway was all cold air and black shadow, a sanctuary—he forced himself to move and lurched forward, trying to get inside before he blacked out.

"Hold it right there!" the man called out, from somewhere farther back in the room. "Don't come any closer! I don't know who you are!"

But Gavin knew only that he had to get inside, into the cool. He kept moving.

"Stop," the man cried, "oh God, please," but Gavin didn't. He heard a dull sound but didn't immediately understand what it had to do with the sudden pain singing out from his left arm, his rapidly numbing hand. He fell to his knees.

"I think I have heatstroke," he mumbled, to no one in particular. He fell forward then and closed his eyes, soft carpet. His shirt was wet and he was impossibly tired. It seemed like a good moment to sleep, and he drifted off into a confused dream about New York City, Sasha, the pleasant chaos of the *Star* newsroom, a trumpet.

Nineteen

The Lola Quartet's last concert:

Anna threw the paper airplane and took a step backward, dry leaves breaking under her shoes. The quartet was playing on the back of Taylor's dad's pickup truck in the night heat with dancers all around them. Daniel was playing with his eyes closed. She watched the airplane rise through the air and descend, the way Gavin looked up a moment before it landed at his feet. The bass solo was ending. Gavin lifted his trumpet to his lips and he half-smiled at her around the mouthpiece before he blew the first note, but she couldn't bring herself to smile back. In a moment he would unfold the paper airplane and read the two-word message it carried, but at this instant he was playing "Bei Mir Bist Du Schön," the quartet's signature piece, the horns in perfect unison, and Taylor was singing again. Gavin let Jack's saxophone take over the brass line. He stooped to pick up the airplane, but Anna couldn't bear to watch him read it so she stepped behind a bush. A childish desire to hide, to disappear for a moment. When she was little she used to stay for hours under her bed.

She heard footsteps approaching. Gavin walked close by her where she stood against the leaves, but he was coming from a haze of light into darkness and he was momentarily a little blind. She kept still, almost not breathing. Gavin called her name, but he didn't look back. He was moving quickly, his trumpet in his hand, and he receded into the trees and bushes until she couldn't see his white t-shirt anymore.

She waited a moment before she turned back toward the lights. The song was done, everyone tired and a little high, people dispersing and picking up water bottles and beer cans from the grass. Jack was standing by the truck, flirting with a twelfth grader whose name Anna didn't know. She saw Taylor looking at her, but Taylor's boyfriend whispered something in her ear just then and they both turned away from Anna. Sasha was packing up her drum kit and this was the hardest thing, not going to her at that moment, not telling her about her departure. Anna and Daniel had agreed that even Sasha couldn't know where they were going, not yet. She would call Sasha when they were settled in Utah. Daniel wrestled his bass into its enormous carrying case, lowered it down from the truck and jumped after it.

"I'm glad you're here," he said. Anna knew he hadn't seen the paper airplane—he played his solos with his eyes closed—but she still felt like a traitor. She wasn't sure in that moment what she'd hoped to accomplish with the airplane note. She couldn't tell Gavin she was leaving, she couldn't tell anyone, everything had all been decided in these past two weeks, long afternoons of cutting school and sitting in Daniel's basement talking about the plan, which was at first so wild that two weeks was how much time they'd needed to talk it into reality.

"Did you see where Gavin went?" he asked. "Did he see you?"

"No," she said. "He didn't see me." She looked back at the trees, where Gavin had disappeared. She wasn't sure how far back the woods went, if it might be possible to get lost in them.

Daniel glanced around. The others were drifting away in twos and threes, no one paying attention to them.

"Why don't you get your bag," he murmured.

Her duffel bag was waiting at the base of a tree. She felt piercingly lonely and in that moment she wanted nothing more than to see Gavin again. She stood for a second at the edge of the shadows, but Gavin didn't emerge and Daniel was waiting for her. They walked together away from the pickup truck where Jack and Sasha and Taylor and a half-dozen others still lingered, their voices fading into sounds of frogs and crickets. Anna and Daniel turned the corner around the side of the gym and she felt safer then, out of sight, fireflies rising silently from the grass all around her.

Daniel had parked his station wagon at the far end of the student parking lot. He struggled to fit the bass into the back while she sat in the passenger seat, staring out the side window at the pavement bright with moonlight, the lights of the school. A thought: I might never see this place again. This didn't make her as wistful as she'd thought it would. It stirred nothing in her except a vague unease. Daniel dropped into the driver's seat.

"Ready?" he asked.

"Yes." She was impatient with the question. What had she been doing these past two weeks, spending time with Daniel and avoiding Gavin, if not readying herself for this? The passing streets were dense with memory. It was unfathomable that before morning they'd be across state lines, like imagining driving off the edge of a map. She had never left Florida before.

"You'll get to come back someday," Daniel said, as if reading her thoughts. "Once this all blows over. This doesn't have to be forever."

Anna only nodded. She didn't feel like talking anymore. She

realized then why she'd sent the paper airplane sailing through the air to Gavin: it was too late for anything to change now, the plan was already in motion and it was the only plan she'd been able to come up with that she thought might save her and keep her child out of foster care, they were going to Utah and she risked everything if Gavin or anyone else knew, but she at least wanted him to know she was sorry. She wished now that she'd written more.

They drove all night. Daniel was nervous, talking to fill the silence. His aunt was a good person, he said. He'd been visiting Utah in the summertime all his life and he knew for a fact that his aunt didn't talk to his parents, who he thought would probably cry if they knew he'd fathered a child out of wedlock. He'd told his aunt about the situation and she'd said they could stay at her house, he said. The aunt just wanted to help, because that's what good people do in situations like this, they help, and if there were more people like that in the world—

"Daniel," she said, "it's okay. We're going to be okay."

"He's your boyfriend," he said after a moment. "I don't like to think of myself as the kind of guy who steals girls from their boyfriends."

"You didn't steal me," she said. She was tired. It was all too much, actually. She was feeling queasy again. The radio was off. They moved in silence up the interstate. Daniel was looking straight ahead, his face illuminated only occasionally by passing lights. He was wearing his hair in an Afro that year, and it turned briefly into a halo each time a set of headlights passed. "Daniel," she said, "I'm going to try to sleep for a bit."

"Okay." He sounded scared and uncertain, and it occurred to her as she was drifting off to sleep that both of them were very young. She was looking at Daniel's dark hands on the wheel and thinking, Please, oh please let the child be black.

.   .   .

WHEN ANNA thought about Utah she had an impression of desert and also an impression of ski slopes, and the two images didn't fit together in her mind. But in the car with Daniel she imagined a house, orderly and large, with a couple of rooms set aside for her and Daniel and the baby. Their own bathroom maybe. A suite! It was a long drive, two days broken up by roadside motels, and there were moments when she wished they could travel forever. A state of suspension, sitting still in the passenger seat while the landscape changed all around her. Daniel did all the driving, because Anna didn't know how to drive—her parents shared a single car that she'd been forbidden to go near—and Daniel didn't like anyone driving his car anyway, even though it was just an enormous old station wagon that his parents had given him when they'd upgraded. On the long drive out of South Florida Anna was free to close her eyes in the passenger seat and imagine being a different kind of person in a different kind of life.

At the end she woke from a long nap and the quality of light had changed. They were on the outskirts of Salt Lake City. The sunlight here had a hard high-altitude brilliance. The landscape had been distilled into the barest palette of colors—brown mountains tinged with green under a blue-white sky, the gray of the highway ahead, white light.

"Are we getting close?"

"We're almost there."

"Daniel," she said, "I don't know how to thank you. Most people wouldn't have done this."

"Look, Anna, there's something I should tell you."

"What?"

"My aunt doesn't have a lot of money," he said. "She and my uncle got divorced a few years back, he's the one with the construction firm

I told you about, and it's the kind of situation . . . look, you'll be safe there, she's a trustworthy person. But it's not a really nice place or anything."

"Oh," Anna said. "It's okay. It doesn't have to be nice." She carefully replaced her vision of the large house, the suite, the deep white carpets with a modest but still cozy house, a spare room.

"I'm glad you don't mind," Daniel said. "I wish I could take you somewhere nicer."

"It's okay," she said.

They were passing through suburbs now. There were things here that were different—mountains rising up at the edge of the sky, an absence of palm trees, less-green lawns—but these suburbs weren't really different from the place where she'd spent her entire life, endless similar houses and cul-de-sacs. She was left with an unsettling sense that they hadn't gone anywhere, that this was only a variation on the place where they'd started. Daniel pulled into the driveway of a low single-story house with peeling white paint. A run-down street bleached by high sunlight, a neighborhood of brownish lawns and toys left out in yards.

"Well!" Daniel said, too brightly. "Here we are!" She stepped out of the car into the thin bright air. Daniel pulled their duffel bags from the backseat and came to stand beside her.

"It's nice," she said.

"Wait till you see the inside." He seemed nervous, trying to keep his voice light but she understood his strain. The same fear she'd felt every time she'd ever brought a friend home, Please oh please let everything be calm inside the house today. She took his arm as they approached the front door.

"It's okay," she said, while they stood waiting for someone to answer the doorbell. "Even if it isn't good, it's better than what I left, isn't it?"

"I don't know," he said. "I hope this was the right thing."

. . .

Daniel's aunt was a thin nervous woman who worked as a hotel maid near the convention center. Delia was kind but tired, distracted by worry. Her hair was caught up in a hundred tiny braids with beads on the ends. She had a daughter in college and she'd taken in subletters to help with the tuition. Anna gathered that Daniel hadn't been aware of this fact. This meant that another family was living in the basement, and there was, it seemed, nowhere for Anna and Daniel to stay.

"I thought you could maybe take Tanya's old room," Delia said, but her daughter's bedroom was being used for storage, stacked high with boxes filled with things that Delia and Tanya were trying to sell on eBay. The people downstairs were playing loud music. Anna stood in the hall listening to Daniel and his aunt, and she felt the rhythm coming up through the walls. She was mesmerized by the movement of the beads at the ends of Delia's braids, the soft musical clicking every time she turned her head.

"Tanya's room looks kind of full, actually," Daniel said, in a tight voice that made Anna shiver. She was acutely sensitive to oncoming storms. She pressed the palms of her hands to the cool wall and felt the bass coming through in pulses. Thinking about the other times she'd run away, about how much less complicated running away was when it was only you and you were only going a few miles from home and no one else's family was involved.

"And she'll be home over the holidays," Delia said. "Maybe you could stay in the living room?"

But the living room was tiny and open to the kitchen, almost entirely taken up by an overstuffed sofa. It was clearly the room where Delia spent most of her time when she was home. There were magazines and half-completed crossword puzzles open on the coffee table, an ironing board set up with a neat stack of pressed clothing folded at the end of it, a gray cat sprawled asleep on the sofa. A TV blared commercials into the air.

"I wonder if you'd mind waiting in the car for a few minutes," Daniel said to Anna, and by this Anna understood that they were leaving again. She sat for a long time in the car with the seat reclined, staring at the mountains. She felt hollow and worn thin. It was obvious to her at that moment that their plans would end in catastrophe. The sunlight through the windshield was too bright.

"We're going to my friend's place," Daniel said when he came to her. He looked flushed and spent, as if he'd been shouting. She looked past him at the house. His aunt was standing in the open doorway, wiping tears from her face. "He doesn't live that far from here."

"What did you say to her?" Anna asked, but Daniel pretended not to hear. He pulled out of the driveway and when she looked back the front door was closed.

His friend lived in a sprawling ranch house on a cul-de-sac with the same reduced color palette as the larger suburbs: white houses, blue sky, green-brown lawns. This sheer white light.

"Why don't we just go to your uncle's place?"

"Because he lives in a small apartment and my friend's got an entire house to himself."

"What's your friend's name?" she asked, on the way up the driveway. Daniel was walking ahead of her with the bags.

"Paul," he said. "We worked together when I was here last summer."

PAUL WAS a wiry man in his early twenties, with blond hair and an earring and a tattoo on his neck, a splash of orange. He took them on a tour. The house seemed to have at least three bedrooms, closed doors along the upstairs hallway. Paul had friends who came to stay with him sometimes, he said. A roommate who was here every couple of weeks. He showed them the garage, where an expensive-looking silver car was parked next to a motorcycle.

"One rule," Paul said, when he showed them into the storage room beside the garage. He was sorry that this was the only room he could give them, he'd said. All the other rooms had other uses. "You can't ever go into the basement."

"I think he's a dealer," Daniel said later, when he and Anna were alone. He had lapsed into a deep silence. She was surprised to hear him speak.

"But when you knew him, last summer . . ."

"He was working construction," Daniel said. "Looks to me like there's been a career change."

The storage room wasn't large. There was a foldout sofa, a layer of dust on the linoleum floor, a bare lightbulb overhead. Daniel was embarrassed, it was obvious to Anna, and she wanted to say something to make it better but didn't know what she could possibly say. She sat on the sofa looking out the window at the backyard, the brownish grass and falling-down fence. Daniel seemed to be having some difficulty looking directly at her. In those last two weeks in Florida they hadn't talked much, she realized, about the actual circumstances in which they'd live after they ran away. He'd told her his aunt had room for them and she had imagined a mansion.

She wanted to leave but she had no more than eighty dollars to her name. She was here and there was nowhere else she could go.

THE DAYS in the house were long and empty. People came and went, cars pulling in and out of the driveway. She heard voices upstairs

and on the stairs to the basement. The day after their arrival Daniel
went to work at his uncle's construction firm. A house was going up
across town, Daniel told her, lying beside her at night. A huge sprawling McMansion of a place with pillars and a portrait of Joseph Smith
carved into stone above the door. Daniel said it was creepy, actually. He'd been raised Catholic, but he wasn't about to litter any house
of his with religious iconography. Anna tried to imagine what their
house would be like, if they ever lived in a house that was theirs. The
thought of living with Daniel indefinitely was somehow awkward. He
was working overtime and went jogging in the evenings. She didn't see
much of him.

Six voice mails came in from Gavin, like dispatches from a foreign
country. Pleas for information, questions about her whereabouts, invi-
tations to the prom. She listened and then deleted them. She sometimes
cried at night.

Before the pregnancy began to show she got a job in a doughnut
shop. It was down on a main street, a twenty-minute walk. She'd never
had a job before but the work was easy and the manager liked her. It
was a pleasure to escape from the silent house. She didn't mind it, although the smell of doughnuts made her nauseous some days. She
served coffee and counted change through long afternoons while the
question of paternity hung overhead like a cloud.

On their third or fourth week in the house she woke at three in the
morning, thrown out of sleep by an unremembered sound. Daniel
was standing by the storage-room window, staring out at the backyard through the smallest possible opening in the curtain. He looked
stricken.

"What time is it?" she asked.

"You don't want to see this," he said, without taking his eyes away from the window, but he didn't object when she came to stand beside him. That was when she heard the sound again, a sharp cry from outside.

She was aware first of movement, a confused motion in the middle of the lawn just at the point where the light cast from the house met darkness, two figures moving on the edge of visibility. It took her a moment to decipher the scene.

There were two men in the backyard. For a moment it was almost a balanced fight, both men punching, but then one fell to his knees and seemed to retreat into himself, curled up on the grass in a ball, and the other—Paul, she realized—struck the fallen man again and again and again.

"He's going to kill him," Anna whispered.

"He won't," Daniel whispered back. His eyes were very wide. "The last thing a guy like him wants is to get in trouble with the law."

"We have to stop him," she hissed, but neither of them moved and the blows continued until Paul gave his victim a final vicious kick and turned toward them, stalking back to the house, sweat shining on his face and soaking through his shirt. Knuckles bleeding and eyes bright, his tattoo slick on the side of his neck. Daniel pulled her away from the window.

Anna woke late in the morning and wondered if it had perhaps been a dream. Daniel had left for work already. She looked through the gap in the curtains, half-expecting to see a body on the grass, but the yard was empty. When she went outside she saw the blood, spattered here and there, less than she was expecting for the violence she'd seen. There was a pine tree in the back corner of the yard by the fence, a wooden picnic table beneath it, and she liked to sit out there sometimes when the air in the house was too close. Today she walked past the blood and lay on her back on the table, numb, staring up at the patterns of pine needles and branches against the overcast sky. She closed her eyes and still saw the patterns on the inside of her eyelids.

"What are you thinking of?"

Anna hadn't heard Paul's approach over the dead grass. She started when she heard his voice and sat up on the table.

"Nothing," she said.

It was difficult not to look at his hands. He'd wrapped both knuckles in gauze and she remembered the impact of fists on ribs, the fallen man's cries.

"I've seen you out here before," he said.

She shrugged.

"So you just lie there on the table by the hour, thinking of nothing?"

"Yeah," she said, "that's sort of the point."

"Cigarette?"

"Yes please."

He hesitated a moment before he lit it for her. "You supposed to smoke when you're pregnant?"

"No." She inhaled slowly. "But I figure the occasional one can't hurt." He shrugged and sat down on the other end of the table. "I like your tattoo," she said. Perhaps this was adulthood, this feeling of danger, smoking a cigarette far from home with a man who'd beaten another man almost to death the night before.

"Thank you."

She hoped he might have a story to tell her, but he sat smoking in silence until she asked, "Why a goldfish?"

"My best friend drowned when we were kids," he said. "I got the tattoo of a fish to remind myself to fear water."

"Oh," she said. "I'm sorry."

"It's okay. I thought, I'll put it on my neck, where I'll never be able to forget it's there. Other tattoos, you put on a long-sleeved shirt and forget about them."

She wanted to ask for the rest of the story—Did your friend fall into a river, swim too far out into the ocean, hit his head in the bathtub?—but it seemed rude to pry, so she just smoked her cigarette and wished Daniel were there.

"So you're from here, then?" she asked, just to break the silence.

"I'm from Spanish Fork. You know where that is?"

"No."

"Gary Gilmore lived there for a while."

"I don't know who that is," she said.

He didn't seem to want to tell her. He blew a series of smoke rings into the cool air. "And you," he said, "I hear you're from Florida."

"Sebastian," she said.

"Where's that?"

"Near Boca. North of Miami."

"The whole state's north of Miami," he said. "Your parents know where you are?"

"I doubt they've noticed I left," Anna said.

"I have parents like that."

"It's a big club." She stubbed out her cigarette on the silvery wood. "You have a nice house," she said, but as soon as she said this it seemed like a stupid thing to have said. She had no idea if the house was Paul's or if he was just renting it, and it wasn't really all that nice.

He laughed and glanced at the house—gray stucco, pale in the dead brown lawn. "It's not a nice house," he said. "What it is is inconspicuous. I've come to value that more than niceness." He blew another series of smoke rings. She watched them dissolve into the air and thought of Sasha. "Don't take offense," he said, "but I look at a girl like you, pregnant, fifteen or sixteen or whatever, and I just have to wonder, what's the plan? What brings you to the Kingdom of Deseret?"

"I'm not sure what you mean." She didn't know what the Kingdom of Deseret was.

"Sure you do. You finish high school?"

"I've only got a year to go. I was thinking I'd get my GED."

"Yeah, and then what? You'll work at a McDonald's?"

"I always thought I'd do something with music. Maybe be a music producer or something."

"Come on. With a GED?"

"I don't know," she said. She found herself on the verge of tears and had to look away quickly. "I don't know what I'll do. I'll think of something."

"Sorry, I didn't mean to upset you. I see a girl like you, it's just something I wonder about. Who am I to talk, right? It's not like I ever went to college."

"What happened to your hands?" It was a bold question and for an instant she thought she'd made a horrible mistake, her stomach sank, he'd probably buried the man from last night behind the garden shed and now he'd kill her too and no one would ever know what had happened and Sasha would never see her again, Daniel would come home from work and she'd have disappeared into thin air, but he only smiled and looked at the bandages.

"I took care of a problem," he said. "Messy work."

"I should probably go," she said.

"You got somewhere to be?"

"I have to get to work soon."

"Where do you work?"

"The doughnut place down the street," she said.

"I'll give you a ride." He stood up from the table. She didn't want to be in a car with him, but she didn't know how to politely refuse. He waited for her while she went into the house and changed into her uniform, the regulation t-shirt tight across her body. "How far along are you?" he asked, on the short drive down the hill.

"Four months."

"Boy or girl?"

"I don't know," she said. "I wanted it to be a surprise." In truth, she didn't care if it was a boy or a girl. All she cared about was the shade of the baby's skin. She caught herself looking at Daniel's skin at odd moments—his exposed back as he turned away from her to put on a clean t-shirt, his hand holding a spoon, the side of his face as he spoke on the phone to his parents—and whispering the same silent prayer over and over again: Please, please, please let the baby be black. She whispered the prayer to herself when she first felt the baby kick, when the first pain shuddered through her on a late afternoon in the doughnut shop four and a half months later, when she sat holding herself in the passenger seat of Paul's car as he sped toward the hospital with Daniel on his cell phone, while she lay on her back on the bed looking up at the lights with strangers shouting at her to push, please, please, please. But even before she had a good look at the baby she saw the way the nurse looked from the child to Daniel and then to Anna, the way Daniel's eyes filled with tears as he turned away from the bed. He left the room then and she was alone with the nurses, with the machines, with the baby who cried out and clung blindly to the soft blanket with hands that were very small and very pink.

Twenty

"You still with me, Gavin?" Daniel asked softly.
The air singing with electric blue stars.

THERE WAS something wrong with the ceiling. It was mostly white, but the texture of the tiles made constellations of gray that swarmed and changed shape the longer Gavin looked at them. His arm was a frozen, inert thing, pain seeping through the drugs. He was aware of sound: a nurse pulling the curtain around the bed, metal rings jangling; a beeping machine; soft footsteps.

The room was flickering. He kept falling in and out of sleep, if sleep was what this was. It felt lighter than unconsciousness. Intervals of twilight. Vertigo, a terrible shifting movement, the bed's a boat on rough water, I am going to drown.

"Was I really shot?" Gavin murmured. "Was that really what happened to my arm?"

"He panicked," Daniel said. Daniel was an unsteady silhouette beside the bed, a blurred figure wavering. How long had he been there? "He thought you were someone else."

Gavin's ears were ringing. He closed his eyes again.

"I'M NOT someone else," Gavin said. He was confused and his voice was a mumble. He wasn't sure how long he'd been talking to Daniel, how long he'd been awake. His throat was dry. The texture of the ceiling above the hospital bed. Dizzy.

"He thought you were after Anna."

"I am after Anna. I've been looking for her." The drugs were a weight in his bloodstream, a fog behind his eyes. Antibiotics, the remnants of general anesthesia, whatever they were giving him for his arm. Was this how Jack felt through all the days of his life? He remembered being wheeled into surgery, flashes of sound and light.

"If you care about her," Daniel said, "I'd suggest you stay away from Deval." Was Gavin dreaming? He had the impression of swimming. Daniel's face wasn't entirely in focus.

"Or he'll shoot me again?" Gavin murmured. Talking nauseated him. He closed his eyes.

"LISTEN," DANIEL said, "I'm here in my official capacity."

Gavin was awake again. Had he been awake the whole time? Nothing was certain. He'd been dreaming of a trumpet.

"I don't understand," he said.

"I'm a detective on the Sebastian police force, and I'm here interviewing the victim of a crime." Daniel was speaking very quietly. "This is what my report will say: you were visiting a friend in the motel, but you got the wrong room and the drug fiend on the other side of the door shot you and fled. Do you understand why I'm going to write that?"

"Not really," Gavin said. "I don't really understand any of it." He hazarded opening his eyes again. The ceiling was still moving so he looked down at the blanket and sheet instead, but the texture of the blanket had a way of telescoping in on itself. He wanted to put his hand over his eyes, to block the light and the queasy motion of everything around him, but his left arm seemed unmovable and the IV was in his right. "To protect Liam Deval?"

"Not Deval. Anna."

"Can you please just tell me what happened to her after high school? I know you know, and I'm so goddamned tired of asking." Gavin closed his eyes. "I am so dizzy," he said, to no one in particular.

"You lost a lot of blood," Daniel said. He was quiet for a few minutes, and Gavin had almost slipped back into sleep before he spoke again. "How did you know he was in the Draker Motel?"

"I used to be a reporter," Gavin said. "I can follow a story. Do I have to ask the question again?"

Daniel sighed. "Look, she was pregnant," he said. "Sixteen years old."

"Yes, I figured that part out already. She was pregnant and sixteen, and then what?"

"This isn't something I'm proud of. You do stupid things in high school. I made a mistake. But listen, she was pregnant, and she told me the kid was mine."

Gavin opened his eyes. Daniel's face was dim, hard to make out in the swarm of stars. "So what did you do?" he asked.

"I drove her to Utah. We were going to live with my aunt until we could get our own place."

"Why would she go with you? What did you offer her?"

"What do you think I offered her? A getaway car," Daniel said. "If you'd had a car and a place to take her, she'd have said the kid was yours."

"I didn't think she was . . ." He couldn't focus his thoughts. "I thought she was different than that."

"She was desperate. People are capable of anything when they're desperate. Look, I don't flatter myself. She wasn't in love with me. But you must have known what her family was like. I offered her a lifeline and she took it."

"She never wanted a lifeline," Gavin said. "I was always offering—"

"No, you were always threatening," Daniel said. "You were always threatening to call the authorities, every time she showed up at school with a bruise. That was your idea of helping her? Calling Family Services? They knew all about that household. She spent a year in foster care when she was a little kid. They were at that house all the time."

"She never told me that."

"They could easily have taken her child away from her. She was afraid of being separated from the baby."

"But she always said she didn't want any help." The whole thing was too much for him. The room was tilting, so he closed his eyes again. His throat was dry.

"If someone's drowning in front of you and they say they don't want to be saved, do you take them at their word or do you pull them out of the water? The way you stood by and did nothing."

"I didn't know—"

"You weren't paying attention."

"I need some water," Gavin whispered. "My throat . . ."

There was a plastic cup of water by the bed. Daniel lifted the cup and guided the straw to Gavin's lips. The water was warm.

"You took her to Utah," Gavin said. "What happened then?"

"The baby wasn't mine. We broke up. She left. She got in some trouble, ended up with Liam Deval."

"Why do I get the impression you're leaving out details?"

"Gavin, does it matter? This was all a decade ago."

"Everything matters, Daniel. Didn't you used to say that in high school?"

"I don't remember saying that."

"If you'll just tell me how to find Anna, I'll stay out of your way. I'll even forget who shot me. I don't know what you and Deval are doing, or why you're helping him. I actually don't even really care, so long as no one shoots me again and Anna and Chloe are safe."

Gavin heard footsteps in the corridor, Eilo's voice. He registered dimly that she'd been here earlier.

"Hello," she said from the doorway. Gavin smiled as best he could. Daniel turned to look at her, and Gavin saw that she didn't recognize him.

"I'll just be another minute, ma'am," Daniel said. He leaned over the bed. "Do I have your word?"

"Yes."

"Go to the Starlight Diner on Route 77," he said softly. "Her sister works the night shift. Maybe she'll tell you where to find her."

"I don't want to talk to Sasha. I want to talk to Anna."

"She switched motels last night. Sasha's the only one who knows where she is."

"Was she there when I was shot? In the room, with Deval?"

"No." Daniel was looking at the floor. "I'm sorry about what happened," he said. "All of it." He stood then and turned away from the bed.

.   .   .

On his first day home from the hospital Gavin lay on the sofa in Eilo's living room looking up at the underside of the freeway across the yard. The bullet had struck the bone between his elbow and his shoulder. His arm was fractured. He would have extravagant scars. A little higher and he would have been crippled. "There's not a surgeon alive who can repair a shattered shoulder socket," a doctor at the hospital had told him. "You're a lucky man." He knew he was lucky but every movement was painful. Eilo came in sometimes to see how he was. He heard the sounds of distant telephones from the office, the soft percussion of Eilo's fists against the heavy bag.

After two or three hours on the sofa he forced himself to sit up, and in the swampy shadows under the freeway he thought he saw something move. A quick inhuman movement, a lizard perhaps. He was thinking of Nile monitors, of anacondas, of the extremities of nature, William Chandler in the swamps. This place is slipping away from us, Chandler had said. These new animals. This sure as hell isn't the Florida I grew up in.

"I don't understand what happened," Eilo had said. Speaking cautiously, the way she almost always spoke to him now. The bullet had pushed him into a different world, one she didn't inhabit, and he could see her calculations every time she looked at him: if he had been shot he must be involved in something. If he was involved in something, perhaps it would follow him here. She had taken to double-checking that the doors were locked.

"It was a mistake," he'd told her. "Someone thought I was someone else and shot me by accident. I just got the wrong room."

"But why were you there?"

"I thought a friend from New York was staying at the motel. Did you see the police report?" But he saw the doubt in her eyes and he knew she was thinking about the *New York Star.* Liar. Liar. "Tell me about my medical expenses," he said.

"Don't worry about that," she said. "I've made some money."

"Eilo, you can't . . ."

"I've always tried to take care of you." Eilo was quiet for a moment, sitting on the edge of the sofa. "Why were you at the motel?"

"I was looking for her."

"For Anna?"

"Anna and the little girl."

"Did you find them?"

"No," Gavin said.

"And it was a coincidence that you were shot?"

"It had nothing to do with anything. I just got the wrong room."

She left him alone then, and a few minutes later he heard the muted sounds of her fists hitting the heavy bag.

HE WOKE on Eilo's sofa at two in the morning. The freeway was a blaze of light high over the lawn. He lay for a while in the half-light, got up with difficulty and went to the bathroom to splash cold water on his face. He hadn't shaved in a few days but he thought he didn't look too bad, except for the pallor and the dark circles under his eyes, and anyway the thought of shaving was exhausting. His car was at his apartment, he realized, and it occurred to him that he wouldn't want to drive it with one hand anyway. He called a taxi company and went outside to wait on the front lawn. At this hour the neighborhood was silent and the taxi almost silent too, the only car on the street when it came for him. The letters on the side door read *Greenlight Taxi Co.* The car was the color of a lime.

"Do you know the Starlight Diner?" Gavin asked. "Route 77?"

"Sure," the driver said. "Good pancakes there."

The Starlight Diner was some distance from Eilo's house, not far from Gavin's apartment. There are certain restaurants meant to be viewed at night and the Starlight was among them. A gleaming chrome-and-red-Naugahyde interior visible from the parking lot, a neon sign shining over a bank of flowers near the front door. It was close to three a.m. when the taxi dropped him off. He opened the door of the diner awkwardly—the sling made everything difficult—and glanced around, but he didn't see anyone who looked like Sasha. Daniel had said she worked the night shift, but perhaps there was more than one night shift, or more than one Starlight Diner on Route 77, or it was her night off.

"Anywhere you like," a waitress said. She was fiftyish, eyes bright with caffeine, bleached hair piled on top of her head and turquoise eye shadow.

He chose a booth by the window where he could see the street, ordered a coffee, and realized as he drank it that he wasn't going to sleep again that night. Gavin had brought a newspaper with him, but it was difficult to concentrate. The pain was a dull constant throb from his elbow to his shoulder but when he gave in and took a Vicodin he thought of Jack, so he'd been trying to get by on aspirin. It wasn't working very well. He looked out at the lights of passing cars and his thoughts wandered. He was thinking of the last time he'd seen Deval and Morelli play together at Barbès, the apparent falling-out at the end of the set, Deval stalking out of the room and Morelli glaring after him. Why had Deval come to Sebastian, if not to play his canceled gig at the Lemon Club? He felt that he was on the periphery of some great drama, trapped on the wrong side of the locked stage door while the action transpired just out of sight. He didn't understand the story. He

was distracted by the pain. He'd been shot four days ago and it had occurred to him that it was a nice thing, actually, that he'd been halfway
unconscious from heat exhaustion and sunstroke when it had happened. He was lucky, he thought, that he had no memory of facing a
gun. But even so, he'd noticed that loud noises rattled him. The man
slamming a car door in the parking lot, for instance. Gavin tensed but
it was just another man, no one he knew, coming in for a doughnut and
a cup of coffee to go.

"Gavin?"

He looked up with a start. Sasha was sliding into the booth across
from him. It took him a moment to recognize her. He hadn't seen her
since she was eighteen years old. "I thought that was you," she said. "I
just came back from my break and saw you here." She'd brought two
cups of coffee. "Cream or sugar?"

"Both. Thank you."

"You're welcome." She carried a faint aura of cigarette smoke. The
preceding decade had been hard on her. She carried the kind of exhaustion that he'd seen only rarely in a woman so young, and mostly
only in his time as a reporter. She had the look of women who've worried too much, smoked too many cigarettes, been too poor for too many
years, and worked too hard for long hours. She was studying him.
"Gavin," she said, "you don't look so good."

"I've had better weeks."

"Are you trying to grow a beard?"

"Not on purpose."

"Well, what brings you here?"

"You know," he said. "Anna."

"Don't tell me you're involved in this."

He nodded carefully. She sighed.

"I don't like it," she said. "Anything about it."

Gavin wasn't sure what to say, so he just watched her. A trick taught to him by an older reporter at the paper: Sometimes if you're silent they'll just keep talking.

"I just can't stand the way they're using the girl," she said.

"Perhaps it's the only way to do it," Gavin ventured, when it became clear that she was waiting for a response. The girl? Could she possibly mean his daughter?

"It's a terrible plan," she said, "and has been from the beginning. If it were up to me it wouldn't be this way. What happened to your arm?"

"Just a stupid accident," Gavin said.

"God, I'm sorry, I'm usually not this rude." Sasha glanced out at the parking lot. She seemed ill at ease. "I haven't seen you in ten years, and all I can talk about is the goddamned plan. This week aside, Gavin, how's your decade been?"

"Good and then bad. How was your decade?"

"Difficult," she said, "but there were a few good moments. Didn't you go to New York and become a reporter or something?"

"I did," Gavin said. "I became a reporter, and then I got fired, and now I'm working for my sister."

"Here in Sebastian?"

"Here in Sebastian."

"Why were you fired?"

"Fraud," he said.

She sipped her coffee, her eyes on his face. "I heard you were engaged."

"I was," Gavin said. "I'm not anymore." He hadn't thought of Karen in a while, but her presence once summoned hadn't dulled with time. Karen's smile, Karen moving through a room, Karen brushing a strand of hair from her forehead as she read the Sunday *Times* over coffee in their sunlit kitchen in Manhattan. He wondered where she was tonight.

"I'm sorry," Sasha said. "It sounds like you've lost some things."

Gavin didn't know what to say, so he nodded and said nothing. They sat together for a moment in silence. "I heard you went to Florida State," he said finally.

"I did. I was studying English lit." She seemed disinclined to explain how she'd gone from studying literature to working the graveyard shift in a roadside diner, and Gavin didn't know how to ask without being rude. "If you know the plan, you've spoken with Daniel since you've been back," she said. "Tell me something, has he seemed strange to you lately?"

"Strange in what way?"

"Like something's horribly wrong," she said. "I don't mean to be melodramatic."

"I don't know," Gavin said. "He seems to have changed considerably since high school."

"Do you know if the time's been set?"

It took Gavin a moment to understand that she was talking about the plan again, and he wished more than anything at that moment that he could shed the pretense and just ask her what she was talking about.

"I haven't heard anything about that."

"Well, Daniel or Liam will let us know, I suppose. All I know is it's going to be sometime between one and three in the morning." She was looking out at the parking lot again, her eyes moving over the few parked cars. It wasn't just that she was ill at ease, he realized. She was frightened.

"Right," he said.

"Well," she said, "I should get back to work. Are you sticking with coffee?"

"I'm not that hungry. Sasha, could you tell me about my daughter?"

"How long have you known about Chloe?"

"Not long," he said. "Why didn't Anna ever tell me?"

"I don't know. I think she was embarrassed about running off with someone else."

"Is there anything you could tell me about her?"

Sasha smiled. "About Chloe? You'd like her," she said. "She's a good kid. Polite, good grades at school. She wants to be an acrobat when she grows up. She likes to draw."

"What does she draw? If you don't mind me asking."

"Houses," Sasha said. "Flowers, people, trees, the usual kid things. Suns with smiley faces. Bicycles."

"And she's—is she okay?"

"She's fine. Well, I don't know, actually, she's staying in a motel with Anna. I assume she's fine. I haven't seen her in a while."

"Thank you," Gavin said. There was a tightness in his throat. "Could I possibly talk to Anna?"

"Not till this is over," she said. "You've no idea how nervous she is."

"Will you tell her that I asked about her?"

Sasha was standing now, smoothing imaginary wrinkles from the front of her apron. "I will. I'll tell her."

"Wait," he said. "Can I borrow your pen?" She gave it to him and he wrote his address and cell number on a corner of the place mat, tore it off and gave it to her. "If you wouldn't mind," he said. "In case she wants to know where to find me."

"I'll give it to her," Sasha said. He watched her move away across the room.

Part Three

Twenty-One

Sasha was raised on stories of brave children entering magical countries. Narnia was behind the coats in a wardrobe. Alice fell down the rabbit hole. There was another story whose name she couldn't remember about a brother and sister picking up a golden pinecone in the woods and in that motion, that lifting of an enchanted object from the forest floor, a new world rotated silently into place around them.

"Once you step into the underworld it's hard to come out again," she said to William Chandler. This was a few months before Gavin appeared in the Starlight Diner with his arm in a sling. Sasha and William met in the diner a few times a month to drink coffee together before the start of her shift. William wasn't her official sponsor at Gamblers Anonymous, her official sponsor had left town a long time ago and Sasha wasn't sure what had become of her, but they had gravitated toward one another over years of meetings and he often seemed more like a sponsor than a friend.

"Don't be melodramatic," he said. "You were never that far in."

But she knew it wasn't really a question of how far in she'd gone. It was true, she'd never sold herself to pay her gambling debts or been physically harmed. The meetings were full of lost marriages and personal bankruptcies and parents who had lost their children forever and women who'd turned to prostitution to finance their debts. She'd played poker a few times in high school, gathered with friends in someone's parents' basement on boring Friday nights. The game made them feel like adults, even if they were usually just playing for pennies. She'd begun playing regularly in her first semester of college, just to have something to think about other than English literature and finance.

It would have been impossible to imagine the slide that followed. By the end of the first semester she was playing almost every day. She'd lost a student-loan payment and had to leave school. She'd stolen money from two previous jobs. She'd taken her father's car and sold it in a parking lot and now he didn't talk to her anymore. She'd lived in terror of a particular loan shark. She'd skated across a dark surface, but the surface was all she'd needed to touch. Sasha could always find the door in the back of the wardrobe after that, she was always already halfway through—"I'd like ten lottery tickets," a man murmured near her in a dusty convenience store on Caroline Street, and there was that shadow angling over the day again. Traces of her old world were everywhere. She saw it in glances, in people sitting together in parked cars, in exchanges of envelopes outside closed businesses. She was aware of it all around her, as if all the off-track betting parlors and basement poker and scratch-and-win tickets were part of the same game, a never-ending continuous transaction of currency and numbers and cards that she could sense in the air but no longer touch. When she drove the streets of Sebastian she always knew where the casino was, where she was in relation to it. She was constantly aware of the casino's gravitational pull, dark star.

Sasha shuffled and reshuffled a deck of cards in the evenings in front of a television set, almost without noticing anymore. She felt tainted but also she wanted to slip back in again, back to the beautiful casino poker room where she'd always been on the verge of winning everything, everything, the patterns of cards unfolding around her and the night so bright sometimes, evenings of ice cubes glinting in glasses and hard chips and money.

"You're getting better," Anna said. "When was the last time you lost any money?" She'd been living with Sasha for years now, ever since she'd broken up with the guitarist and come back down from New York with her daughter and enough money to pay off Sasha's gambling debt. Sasha had known that night that never again in her lifetime would anyone show up on her doorstep with eleven thousand dollars in cash. She'd known that this was her last chance and she'd fought every day since then to not gamble, but she could never bring herself to think of it as a disease. She'd had arguments with William about it.

"If I had pneumonia," she'd said, "I wouldn't be able to will myself to get better. There's no such thing as Pneumonia Anonymous. There's a difference between a disease and a character flaw."

"It's thinking like that that keeps treatment programs under-funded," he'd said, and changed the subject. He'd never felt he stood a chance before the poisonous allure of horse racing. Now, sitting in front of the television set shuffling a card deck over and over again, Sasha looked up from the cards and didn't know what to say. Anna was watching her from the doorway. Cards made Anna nervous.

"I don't know," Sasha said finally, because she had to say something. "I can't remember the last thing I lost."

"That's good," Anna said. She was a little bleary-eyed. She'd slept for an hour between work and night school and was on her way out again. Chloe was at the babysitter's house. "Are you hungry? There's a pizza in the freezer."

"Thank you," Sasha said. There were nights when it was easy, but she knew this wasn't going to be one of them. "I'm leaving for work soon."

THEIR SHAKY mother married twice. Sasha and Anna had different fathers and different last names and different clothes, and one was luckier than the other. "Your mother dresses that kid like a whore," Sasha's father muttered once when Sasha was thirteen or so, picking her up from her mother's house where Anna waved good-bye on the driveway in high cut-off shorts and a too-small tank top, and Sasha felt bad about him saying this but she couldn't disagree. People didn't know they were sisters and it was the shame of her life that she sometimes didn't mind this and sometimes even let it slide. Anna wore clothes that Sasha wouldn't have left the house in. Anna often had bruises and did poorly in school. Anna was suspended twice for fighting, once for graffiti. Anna ran away for days at a time. Her friends were mostly drug addicts and dropouts until she changed schools and found the jazz quartet.

Sasha hadn't minded Anna hanging around on the outskirts of the quartet but she'd always secretly thought of Anna as a bit of a basket case, wayward child, lost girl. When things were bad at their mother's house, during Sasha's increasingly infrequent visits, she tried her best to protect Anna because she thought it was her duty. She'd told Anna to go upstairs and she'd faced their mother and Anna's father on her own, scared but also a little virtuous about it, and it was shocking that after all this Anna had been the one to save her. Sasha had owed ten thousand seven hundred dollars to a man named Lizard who was threatening to beat her and then Anna appeared one night on her doorstep with Chloe and eleven thousand dollars, all that remained by then of the hundred and twenty-one thousand from Utah after three years of rent and groceries and the production of Deval & Morelli's first album. Sasha had just got off the phone with Lizard when the doorbell rang. Anna stood on her doorstep holding the tired three-year-old's hand and asked why Sasha was crying, and by late afternoon the next day Sasha's gambling debts were erased. Anna tried to pretend it was nothing. "You'd have done the same for me," she said, and through all the days of her life Sasha hoped this was true.

SASHA HAD been working the graveyard shift at the Starlight Diner for four years now. At first just because she was new and had no say in her schedule and they needed someone for the night shift, later because she liked it. She felt too jangled there in daylight, overexposed in the clatter of plates and voices, always falling behind. She arrived every night in time for the dinner rush. It was the time of day she most hated, but she knew it was necessary. The diner served decent dinner entrees, and it was a popular destination. The tips from the dinner rush were what made the night shift financially viable, and beyond the rush lay the promise of long quiet hours.

The nights were serene. Usually just she and Bianca or sometimes Jocelyn, Luis and Freddy in the kitchen. Bianca was in her fifties, Jocelyn forty-three. They had both been working nights for years and had identical looks of permanent tiredness. They'd told Sasha they didn't want to work days, though, and Sasha understood. It was Sasha's first night job but she already knew she didn't want to work in daylight again either.

The best part about working at night was the silence. She stepped out of the diner for a cigarette sometimes in the quietest hour, between three and four in the morning, stood alone at the edge of the shadows out back listening. Not that the silence was ever complete—cicadas, frogs in the canal across the street, rustlings in the bushes, the occasional passing truck or car—but daylight was cacophonous by comparison. The diner was never crowded at night. The pace was calm, and calm was the state that Sasha most longed for. A few coked-out nutjobs or shadow-eyed meth addicts seized by sudden excitable cravings—a strawberry milkshake! Chocolate mud pie!—staring down their forty-eighth consecutive hour without sleep, but mostly just a steady stream of truckers and strippers and insomniacs, a few night staffers from St. Mary Star of the Sea Hospital a mile away. This is what a steady life looks like, she told herself sometimes, when she was driving home in the early morning, and took pleasure in the thought. It's just that it happens at night. She liked watching the progression of darkness into first light into morning.

Daniel came in sometimes. She'd take a quick break—no managers at night, that was the other nice thing, just Sasha and one of the sympathetic night-shift veterans, either Jocelyn or Bianca—and sit with him for a few minutes. He'd started coming here about a year ago. His grandmother was in and out of St. Mary Star of the Sea. He came for dinner after visiting hours. It was startling, how much he'd changed in the years since high school. She hardly recognized him the first time she saw him after all these years, almost didn't know where to look.

"What happened to you?" he asked, the second or third night he came in, and it could have been a cruel question but he spoke so gently, he was looking at her with such kindness and sympathy that there seemed no reason not to tell the truth—he was *Daniel*, they'd played music together in competitions in the days of band and orchestra and the Lola Quartet, she'd known him since the eighth grade even if years had gone by when they hadn't seen one another—so she poured herself a cup of coffee and told him about the lost student-loan money, the frantic bets and the almost nightly poker games, the enormous sums of money won and lost and lost further, the boyfriends who thought she was fun at first, a novelty, a girl who drank whiskey and loved poker, until they saw that it was pathological and finally left her when they realized she couldn't stop and that their watches were missing, the miserable long slide, but she stopped when she got to the part where Anna had reappeared in Florida because she remembered that Anna was where their stories intersected. She looked at the table, flustered.

"I have no right to ask," he said, "but how is your sister?"

"She's fine. She moved in with me a few years back. We live together, the three of us."

"You and Anna and the little girl."

"Chloe. She's a good kid."

"Interesting family."

"Family's always a provisional arrangement. But what about you?" she asked, suddenly emboldened. "What happened to you?"

"You know the first part of it already," he said. "I ran off with your little sister. I said something stupid that scared her, she stole money from our scumbag roommate and then took off with the baby. But you knew that part."

Sasha nodded. She knew that part. It was the part that always made her perversely jealous. She'd been spinning down into a tedious glazed-eyed oblivion of scratch cards and poker and Anna had been fleeing across the country with a baby and a gym bag full of money, Anna had been falling into the arms of jazz musicians and evading villains across the continental United States. Anna insisted that this life had mostly been a dull grinding shadow existence but there was a small part of Sasha that didn't entirely believe it. That life did sound horrible, but also—and she was shot through with guilt whenever she let herself think this—it sounded more exciting than Sasha's life had ever been.

"What's the part that comes next?" Sasha asked.

"Next? Then there were two marriages in five years," Daniel said. "Four children between the two of them. Two divorces, police academy, police work, a number of promotions, a thyroid condition, and a decade of crushing guilt. Nothing about my life is exceptional except my children. May I have another cup of coffee?"

"Of course," Sasha said. She crossed the room to the coffee station and refilled two cups. Bianca nodded at her from behind the cash register. They'd been working together for years and had an understanding: unlimited breaks when the restaurant was this slow. There were only two active tables just now, both Bianca's, both eating dessert.

Daniel stirred his coffee, tapped the spoon on the cup. "The girl's father," he said, without looking at her. "It's Gavin Sasaki, isn't it?"

"Yes."

"Mr. New York," Daniel said with unexpected bitterness. "Does he know?"

"I've told Anna she should try to get child support, but she says she doesn't think Chloe needs more than one parent. I think she's embarrassed that she left him and ran off with you. I don't know," Sasha said, "he had to have known she was pregnant. There were so many crazy rumors flying around about Anna just before you two left for Utah, and then he ran into me buying baby clothes. I heard he's a newspaper reporter or something now."

"A newspaperman," Daniel said. "Some of us get the lives we want, don't we?"

He came in once or twice a week after that and they talked about Anna, about Daniel's kids, about Chloe, about nothing. It wasn't romantic. It was nice to just sit with someone for a half-hour or so. She felt that he understood her; he'd fallen too. She didn't really have friends besides him and William Chandler, and she was never entirely sure if William Chandler was her friend or her sponsor.

THEY WERE sitting together the night Anna called. Daniel's grandmother was in St. Mary Star of the Sea Hospital for the duration now, living out her final days on morphine, and he'd been coming here almost every night for the past week.

"Someone came to Gloria's house and took Chloe's picture," Anna said, without saying hello first. There was panic in her voice.

Anna was going to night school three nights a week to qualify as a paralegal, and on those days Chloe went from school to Gloria's house. Gloria was Liam Deval's mother, the closest thing Chloe had to a grandmother, and she'd moved from the suburbs of Miami to the suburbs of Sebastian a few years earlier. Gloria had visited Liam and Anna a few times when they'd lived together in New York and seemed to consider Anna and Chloe part of her extended family.

"Calm down." Sasha glanced across the table at Daniel, who was looking at her with mild concern. "It's probably nothing. Tell me what happened."

"I had night school," Anna said. She was crying. "So I didn't pick Chloe up until nine, and Gloria told me this woman had come by to appraise the house or something, but while she was there she took Chloe's picture."

"What did Chloe tell you?"

"She said the woman asked her how old she was, and her name."

"Jesus," Sasha said. "Who was this woman?"

"I don't know," Anna said. "She told Gloria she was a real estate agent, but she didn't give her a card before she left, and now Gloria can't remember what her name was. We don't know who she was. She said she was from a real estate company, then she said she was with the bank—"

"Well, we knew Gloria was getting foreclosed—"

"But what kind of a real estate agent takes pictures of someone else's child? Asks her questions? They've found us, Sasha, they've *found* us—"

"No one's found us," Sasha said. "There's no *they*." She was looking at Daniel now. "There's just a *him*. One person. Who probably hasn't left Utah." Daniel was expressionless. "Who probably has no idea where you are and probably stopped looking years ago. Everything will be fine. Listen, Daniel's here." Anna made an indecipherable noise. "Let me talk to him about this."

"What the hell can he do?" Anna asked. "All he's ever done is—"

"He's a cop," Sasha said. "Snap out of it. I'll call you back." She disconnected and watched the call fade from her cell-phone screen. "A stranger showed up and took a picture of Chloe," she said. Saying the words aloud made the story real, and she began to be afraid.

"It might be nothing," Daniel said, when she told him the story about the real estate agent. "A misunderstanding."

"But it might not be."

"It might not be," he agreed, and she thought she'd never seen anyone look so tired.

"Do we go to the police?"

"Of course you can't go to the police." Daniel spoke softly, looking into his coffee. "The only police you can tell is me, and that's only because I'm your friend." He stood up from the table and left some money next to his coffee cup. "Let me think about this. I'll be back in tomorrow or the next night."

She almost asked why they couldn't go to the police, but she understood as she watched him leave. Anna was in trouble because she'd stolen a hundred and twenty-one thousand dollars. Anna was the criminal. Once you've slipped into the underworld, it's difficult to come back out. Shadows slanting over everything.

ANNA WORKED full-time as a file clerk at a law firm. She never missed a day of work but when Sasha came home that morning she was still in her bathrobe, red-eyed at the kitchen table with a mug of coffee in her hand. She'd been crying. Sasha wanted to go to bed but she sat across from Anna instead.

"You're usually home earlier," Anna said. Her voice was very small, and all of Sasha's old instincts—to protect Anna, to shield Anna from everything bad—flashed through her.

"There was an accident on Route 77."

"An accident. That's awful." Anna was smoking, which was startling—she had always been vehement that no one was allowed to smoke in the house, not with a kid living here—and she stubbed out her cigarette in the ashtray as she spoke. "Was anyone hurt?"

"I think so," Sasha said. "There was an ambulance. You look tired."

"I've been up all night."

"Me too," Sasha said. "You have to stay calm."

"He has a *picture* of her, Sasha."

"You don't know that."

"Even if he doesn't," Anna said, "he's always out there. He'll always be out there. And I don't have the money anymore. Any of it."

Sasha looked away. There were moments even now when she wanted to drown. Walk out the door, drive to the casino, play poker until her chips were gone and then dive into the ocean and swim away from the shore.

"I'm sorry," Anna said quickly. "I didn't mean it like that. I was happy to help, you know I was. You were sick."

"This language of disease," Sasha said, but she was too tired to finish the thought.

"Sasha, I'm sorry."

"It's okay. I'm sorry too. What do you want to do?"

"I called Liam. He's coming down here."

"Liam Deval? Why would you call him?"

"Because he's my best friend," Anna said. Sasha had never understood this. She found it unnatural. All of her own relationships had ended in disaster and she couldn't conceive of being friends with any of her former boyfriends. "Because he said to call me if I was ever in trouble, and we talk all the time anyway. And because Gloria's his mother," Anna said. "It's his mother's house. He needs to know."

"This woman, she was probably just who she said she was. You don't know—"

"A real estate agent who takes pictures of kids? Asks them their names, *identifies* them?" A high edge of hysteria. She lit another cigarette.

Sasha sighed and dropped her head into her hands. Every cell in her body was straining toward sleep.

"What do you want to do?" she asked, again.

"I don't know," Anna said. "I just want this to be over."

"Are you going to work?"

"I called in sick."

"Where's Chloe?"

"In her room. She's not going to school today. But maybe even that's not safe. I keep thinking, what if he knows where we live?"

"Anna, I have to get some sleep. Let's talk about this later." Sasha stood and left her sister alone in the kitchen. Theirs was a very small house on a street of small houses. Two bedrooms, a kitchen, a living room. But the basement was finished and she had it to herself, which suited her. It was a large room with her own small bathroom and a cool cement floor, easy to darken completely against the daylight. She drew the blackout blinds, locked the door and undressed, turned on the air conditioner and lay still on the bed. The ceiling was creaking softly, Anna pacing overhead. She heard Chloe and Anna talking but couldn't make out the words. She fell asleep and dreamed of snow.

S ASHA WOKE at two in the afternoon. The movement upstairs had ceased. She opened the door to the stairway, blinking in the light from upstairs, and the silence of the house came over her. There was a note on the kitchen table. *Liam arrived in town. We're staying with him in his motel for a while. I'll call you. Love, A.*

Her first thought was that now it would be easy to gamble, and the fact of that having been her first thought made her shiver. She went through the mechanical motions of coffee and breakfast, and even though she was almost always alone at this time of day—Anna at work, Chloe at her after-school program—their absence from the house was overwhelming. The light through the windows was too bright. She drank two cups of coffee, spent a long time in the shower, tidied the basement. She moved slowly, willing the time to pass, but when she was done with all of this she was still alone, there were still hours to get through before she could go to work. She called Anna, but Anna didn't answer her phone.

Sasha did a load of laundry, sat in the basement watching the dryer spin. Four fifteen. She did the ironing, hung up two clean uniforms and went outside. She stood on the front steps for a few minutes, unsure what to do with herself. It was going to rain later but for now light still hung in the air outside. She found her deck of cards and sat in front of the television set while the afternoon faded outside the window, shuffling and reshuffling and playing solitaire until her cell phone rang at four forty.

"Is tonight still good for you?" William Chandler asked. She'd forgotten that it was one of their regular coffee nights.

"Tonight's fine," she said. The relief of being saved from solitude. "You'll come after the dinner rush?"

"I'll be there," he said.

The television couldn't mask the emptiness of the house all around her. When she'd disconnected the call she went from room to room turning on every light, but it wasn't enough, so she left early and spent a half-hour drinking coffee and reading the paper in a booth before her shift started.

After the dinner rush she clocked out on break and returned to the same booth with her dinner. The rain had started. William Chandler shook his umbrella under the awning, a spray of silver droplets flying out through the air, and set it down in the foyer before he came to her.

"You seem distracted," William said.

"I am." Sasha hadn't turned the lights off before she'd left because the thought of coming home to a black and empty house was unbearable, but now she was worried about the electric bill. She thought of the house with every window ablaze through the night, a beacon on the darkened street. Rain was streaking the diner windows, light slipping down the glass. She found herself wishing for a real storm, for a hurricane, a reason to get in the car and drive away from this life. She'd read that the evacuees of Hurricane Katrina had dispersed to every

corner of the country, a New Orleans diaspora from Washington state
to Boston to California. Couldn't she join them? There were moments
when she wanted to leave everyone, even Anna and Chloe, strike out
alone into a new state and a new way of living. After everything Anna
had done for her.

"Have you been gambling?"

"No." She felt sick. "A little. Yes."

"A little?"

"I bought a couple of scratch-and-win tickets before work today."

"Just two?"

"Twelve," Sasha said. It had been so easy to slide back in. The tickets were so bright and as she'd carried them out to her car they'd
seemed almost like *real* tickets, like slips of paper that might transport
her to another place. The colors vibrating with possibility.

"Well," he said. "First time in a while. You have them with you?"

He knew her well. She'd kept them in her apron pocket. She laid
them out on the table, iridescent rectangles with gray smudges where
she'd scraped away the film to reveal the numbers. Across the room she
was aware of Bianca watching her with concern. They'd been working
together for years now and Bianca knew about the Gamblers Anonymous meetings, about the tickets, about Sasha's ruined credit rating
and her fallen-down life. They'd talked about scratch-and-win tickets.
Bianca had had a drinking problem when she was younger and said
she understood.

"You won twenty-one dollars," William said. "Congratulations.
Was it worth it?"

She'd seen it as a sign, but of course she couldn't tell him that. One
hundred twenty-one thousand, twenty-one, the mirror of twelve,
twelve tickets, if this wasn't a pattern then what was? But she knew
where the rabbit hole led and so she looked away from the twelve rect-

angles on the table and said, "Could you please take these away from me?" and when she looked back they were gone.

"What time do you get off work?"

"Six a.m.," she said.

"Seriously? That late?"

"I work twelve-hour shifts a couple times a week."

William was flipping through his notebook. It was a worn leather scrap of a thing that he carried everywhere. Sasha saw it as an affectation—who still carries a leather notebook?—and sometimes found it obscurely irritating.

"Here," he said, "there's a meeting up on Lakeview Crescent at seven." He wrote an address on a notebook page, tore it off and gave it to her. "I won't be there. Seven a.m.'s when I get my kid up for school. You'll go, won't you?"

"I will. Thank you."

SHE WAS tired at six a.m. but the suburbs were beautiful, the heat already rising and the sky streaked with pink, streetlights fading out as she drove. She was frightened but she had some hope. Daniel had come in after William had left and told her his plan. His grandmother was very close to death, he said, and he didn't like to think of death in these terms but the fact was that he was expecting an inheritance. He was going to go to Utah and negotiate with Paul. "People like him don't really want to draw attention to themselves," he'd said. "There's no reason why he wouldn't be willing to talk." She could have wept for happiness, but she'd settled for kissing him on the cheek. He was leaving for Utah the next morning.

Lakeview Crescent was in a planned development, the houses set at angles around a man-made lake with palm trees all around it, small piers out into the water. The meeting was being held in a private home. She drove slowly with the scrap of paper William had given her in her hand, reading numbers on mailboxes, but even before she read the street address of the meeting house she saw the cars out front.

In the chilled air of the living room Sasha picked a chair facing the floor-to-ceiling windows. The lake was brilliant in the early light.

"It's stocked with fish," a woman, Loreen, said. It was her house but she seemed anxious and out of place in it. She wore a white blouse and jeans and her hair was spiked up. The impression was of a punk rocker trying to impersonate a housewife. There was a white guitar leaning against a wall at the end of the room. The sleeve of her blouse slipped up as she passed Sasha a cup of coffee, and Sasha saw the edge of a tattoo—the letters "ocks" in gothic script, blurred and faded with time and sunlight. She wished she could ask to see the rest.

There was the usual round of introductions. She found herself looking out at the water, mesmerized and caffeinated, bone-tired, thinking about swimming. She wasn't a strong swimmer but she'd always enjoyed it, the shock of a new element, the moment of plunging when the water closed over her and she was suspended. She felt a little feverish, as always happened when she was exhausted, sweat between her uniform and her skin, and she realized that everyone was looking at her and that she'd heard her name at least once.

"I'm sorry," she said. "I just got off the night shift." There were sympathetic smiles but most of the people here were day workers, well dressed and polished, going to an early-morning meeting because after this they were driving to their offices, and she saw that they didn't really understand. "My name's Sasha," she said. "I used to gamble. I lost everything of value."

"What did you lose?" This from a man whose name she couldn't remember, thirtyish in a linen suit and expensive-looking glasses.

"I spent a student-loan payment on Lotto tickets and poker games," Sasha said, "so I had to drop out of school after a semester. I was studying English literature and finance. I know it doesn't matter anymore, but my grades that first semester were really high. I stole some watches. I stole my dad's car." She'd told the story so many times that it sounded flat to her now. A recitation about loss and poker games and tickets. "I bought some scratch-and-win tickets today," she said. "I mean yesterday. Before work."

"I did that too," Loreen said. "Just last week." The conversation shifted away from Sasha, toward scratch-and-win tickets and how they were everywhere now, every 7-Eleven and gas station and grocery store, and Sasha's attention drifted back to the lake. "It's all part of the sickness," someone said. Reflections of palm trees shimmered over the water.

WILLIAM CALLED her in the late afternoon, when he knew she'd be up. She was sitting on the front steps smoking a cigarette.

"Did you go to the meeting this morning?" he asked.

"I did," she said. "It was a good idea. Thanks for making me go."

"You sound tense."

"I'm fine." What could she possibly tell him? William understood gambling. He understood what it felt like to slip away from yourself and to move beyond your own control, to turn into someone you never meant to become who did things you never wanted to do, but he didn't know that her sister had stolen over a hundred thousand dollars from a drug dealer. She'd been sitting on the front steps for an hour, because she couldn't bear to be alone inside.

"I've known you for a while now," he said. "I don't believe you."

"Just family problems. No gambling."

"Okay," he said, and this was one of the things she liked best about him, the way he let things drop so easily. "Hope it all works out. You going to our regular meeting later?"

"I think I'll go tomorrow."

After the phone call she stayed on the steps for a while longer looking out at the twilight, restless and utterly alone. There were kids playing basketball in a driveway across the street. She waved when one of them looked at her, but he didn't wave back. There were hours to go before she had to leave for work but she didn't want to stay here anymore. She went back inside for her handbag and a clean uniform, draped the uniform carefully across the backseat of her car so it wouldn't get wrinkled, and left the neighborhood. She was as alone in the car as she'd been in the house, but at least the car didn't echo with anyone else's absence.

Sasha parked at the end of a beach access road and walked down to the water. There were two new scratch-and-win tickets in her pocket from when she'd stopped to get gas. Two was a manageable number. Two wasn't the end of the world. She wouldn't dive into the ocean tonight but it was nice to think that she could. The lights of a yacht shone over the water but other than that there was nothing, only the sea and the sand and the bright stars and Sasha, the tickets stiff and sharp-edged in the pocket of her jeans.

Twenty-Two

The thing about private investigators, Gavin had read some-where—Raymond Chandler? A dim memory of an essay with heavy underlining among his abandoned papers in New York, no doubt dragged out to the curb by his landlord and turning to mush in a landfill now—was that they wore trench coats. It sounds trivial but it isn't, because the profession exploded in the 1920s. These were men who'd been through trench warfare and emerged hard and half-broken into the glitter and commotion of the between-wars world; men out of time, out of place, hanging on by the threads of their uneven souls. The detectives were honorable but they'd seen too much to be good. The hardest among them had seen too much to be frightened. The mean streets were nothing compared to the trenches of Europe. Some of them had lost everything and all of them had lost something, and consequently most of them drank too much.

He'd been shot but he felt more tired now than hard-bitten. At his desk in the rec room of Eilo's house he stared at the flicker of the computer screen and thought of the motel room, the man's voice in the shadows and the soft carpet under his face. His fedora had been lost at the Draker Motel. It was too hot here for a trench coat.

"I brought you some lemonade," Eilo said. Ice cubes clinked softly as she set the glass on his desk. "It's cold."

"Thank you," he said. He was unexpectedly moved. "That's exactly what I wanted." *Wounded private detective Gavin Sasaki is reduced to tears by lemonade.*

"It's a hot day," she said. "There's a pitcher in the kitchen if you want more."

He had been doing desk work for a few days now, typing up descriptions of properties and uploading photographs, updating the website as new properties came in or were sold. Quiet, undemanding work and he didn't mind it, he liked not having to go out into the heat. But he was aware at all times of a story unfolding just beyond the edges of his vision, some terrible drama involving Anna and his lost daughter and Liam Deval and a gun, a transaction whose details remained dangerous and vague.

THAT NIGHT Gavin took a taxi back to the diner and sat by the window again until Sasha came to him.

"You're so pale," she said, when she gave him his coffee.

"I haven't been out much since I hurt my arm." And then, experimentally, "have you spoken with Daniel?"

She smiled. "He told me he has the money," she said. Her voice trembled a little, with fear or relief. "His inheritance came through. It's happening tomorrow night."

"It'll be nice when it's over with."

"It will be like it never happened," Sasha said, and he saw how desperately she wanted this. "We'll pay back the debt and he'll disappear. Are you ordering food?"

"Two hard-poached eggs and multigrain toast," he said.

She nodded and turned away from him. He watched her recede across the restaurant, wondering why, if this whole thing was simply a matter of paying off a debt, Liam Deval was in Florida with a gun.

W HEN GAVIN went back to the diner the following night, Sasha was at a banquette with a girl. His breath caught, but she wasn't his daughter. She was older than the girl in the photograph. He realized as he crossed the room that he'd seen her before, leaning on the door frame of a house where everyone was sleeping, her eyes closed.

"May I join you?" he asked. Sasha had watched his approach. She shrugged, so he sank into the booth across from them. The girl was sitting by the window with Sasha beside her, and it seemed to Gavin that she was dressed oddly. The last time he'd seen her she'd been wearing cut-off shorts and a dirty t-shirt, but now she wore a cheap-looking white-and-pink dress with scratchy-looking lace and bows on the sleeves. She looked like a thirteen-year-old playing at being nine. Her hair was darker than he remembered.

"Hello, Grace," he said.

"You two know each other?"

"I've seen her around."

The girl only watched him. He couldn't read her expression. She was perfectly still.

"She doesn't talk much," Sasha said.

"Probably wise." The girl's silence made Gavin uneasy. "Only gets you in trouble." It occurred to him that she was probably always in trouble anyway. "You dyed your hair," he said. He realized that he had absolutely no idea how to speak to a thirteen-year-old, and he seemed to have said the wrong thing. Grace winced.

"She's being a good sport," Sasha said. "Aren't you, Grace?"

"A good sport?" A plan unfolding all around him while he only grasped at its hanging threads. "What do you mean?"

"You said you knew the plan," Sasha said. "You know exactly what I mean."

"They said if I sat here in this dress by the window," Grace said, in a voice so soft he could hardly hear her, "then I wouldn't face charges."

"Charges," he repeated helplessly. He was so close now but he still couldn't see it, he didn't quite grasp how her presence here fit into any sort of a larger scheme, the story just beyond his reach. "Who said that, Grace?"

"The detective," Grace said. "The detective and Anna."

"Grace," Sasha said, "would you listen to your music for a minute?"

Grace had a tiny plastic purse, suitable for a girl much younger. She zipped it open with difficulty—it was cheap, and the zipper stuck—and pulled out a scratched-up iPod, inserted the earbuds and looked away from them. He could hear the music very faintly but couldn't make out what it was.

"Sasha," Gavin whispered, "I don't know this part of the plan. Could you tell me what's going on here?"

"What do you mean, you don't know this part of the plan? This *is* the plan."

"She's not—you're not giving her to anyone, are you?"

"Of course not," Sasha whispered. "You know that. She's a decoy."

"So nothing will happen to her?"

"She'll sit here as planned, and at a certain point I'll walk her toward the back door in full view of someone who will be waiting outside in the parking lot. That's all."

"Why her?"

"She's a runaway," Sasha said softly. "She's facing drug charges. She's at hand."

"So if she sits here as a decoy, the drug charges go away?"

"All she has to do is remain in full view through the windows while a payment gets handed off in the parking lot. It's not such a bad deal. How do you not know all of this? You said you knew the—"

"What happens to her afterward?"

"Afterward? I'll drive her home."

"The home she ran away from."

"It's an imperfect world. Would you rather have Chloe sitting here?"

Gavin was silent.

"Me neither," she said, "Grace made a deal. She knows what she's doing. Nothing will happen to her."

"Then why not have Chloe here?"

"There's always a risk."

"And you think this girl's disposable." Something was welling up inside him. He reached across the table and pulled the earbuds gently from Grace's head. He heard thin tinny voices. She was listening to rap.

"Grace," he said, "do your parents know you're here?"

Grace reached for the earbuds and turned her face to the window. Sasha was glaring at him.

"Gavin, what the hell was that?"

"She's so goddamn young," he said.

"We all were, at one point or another." Sasha sipped her coffee, watching him over the rim. It struck him, watching her, that he'd never realized how hard she was. "And we all survived our youths, didn't we? She fell into our laps. She's a little old for our purposes, but

she looks young for thirteen and Chloe's almost eleven. It's plausible."
Sasha glanced at her watch. "Are you really supposed to be here
for this?"

"No," Gavin said, "I don't think I am." His arm was throbbing, a
dull sick pain. The floor lurched alarmingly when he stood, the diner
lights too bright. "Will you . . . could you possibly tell me where to
find Anna?"

"I don't know where she is," Sasha said. "She just said she was going
to another motel."

"If she—if you speak with her," he said, "will you tell her I'd like
to talk?"

"I will," Sasha said.

"Thank you." He crossed the room and opened the door with his
good hand, walked out of the air conditioning into the heat and the
darkness of the parking lot. Long after dark but he still felt heat radiating from the pavement.

A taxi was pulling into the parking lot. Gavin stepped between two
cars and watched Liam Deval get out. Deval paid the driver, but he
didn't enter the diner. He was walking toward the back of the building, where shadows hung black and the parking lot faded into bushes
and weeds, and Gavin didn't want to see any more. When he looked up
Grace was still listening to music in the window, her hair falling over
her face. Sasha was staring into her coffee cup.

The diner wasn't far from his apartment, two miles, maybe three.
Gavin slipped between the parked cars and walked quickly away from
there, turned away from Route 77 onto a side street. The beauty of the
suburbs at night, streetlight shining through palm trees, the flicker of
sprinklers on lawns, strange shadows. The pleasure of being alone
outside after all these days of interiors. He was wandering through a
new housing development when he realized he was lost. He didn't

recognize the name of the street he was on. Half of the new houses seemed vacant. At the far end of the development they weren't even finished yet, skeletal beams against the sky. Raw dirt driveways with tall weeds, an abandoned bulldozer silhouetted black. Does a house still count as a ruin if it's abandoned before it's done? Asphalt soft beneath his shoes. He was aware of his footsteps on the silent street.

He crossed an expanse of weeds to the next cul-de-sac, an older neighborhood where the houses had people in them, out onto a wider commercial strip. A 7-Eleven was shining like a beacon ahead. He went in and bought a map. His thoughts were scattered. He didn't think he'd wandered that far from Route 77, but it took Gavin and the 7-Eleven counter guy a solid five minutes to find themselves on the map. All the streets looped and circled back on themselves and crashed up against grids, the grids broke into a spaghetti chaos of freeways and came back together on the other side and then disintegrated into loops again, and also the 7-Eleven guy was stoned.

Gavin found the intersection closest to his apartment after a while, but the loops and circles of the outer suburbs made for a confounding route and the 7-Eleven guy was distracted by the way all the streets *converged*, man. Gavin thanked him and set off in what he thought was the correct direction, but it wasn't easy to tell and all his thoughts were of Anna, Chloe, the girl in the diner. He kept realizing that he'd been walking without thinking, taking random turns. He wandered in and out of three cul-de-sacs. All the houses looked the same to him. Dogs barked occasionally. A shadow in the middle of the street turned into the silhouette of an animal he couldn't identify, then ran off into the bushes. An iguana, he decided a few blocks later, and he wished the street had been bright enough to see its skin.

Gavin lost track of where he was on the map, so he resolved to set his course by the stars. It was a clear night and in theory he was trying to get home again, but it seemed to him later that he'd really just wanted to keep walking and stay alone with his thoughts, away from the diner where at this moment a glassy-eyed runaway in a frilly dress was playing the part of his daughter and a plan that had a gun in it was moving into action. He was trying to understand and something was pulling at him, a memory of a story covered years ago by the *New York Star*, something about a lost child. Gavin found the North Star and kept it over his left shoulder, or tried to, but the streets wouldn't cooperate.

AFTER SOME time Gavin came upon a wider road—a semitrailer roared past in the darkness—and ahead were the bright signs of chain restaurants, a shopping mall that he recognized. The mall had faux-Greek pillars around the entrance, a banner reading SUMMER MIDNITE MADNESS!!! sagging over the glass doors.

Gavin walked blinking into the mall's winter chill and found a bench under a plastic-and-fabric palm tree. It was a mall filled with elevators and mezzanines. He found himself gazing blankly up at the levels of other people, these stragglers under the spell of a late-night summer sale, sales clerks smiling fixedly from store entrances. What was the *Star* story? It had been published years ago but there was something in it that he thought might somehow pull everything together, if only he could remember the details. There had been a lost boy in the Bronx, a transaction. He hadn't worked on the story but he remembered his editor and another reporter talking about it, and what was startling was that after all these months, here under the halogen lights of this distant southern land, in this unrecognizable life, he still had his editor's cell-phone number programmed into his phone. He scrolled through the names, all these ghosts from his vanished life, let her name slide past on the screen three times before he summoned the courage to press the button that sent the call through the satellites to New York.

"I almost didn't pick up," Julie said. He imagined her in the night quiet of the *Star* newsroom, her stocking feet on her desk and her hand on her forehead, the far-off look she always had when she talked on the telephone.

"Hello, Julie," he said. He hadn't seen her since an afternoon months earlier, a different lifetime actually, when he'd risen from a conference-room table with her and the editor-in-chief and the directors of the personnel and legal departments staring at him and walked out of the *Star* building for the last time.

"You know where I work now?" Her tone was studiedly casual. "A *website,* Gavin. There isn't even paper involved anymore."

"You lost your job?"

"Most of us did."

"I'm sorry," he said. "I can't tell you how sorry I am." He could think of nothing else to say. He closed his eyes against the mall's cool light and pressed the palm of his hand against the plastic bench.

"I'm not even going to ask why you lied in your stories, Gavin. Nothing you could possibly say would make it better."

"I wasn't myself," he said. "I came a little undone."

"Just like that," Julie said, but she sounded deflated, the fight fading from her voice. It was, after all, one thirty in the morning. She sighed audibly and he reformatted his image of her into another, imagined office. What kind of space would a website occupy? He pictured a loft, an open workspace, her feet up on a different desk, the ceiling so high that shadows gathered up above her.

"Julie, I have to ask you something. It's about a story."

"You know, I've often wished over the past few months that you'd come to me to ask about stories," she said. "But it seems a little late now, doesn't it?"

"You have no reason to believe me," he said, "but it's important. I wouldn't have called if it wasn't."

She was silent, but she didn't hang up.

"Do you remember two years ago, maybe two and a half, the paper covered a story about an abandoned boy in the Bronx? You worked on the story. I think there'd been a shootout or something, and the kid had somehow been part of it. There was some kind of drug connection."

"Theo," she said, after a moment. "Theo Cordell. He was seven."

"Will you tell me about it? I was thinking about it just now."

"You called me at, what, one thirty-five in the morning," Julie said, "to ask about a story I worked on two years ago?"

"I knew you'd be up."

"You knew I'd be up. Fine," she said, "why not? Let's tell each other stories. A seven-year-old boy was found wandering in the Bronx after a shootout. Turned out the boy's father was one of the men who'd been shot. He'd taken the kid along to some meeting, I can't remember all the details but it was a drop-off of some kind, at the other party's request."

"But why would the other person request that? Wouldn't a kid just get in the way?"

"The deal was, if either the product or the count was off, I can't remember which it was, the other party would take the kid."

"Was it off? The product, or the count?"

"One or the other," Julie said. "I can't remember now. The kid escaped in the confusion."

"So the kid came along to the transaction," Gavin said, "as, what, a kind of insurance policy?"

"Exactly," Julie said. "That's exactly it." She was animated now, the exhaustion fallen from her voice. She had a passion for people, for drama, for news. It seemed to him that she'd perhaps forgotten whom she was speaking to, or perhaps they'd managed to slip back through some invisible doorway into a time when he hadn't yet given her cause to despise him. "The detective told me it's not that uncommon. The theory is that people who'll risk their own lives won't risk their kids."

"Except Theo's father did."

"Well," she said, "you can't choose your parents."

"What happened to him?"

"To Theo? He went into foster care. I don't know what happened to him after that."

"Thank you for talking to me," he said. He wanted the call to end before she remembered who he was and became angry again, and also he was feeling ill.

"Good-night, Gavin."

He disconnected. His head was pounding and his arm was throbbing, an ache that he was afraid might stay with him forever. It was nearly two in the morning. He'd left Sasha and the girl at the diner two hours ago and whatever had happened there was almost certainly over by now. It was too late to do anything but he thought he finally understood.

How does this play out? A man from Utah arrives in a parking lot. Through the window he sees a girl in a white-and-pink dress. She's thirteen but she's small for her age, she could be ten, she could be Chloe, especially in that getup with her hair falling over her face, especially from a slight distance. Someone speaks to him and the arrangements are made. He sees through the diner window that the girl is being led toward the back door, his insurance. Someone's giving him money tonight. He's confident that the amount will be correct because the girl will be standing there when he counts it. And then?

The pain from his arm was overwhelming. Gavin left the mall and in the parking lot he realized that he was closer to Jack's house than he was to his apartment, so he set off walking in the direction of Mortimer Street.

Twenty-Three

J ack had been playing the saxophone on and off for a long time
before he became aware of movement at the edge of the yard.
Gavin was coming through the bushes at the side of the house.
"Don't stop," Gavin said. So Jack continued, eased back into another long loop of melody. George Gershwin's "Summertime." Music
for a place where it was almost always summer. He knew an arrangement that kept the song looping around and around and he improvised
inside it, leaving the melody and wandering away and then coming
back to the tune again, *and the living is easy*, long and slow and meander-
ing, soft and low under the orange tree. Jack always imagined a singer's
voice when he played this song, a woman soothing a child to sleep on a
porch in the southern lands that lay north of Florida, Alabama, Missis-
sippi, a summer afternoon with the air heavy around them, a breeze
through tall grass. He stopped all at once because the daydream and
backyard had converged and he was momentarily disoriented, caught
between the two. There was a soft wind moving through the grass
around him, and the lawn hadn't been mowed in so long that the grass

rippled. Gavin was watching him with that look he always had
since he'd come back from New York. Anxious, something desperate
about the eyes.

"That was beautiful," Gavin said.

"Thanks." The instrument felt inert in Jack's hands now that the
music had left it. He tried to lean the saxophone against his lawn chair
but it toppled over and fell into the grass, an empty shell. He decided to
leave it there for the moment. There was a high silent whine in his
bloodstream, sweat on his forehead, he needed another pill. Gavin
sank into the chair beside him and closed his eyes.

"What happened to your arm?"

"Bar fight," Gavin said. "You should see the other guy."

It seemed to Jack that there'd been a time when Gavin would have
just answered the question. "I miss everything sometimes," he said. He
meant high school and the Lola Quartet, his life before South Carolina,
but he realized as he spoke and as the flicker of confusion crossed
Gavin's face that he didn't want to have to explain all this, so he spoke
again quickly. "You like that song?"

"I always liked that song," Gavin said. "There was a guy who'd play
'Summertime' on his saxophone on the street near Columbus Circle,
Broadway and 61st, maybe 62nd Street. I used to stand there and listen
to him sometimes on my way home from work."

"I knew a girl who thought it was about death," Jack said.

"Death? When I hear that song I always sort of picture a woman
rocking a child to sleep. I always thought it was peaceful."

"That bit in the middle," Jack said. "The lyric about rising up singing into the sky."

"I thought that part was about leaving home."

Jack reached into his pocket. The shivering in his blood was getting worse. "This girl, Bernadette, she knew her stuff," he said. "She studied a lot." He swallowed a pill, quickly. He didn't think Gavin noticed. "She said that part was about dying."

Gavin was silent, looking at nothing or maybe at his distant spired city where men played saxophones on Broadway.

"You can hear it in some of the versions," Jack said. "Not all of them. You ever heard the Nina Simone cover?"

"I'm not sure." Gavin sounded distracted.

"Some versions are pretty bright and harmless, lots of brass. Ella Fitzgerald's recording was like that. But I hear Nina Simone's version and I think the girl was right. The drummer makes a sound like static and then the first note's a growl, the bass line's ominous and it kind of drags, and the melody's on piano but the piano's muted. It sounds fragile. You can hardly even hear the melody at the beginning. Half the song, it's just the piano drowning in the bass line, trying to break through. The singing doesn't start till halfway through, and then when it gets to that part about rising up singing, it's like—" Like a thunderstorm, like disintegration, like a soul rising up, but Jack felt stupid saying these things aloud. "I don't know, you can just hear it in that version."

"Jack," Gavin said, "do you know what's happening tonight?"

"I don't know." Jack wasn't sure what Gavin meant but earlier in the evening he'd been inside and he'd heard a car door slam. Through the living room window he'd watched Grace walk down the driveway to the waiting car. She'd been wearing a dress that reminded him of his little sister's china dolls, and this detail was so strange that he couldn't stop thinking about it, but stranger still was the identity of the driver waiting for her by the car. "What time is it?"

"Two o'clock," Gavin said. "Maybe a little later. I keep thinking, if I'd just known, if I'd known she was pregnant. But then I think, maybe I *did* know, maybe I just didn't do anything about it . . ."

Jack had taken a Vicodin but it wasn't enough, his skin was crawling, so he swallowed another. Why hadn't he called Gavin, all those years ago, when Anna arrived at Holloway College with a baby? He took another pill and sat still for a while before he spoke again, waiting for the substances in his bloodstream to light up. "I think she should have told you," he said. Gavin was looking at him now, a ghost in the dark. A light blinked on in the house and cast complicated blue-yellow shadows over the grass. "But you didn't hear that from me."

"What happened to that girl who was staying here?"

"Grace," Jack said. "I don't know what's happening to Grace. She left earlier in a funny dress." He remembered his saxophone and lifted it from the grass.

"Who did she leave with?"

"Anna," Jack said. "She left with Anna."

"Do you know where Anna is?"

"No."

"I want to talk to her," Gavin said, but Jack thought he was talking mostly to himself.

"Why would you want to talk to Anna? When has Anna ever done anything good?" Jack wasn't sure if he'd spoken aloud. He was floating. The saxophone was warm and clammy in his hands and it caught the light from the house, an ethereal shine down the curve of the bell. He liked looking at lights when he was in this state. All the edges were shimmering. "I'm going to play again," he said.

"Wait," Gavin said.

"What for?"

"Jack, listen, it's none of my business, but it seems like maybe you're taking a lot of pills."

"The thing with this arrangement of 'Summertime,'" Jack said, "is you can just keep it going. There's the first section that everyone knows, and then—"

"What are you on, Jack? Is it Vicodin? Oxycontin?"

"I'm going to play again," Jack said. Playing, he had realized, was something that would preclude talking. He wanted to fall back into music and rest for a while. He started playing "Summertime" at half-speed, almost a dirge, slow light all around him, and when he looked up some time later Gavin was gone. He drifted alone in his lawn chair on the grass.

Twenty-Four

When Gavin reached his apartment he took two Vicodin and flushed the rest down the toilet. He sat for a long time in front of the television. Remembering nothing of the programs he was watching, bone-tired, anesthetized by the flickering blue light. When he allowed his thoughts to wander he imagined an alternative version of events: he arrives in Florida on assignment from the *New York Star*, spends a few days interviewing people about the exotic-wildlife problem, following William Chandler around swamps, writing up his notes in a Ramada Inn in the evenings. Until finally he meets Eilo for dinner in a seafood restaurant, and this is where the fantasy begins: they have a pleasant dinner and he drives back to the hotel afterward, and the difference between this scene and what actually happened is that when Gloria Jones's house goes into foreclosure the bank calls a different broker, not Eilo, so Eilo never goes to Gloria Jones's house and never has a photograph to give him.

. . .

Gᴀᴠɪɴ ᴅɪᴅɴ'ᴛ realize he'd fallen asleep until he heard the doorbell. He started awake and the television was showing a nature special, seagulls wheeling through the air above a rocky shore. He stood up, his heart beating too quickly, and the doorbell rang again. It was four in the morning.

At the bottom of the stairs was his front door, and on the other side of this a dusty foyer where his mail was delivered. The door between the foyer and the street was steel with a dusty spyhole that he'd never looked through. The glass was so greasy that he saw only a vague shadow, a man standing outside with his arms folded over his chest. He couldn't tell who it was. Gavin got down on one knee and called through the letter slot. "Who are you?"

"Liam," the man said. "It's Liam."

Gavin only knew one Liam. There was no reason to let him in except his own desperate curiosity, and the shock of Liam Deval being there at all; here after all these weeks was his story, waiting on the other side of another door. Gavin unlocked the door and opened it a crack.

Liam Deval was shivering in the streetlight. "Can I come in?"

Gavin stood back, and Deval slipped past him into the foyer and up the stairs. In the light of the apartment Deval looked malarial, glittery-eyed and shivering with streaks of sweat down his face. His hair wet against his forehead, sweat coming through his shirt.

"I came to apologize," Deval said. "I'm sorry. I can't tell you how sorry I am." He was looking at Gavin's arm in the sling. Gavin nodded but said nothing. He wasn't sure what a person was supposed to say in these circumstances, what the etiquette was for forgiving or failing to forgive the man who'd sent a bullet into your arm. His bandages itched.

"I never would have done it if I'd known who you were," Deval said. "Why did you let me in?"

"That's a good question. Curiosity, I guess."

"Is it okay if I just stay here for a few minutes?"

"Are you armed?"

"I threw it away," Deval said. "Can I use your bathroom?"

"It's there on the left." Deval stood before the bathroom sink and began methodically scrubbing his hands with soap and hot water. Steam rose and clouded the mirror. Gavin left him there and went into the living room. He turned off the TV and straightened the pile of newspapers, moved his cameras from the coffee table to the lower shelf of the television stand. "Can I offer you anything?" he asked, when Deval emerged from the bathroom. Deval's eyes looked unnaturally bright.

"Do you have any alcohol?"

"Alcohol, no, I've just got juice and orange soda. Or I could make some coffee if you'd like."

"You have any lemons?"

"Lemons?"

Deval nodded.

"Actually, I think I might."

"Would you mind boiling some water," Deval said with curious intensity, "and then squeezing some lemon juice into it? I know it's a strange request."

In the kitchenette Gavin filled the kettle, put it on the stove and began searching one-handed in the fridge. A slightly desiccated lemon was hiding behind a ketchup bottle. "I used to go to Barbès to hear you play," he said, to break the silence. He sensed Deval watching his every move.

Deval's eyes seemed to focus. "Barbès," he said. "Barbès. Really?"

"Before I knew you were involved in . . . in any of this," Gavin said, trying to keep the frustration at the fact that he still didn't know exactly what *this* was out of his voice, all he had to go on was his own wild conjecture, his guesses, his suspicions and his paltry trail of clues. "Whatever you're involved in. I used to go every Monday night. Feels like a different lifetime."

"Barbès," Deval said. "I was just thinking of that place a little earlier."

Gavin heard a noise he couldn't immediately identify, and he realized that Deval's teeth were chattering. Gavin turned off the air conditioner, opened the other window in the living room as far as it would go. Soft sounds of traffic drifted up from the street. The heat at this time of night wasn't terrible.

"I used to stand at the back," Gavin said. He walked past Deval into the bedroom and pulled a blanket from the unmade bed. Deval was staring at him through the doorway, as if Gavin's words were all that kept him from floating off. "I was there listening to you every week for a while, you and Arthur Morelli. I loved your sound."

"I loved it too," Deval said.

"Why did you stop playing together?"

"We had a falling-out." Deval reached for the blanket and pulled it close around him. "It's hard to play with someone for a long time. It's like a marriage. Sometimes it lasts forever, sometimes you get sick of each other, sometimes the other party gets tired of playing the rhythm part."

The kettle was whistling. Gavin found a clean mug and filled it, but the lemon was hard and almost dry. He squeezed as hard he could with his good hand. He could only get a few drops out of it, but Deval didn't complain when he raised the hot water to his lips.

"Thank you," Deval said. The drink seemed to calm him. He sipped, gazing around at the unremarkable room, and his shivering subsided.

"Did something happen to you?"

"I took care of something," Deval said. "I solved a problem." His hands were shaking again. Gavin sat on the other end of the sofa, unsure where to look, trying not to stare.

"Listen," Gavin said. Deval's expression was inscrutable. "The whole time I've been back in Florida, I've been trying to find out what happened to a girl named Anna Montgomery. Do you know her?"

Deval didn't speak for a moment. "Do I *know* her," he said. He made a sound very much like a laugh. "Yeah, I know Anna."

"When did you meet her?"

Deval glanced at Gavin's bandaged arm. "I guess the least I could do is tell you a story," he said. "I met her at a music school in South Carolina. She'd stolen some money and she was on the run with her baby, which was as crazy as it sounds, and she knew my roommate. She just appeared out of nowhere in the dorm one night. She'd had to leave Utah quickly. She didn't really have a plan."

"Why didn't she go to her sister?"

"Because Daniel told her not to. He told the guy she'd stolen money from that she'd never go anywhere but back to Florida, then he called her and begged her to go anywhere else." Deval lifted the mug with some difficulty. His hands were unsteady. "She was thinking of people she knew outside Florida, people who were kind, and she wasn't really close to anyone outside your jazz quartet. She thought of Jack."

"Jack's kind."

"He is. Inept, but kind. It wasn't such a bad choice."

"So she arrives in South Carolina with a baby. Then what?"

"I drove her to Virginia," Deval said. "I know it's crazy, but I was already half in love with her that first night and I liked her kid, and I thought, you know, why not? She couldn't stay in the dorm. There was something about her. I wanted out of the music school anyway, I was young and stupid and thought I was too good to be there. I wanted an adventure, and if you're in a position to help someone, shouldn't you? She had a tattoo of a bass clef on her shoulder and I took it as a sign. I had ideas about what I wanted my life to be. Living with a woman and a child, I liked that, there was something settled about the arrangement. We were together for three years."

"And what brings you to Sebastian?"

"Someone came to my mother's house and took a picture of the kid." Deval leaned forward, his elbows on his knees, and slowly lowered his face into his hands.

"Your mother? Gloria Jones, that woman she was staying with a few months back?"

"Gloria. Yes."

"A picture. That's what started this whole thing?" He felt ill. The picture of Chloe was stuck to his fridge with a magnet.

"You can't imagine how terrified Anna was. She calls me sobbing in New York, tells me Paul's found her. It all just happened so quickly after that. I came down to Florida, plans were made . . ." He sat up, his eyes unfocused. "How far would you go for someone you love?"

"Is that a serious question?"

"Yes."

"I don't know," Gavin said. "Far." Who did he love? Eilo. Maybe Karen, he realized, even now. It seemed paltry, loving only two people in the entire teeming world, but he knew some people had far less.

"Exactly. You never know how far you'll go till you're faced with it."

"How far . . . ?" But he didn't want to know.

"I owed her," Deval said. "I lived off her money for years. She funded the first album I recorded with Morelli." He turned suddenly to Gavin. "I don't want to do the wrong thing anymore."

"I don't want to do the wrong thing anymore either," Gavin said, but he didn't think Deval heard him.

"Are you supposed to just go back to your life, after something like this?" Deval didn't seem to expect an answer. He'd looked away again. He was gazing into the air at the center of the room. "That *sound*," he said. "It was like he was choking."

"What?"

Deval shook his head and swallowed hard. "I'm sorry," he said. "I came here to apologize. I didn't know who you were when you came lurching into the room at the Draker. I didn't realize how sick you were, I thought you were coming at me, I just panicked and there was a gun in my hand." He was standing. He swiped his hand over his eyes and pulled the blanket from his shoulders, folded it into a neat square without looking at Gavin. "Thanks for letting me in," he said.

"There's one last thing. I have a small favor to ask of you."

"What kind of favor?"

"I just want to talk to Anna," Gavin said. "I just want to know that she's okay. Could you possibly tell me where to find her?"

Deval hesitated a moment, looking at the square of blanket in his hands. "Fine," he said. "I suppose I owe you that. You just want to talk to her?"

"That's all."

There was a pen on the coffee table from when Gavin had been doing the crossword puzzle. Deval wrote an address on the corner of a newspaper page. "She gets in late," he said. "Ten, eleven p.m."

"Thank you." Gavin shook Deval's hand and locked the door behind him, listened to Deval's footsteps receding on the stairs. He turned on all the lights. Sleep was out of the question. He felt watched. There was no sound except the distant hum of traffic through the open window. He closed the window, turned on the air conditioner for background noise and then the television set for company, lay down on the sofa with the blanket over him and tried to think of nothing but the screen.

Twenty-Five

A day earlier, the day of the transaction, Sasha started swimming again. She'd rarely taken advantage of the recreation center pool before—it was ten dollars for a pass, and she never felt like swimming at convenient moments—but on the way home from the diner that morning she saw sun glinting off the vaulted recreation center roof ahead and she was struck by an unexpected wistfulness. She hadn't swum seriously since high school, and only occasionally afterward.

When she arrived home the thought of swimming hadn't yet left her. She knew she should be sleeping but the transaction was so close now and her thoughts were racing. She went through all her drawers and found her swimsuit under the t-shirts, threw it into a shopping bag with a towel and went back out. At the recreation center she paid the fee—the attendant glanced at her waitressing uniform but said nothing—and changed quickly in the damp of the locker room. It was seven thirty in the morning, the pool deserted but for two men swimming laps. Sasha dove in and the water closed over her. She swam two laps, which was all she could manage after so long without exercise, drove home with wet hair in the sunlight and fell into a blessedly dreamless sleep.

W HEN SHE woke in the late afternoon she lay still on the bed for a while, feeling curiously light. A faint scent of chlorine rose from her skin in the shower. Tonight was the transaction, tomorrow Anna and Chloe could come back and the house wouldn't seem like a tomb above her, tomorrow the debt would be paid. She drove to the diner and clocked in early, and a few hours passed in a haze of plates and bright lighting. Bianca touched her shoulder near midnight.

"Someone here to see you," she said. "A kid."

Sasha looked past her and saw the girl waiting by the hostess stand. The girl was looking down at her shoes, tugging at a too-tight sleeve of her frilly dress. Beyond the girl she saw Anna, just for a moment, watching her from the other side of the glass door to the parking lot. Anna turned away into the darkness.

"She's my cousin," Sasha said. A part of her wanted to run after Anna. She hadn't seen her in so long.

"Bit late for a kid that age to be out, isn't it?"

"Family problems," Sasha said. It pained her to lie to Bianca. "Bad divorce. I told her, you feel like you can't be at home, you come visit me here, no matter what time it is. Listen, I'm clocking out on break."

Sasha went to the girl and stood before her. The girl's eyes were flat, a greenish shade of blue. An unnerving blankness in her stare that made Sasha wonder if she was entirely well.

"Come sit with me a while," Sasha said.

. . .

Hours later, afterward, when Gavin had come and left and everything had gone exactly as Daniel had said it would, when Grace had finished her milkshake and was dozing off in the booth, Sasha told Bianca she wasn't feeling well and clocked out. At three in the morning she was driving slowly down Mortimer Street with Grace in the passenger seat, reading street numbers.

"Here," Grace said.

"This is where you live?" Sasha stopped the car in front of 1196 Mortimer and she was certain that she'd been here before, perhaps years ago, but she couldn't fix an event in memory. Grace didn't answer. She closed the car door behind her and disappeared around the side of the house.

Sasha cut the engine and got out of the car. She waited for a light to come on in the house, but none did. A window on the first floor was broken; the other windows reflected streetlight but this one absorbed it, a blank rectangle of cardboard or wood. She stood on the street for a few minutes, looking at the darkened house and the shadowed chaos of plants all around it, pale explosions of blossoms in ink-black leaves. The front lawn hadn't been cut in some time. A faint scent of flowers in the still air. She was alone.

Sasha knew she should be exhausted but she wasn't. She drove to an open-all-night doughnut shop and drank coffee for a while, trying to read the paper but too jittery. She was waiting in her car in the recreation center parking lot when the doors opened at five a.m. At this hour fourteen out of fifteen lanes belonged to the swim team, a flock of teenagers and adults in black swimsuits who dove in one after another with hardly a splash and shot through the water with such speed and power that she felt her breath catch in her chest. She slipped as unobtrusively as possible into the unoccupied lane.

Something was troubling her, a memory from a few hours before. As far as she was aware the transaction had gone flawlessly and Anna's debt had been paid. She had been sitting in the diner with Grace when her cell phone had vibrated on the table. A text message from Daniel: *Hi Sasha.* This was her cue.

"Come with me," she said to Grace, who hesitated just a moment and then obeyed. She walked slowly with Grace down the length of the restaurant—all but deserted at this hour—and when they were almost at the back door she'd said "Grace, go in there for a few minutes, will you?" and Grace went as directed into the restroom. Sasha turned her back to the windows. But first she glanced outside—she didn't mean to—and saw a man's pale face looking up at her. He was standing at the very back of the parking lot. She looked away quickly and it seemed that he turned away at the same time, as if both were embarrassed to have met one another's eyes in the middle of all this, whatever this transaction was that they'd found themselves in. But what was strange—and all these hours later she lost her rhythm in the pool, turned over onto her back in the middle of her third lap to look up at the distant ceiling with her breath tight in her chest—was that just at the instant when she averted her gaze he seemed to fall away, as if a trapdoor had opened under his feet or his knees had failed him.

Sasha reached for the edge of the pool and hauled herself gasping up on the side. She sat with her feet in the water, the swim team flashing up and down the lanes before her. She'd walked to the back of the restaurant. She'd looked out the window. The man's pale face, a half-second of descent in her peripheral vision as she'd turned from him.

She left the pool and the clamor of the swim team, washed the chemicals from her hair and put her uniform back on. When she stepped out into the parking lot it was six a.m., bright morning. She drove home and prepared herself for bed, but sleep was elusive. At eleven a.m. she gave up and turned on the light. She wanted to go outside into the fresh air and sunlight, but she knew she could fall asleep again only if she kept the illusion of night.

Sasha had long ago fallen into the habit of reading when she couldn't sleep. Easy to forget sometimes that there were books back at the beginning of everything, that she'd gone to Florida State because she'd loved books and that even in the long fall into patterns and numbers she hadn't lost this. She turned on the lamp in the late-morning darkness of the basement and pulled a volume at random from the shelf above her bed. A translated-from-the-Russian novel that she'd read twice already, *Delirious Things*. She read for a while about the unreliability of memory, about snow and northern lights.

She had never left the state of Florida and had never thought seriously about leaving, but she liked to imagine living under the aurora borealis and she'd looked up pictures of it on the Internet. Sasha sometimes imagined stepping through the front door of the house into a parallel universe where the aurora borealis came south to the Florida skies, a shadowed empty neighborhood with colors shifting overhead. When her alarm clock rang she woke exhausted, the bedside lamp shining and the book fallen from her hands.

Twenty-Six

Gavin woke with a dull headache throbbing behind his eyes, a morning news anchor in a pink suit telling him about the weather. Lights burned uselessly in the unoccupied rooms. It seemed crazy now that he'd found this place haunted a few hours earlier. If it weren't for the blanket he'd slept under, the empty cup on the coffee table, he might not have believed that Deval had been there at all. He considered the cup for a moment, took it to the sink and scrubbed it over and over again with hot water and soap and paper towels, wondering about the tenacity of DNA. At eight a.m. he called Eilo and told her he wasn't feeling well.

The story didn't appear till later in the day, in the online edition of the local paper. A body had been found behind the Starlight Diner. The victim had been identified as Paul J. Harris of Salt Lake City, Utah, shot twice in the chest with no witnesses sometime between the hours of midnight and three a.m. A quote from a detective on the Sebastian police force: while the police were actively pursuing all leads, there were no suspects at this time. Gavin turned away from his computer and looked down from his window at the movement of cars on the street. Thinking of Liam Deval sitting on his sofa twelve hours earlier, his hands shaking around the mug of hot water and lemon juice.

Twenty-Seven

I t was necessary to stop twice for scratch-and-win tickets on the way to work, but Sasha didn't buy many and she managed not to spend very much. She found when she pulled into the diner parking lot that night that she had been expecting the police tape. Her hands trembled on the steering wheel but she felt no surprise. There wasn't much to see. Bright yellow tape blocking the back half of the parking lot, two officers standing around talking in the end-of-day light, a police cruiser. She clocked into the clamor of the dinner rush. Some hours later when the restaurant was quiet she found herself standing next to Bianca, but it was a moment before she could bring herself to ask.

"No one told you yet? It's an awful thing," Bianca said. "You left what time last night? Around two thirty?" Sasha nodded. Around two thirty. "Well, early this morning," Bianca said, "maybe five a.m., Freddy goes out for a cigarette, I hear a yell. He comes running back in here, pale as a sheet, says there's someone lying in the parking lot out back, says it looks like he's been shot in the chest. Well, you know that detective comes in sometimes, friend of yours?"

"Daniel?"

"That's the one. He came in last night after you left, and he was lingering, drinking coffee and reading the paper. Told me he couldn't sleep. Anyway, he goes out back to see what Freddy's talking about, makes everyone stay inside so they don't contaminate the crime scene, next thing you know there's cops everywhere."

"Do they know who it was?"

"I heard a few of them talking. They said it was some criminal from Utah, some guy with a drug record."

"From Utah? Are you sure?"

"You look pale, sweetheart."

"I didn't sleep well." A new group was coming in, four men in hospital scrubs from St. Mary Star of the Sea Hospital, and Sasha crossed the room unsteadily to greet them. She gave them menus and a forced smile, took orders for drinks and moved on autopilot through the motions of her exhausting profession. There were moments that night when disaster seemed so certain that she found herself paralyzed, concentrating on breathing because breathing was all that was left, but sometimes she was above this kind of panic and floated through the hours in a state of suspended hope. The smooth surfaces of the tickets in her apron pocket every time she reached for change.

"You okay, doll?" Bianca was watching her.

"Fine," she said.

"You don't look it, hon." Bianca's voice would be Anna's voice in a few decades, the low rasp that follows a lifetime of cigarettes, and it reminded Sasha of her stepmother's voice, silent now, rest in peace, her father alone. Her hand hovered in the air for just a second and then she punched in the hamburger, the fries, the macaroni and cheese, the Diet Coke and 7-Up, and on the other side of the thin adjoining wall to the kitchen an efficient small machine spit out a receipt with the order and

Freddy tacked it up on the counter, the machinery of the restaurant moving into motion and Sasha at the middle of it. She was if nothing else an excellent waitress.

"That's not nothing," Anna had said a few months ago, "and surely there's more than that." There was. This evening Sasha looked out over her tables of customers and tried to remember all the things that were transcendent. Swimming, clean passage up and down the lanes. Chloe, a delight, an elf in the school Christmas play, sitting cross-legged on the sofa reading magazines, doing backflips and cartwheels in the backyard, careening down the street on a secondhand bicycle. A bell from the kitchen: an order was ready. Sasha carried the tray of food out into the dining room.

AT ELEVEN o'clock Sasha went outside to make a phone call. She usually went out back but that was impossible now that the space behind the diner was a crime scene, so she left through the front door and stood by the restaurant's neon sign, its bluish light flickering over the gardenia bushes. She counted thirty-eight flowers while she waited for Anna to pick up.

"Anna," Sasha said. She'd been so breathless since Bianca had told her, since she'd seen the police tape. "Am I calling too late?"

"You sound strange." Anna's voice was muffled and sleepy.

"Anna, they found a body behind the restaurant. They said—" and there were tears now, humiliating but at least Anna couldn't see her and she struggled to steady her voice—"Bianca, my coworker, she said a cop told her it was some drifter from Utah."

"From Utah?" Anna spoke a beat too late. She sounded fully awake now. "Really?"

"Anna," she said, but it wasn't possible to ask the question. "Anna . . ."

"What are you asking me?" An edge in Anna's voice that Sasha had heard only once before, a decade ago, when Anna had called her from Utah months after Sasha had seen her last, before Sasha had even realized she'd left town—I'm going to have a baby and I'm not sure if it's Gavin's or Daniel's, do you think I'm awful Sasha? I've run away and I couldn't tell Gavin and please don't tell him either, I'm so scared—and Sasha had done her best to soothe her over the staticky connection, Shh, of course you're not awful, everything's going to be fine, Anna, we'll work it out, and after she'd hung up she'd gone to buy baby clothes at the mall in a gesture of what? Acceptance? Love? Guilt, because her sister had been gone for three months and Sasha had been too caught up in the theatrics of her own life that summer to really notice. She reminded herself that they'd been living in different houses, each with their respective fathers, but still; it was shocking, actually, how easy it had been for Anna to leave town undetected, and Sasha always knew afterward that she should have been paying more attention.

"Are you still there?" Anna asked.

"I'm here."

"Then what are you asking me?"

Sasha found herself at a loss for words. What am I asking you? I'm asking you if I was complicit in something unspeakable, because Anna, Anna, I already carry so much. The tears hot on her face.

"That's a good question," she said. "I don't know, Anna. I don't know what I'm asking you." She disconnected and when she went back inside she put her phone in her handbag in the staff room, where she wouldn't be able to hear it ring. For just a moment she felt unreachable and protected, but of course everyone who knew her also knew where she worked.

. . .

Daniel was there at two in the morning, slump-shouldered and harrowed in the corner of a booth. Sasha poured two cups of coffee, milk and sugar for him, black for her. She set the coffee in front of him. He was changed, smudges of exhaustion under his eyes, a tightness around his mouth that she hadn't seen before.

"Hell of a thing," he said after a few minutes of silence, and it was so inadequate that she laughed out loud. She felt a little giddy. He gave her a look that she recognized from gambling. It was a look she'd seen across poker tables on the faces of men and women who'd been dealt poor hands and hadn't decided whether to bluff or not. Daniel was sizing her up, but he was also afraid. They had, she realized, something in common at that moment: neither of them knew what she was going to do.

"Sasha," he began, but stopped.

"Yes?"

"Sasha, I spoke with Anna earlier. She said you were a little . . . she said you seemed . . ." He had run out of words again. He looked at her helplessly for a moment and then turned his focus to pouring a third packet of sugar into his coffee and stirring it for longer than necessary.

"How's your investigation going, Daniel?"

"Investigation?" He looked up as if startled.

"The body behind the diner last night. The drifter from Utah."

"Well, it's not my investigation, but in my understanding there's no weapon, no suspect, and no motive."

"Not much of an investigation, then, is it?"

"Sasha," he said.

"Where's Liam?"

"Gone."

"*Gone* gone?"

"Jesus, Sasha, he just left town. People do that sometimes. He said he was leaving for Europe."

"Daniel," she said, "you told me not to worry about where the money came from."

"What?" That miserable fugitive look. It wasn't just exhaustion. He looked eaten alive.

"When you came back from Utah," she said. "All those weeks ago. You told me you'd talked to the dealer, arranged repayment of the money Anna took. I asked where the money was coming from, and you said you'd recently come into an inheritance. Do you remember telling me that?"

"I remember." He wouldn't meet her eyes. "A man like that has a lot of enemies," he said. "Would you believe me if I said I see this all the time?"

"Yes," she said. "People who think they're getting a payment and get shot instead, because there was never any money at all. Why did I believe you when you said there was money? I wanted so much to believe that this could actually be over, but—"

"Sasha, think about what you're saying."

"What am I supposed to say?"

"Think about how the things you say might affect other people," he said. "Think about your niece."

"I *am* thinking about my niece. My niece is the only reason I haven't gone to the police yet."

"Who would believe you if you did?"

"Daniel . . ."

"But suppose you did go to the police," Daniel said. "Suppose a troubled and unreliable woman with a long history of compulsive gambling did go to my colleagues and tell an improbable story about a detective with an impeccable record, even if that story was somehow believed, I was thinking of something earlier. That girl who was here last night, Grace. Did you know she's a runaway whose mother's in prison?"

"So?" But she understood, and she felt a chill down her spine.

"So you could turn Chloe into Grace, just by saying the word. You could take a little girl who lives happily with a mother who loves her, and you could set her adrift." He was speaking very quietly, leaning close across the table. His voice was flat but his eyes were shining. "Grace has been arrested three times, Sasha. She's a runaway living with a stripper and a drug addict. I'd say there but for the grace of God goes Chloe, but it isn't really God who gets to decide this one, is it?"

"You know that isn't what I want."

"Then let this blow over," Daniel said. "Let this go."

"Is that what you've done, Daniel? Let this go?"

But Daniel paid and left without answering her.

SASHA WENT home in the morning and took two sleeping pills that held her only just below the surface of sleep. After three hours she was awake again in the silence of the basement. *A troubled and unreliable woman with a long history of compulsive gambling.* The sleeping pills had left her dizzy and drugged. She was aware of the weight of her skeleton, her sluggish heart. She lay still for two more hours before she gave up on sleep, turned on the bedside lamp and tried to read but her thoughts were scattered. She showered and dressed and went upstairs into the violent daylight, sat on the front step and called William.

He answered through a burst of static. She knew this meant he was far out in the field, in the swamps beyond town where reception was spotty.

"Can you meet me?" she asked.

"How soon?"

"As soon as you can."

"I'm at work all day," he said. "I could be at the diner by six."

She wished she could go swimming but she was far too tired; she closed her eyes in the sunlight and thought for a moment she might fall asleep. Daydreams of swimming laps and weightlessness.

Hours later in the diner she sat across a table from William, who was still in his Parks Department uniform, and it was all she could do to stay awake.

"How was work?" she asked.

He shrugged. "I was hunting," he said. William was only supposed to track the Burmese pythons, he was supposed to log their where-abouts and report sightings, but he'd confessed to Sasha that he'd taken to killing them. He knew how dangerous they were. He thought of those kids who lived near the canals and his heart just constricted. He was afraid of opening the paper one morning and seeing that one of the snakes had swallowed a four-year-old. He followed them through swamps with the radio transmitter, a quick loop of wire around the fleshy throat. His boss was turning a blind eye.

"You seem agitated," he said.

"I've been thinking about leaving town." Sasha glanced out the window. The crime scene had been dismantled, the police tape gone from the parking lot.

"You in trouble?"

"I haven't been gambling. Just the tickets."

"That's not what I asked."

"I don't know," she said. "When you were gambling, or anytime else in your life, did you ever . . ." She tried to find the right word while William watched her. "Did you ever witness anything?"

"Sasha, what are you talking about?"

"I think I saw something," she said.

"Are you saying you witnessed a crime?"

"Two nights ago."

"Have you gone to the police?"

"I can't."

"Why can't you?"

"I just can't," she said. "William, I need your help."

"What can I do?" He had set his coffee cup down on the table.

"I have to leave town," she said. "I have to get out, and I only know one way to raise money."

"Don't be crazy," he said.

"Can't you see I have no choice? I *saw* something." But what had she seen? A man's face tilted up toward the window, something almost plaintive in his look, a possibly imagined instant of falling as she turned away. It didn't matter what she'd seen. She'd lifted her cell phone from the table and obeyed a text message that had perhaps helped send him on his way to the next world.

"If it saves me," she said, "then isn't it worth it?"

He was looking at her as if he'd never seen her before.

"When you were gambling," she said, "it was only horses, wasn't it?"

"*Only,*" he said.

"I'm sorry. I just mean that that was the only kind of gambling you ever did."

"That was the only kind that was a problem."

"William, I need you to come with me to a poker game."

"Sasha, please."

"I need you to come with me to a poker game, and pull me away from the table if I'm losing too much."

"Think about who you're asking. I can't."

"I can't ask anyone else, William. I'm sorry." She was finding it difficult to meet his eyes. "William," she said, "I have to leave town soon, and I'm going to go to the casino before work tomorrow whether you'll meet me there or not. But I hope you'll meet me, because I need your help."

"I can't help you," he said. "You're asking too much."

In the casino it was always night. Sasha stood for a few minutes near the door, afraid to go further, adrift on the wild patterns of the carpet. She had slept for only three hours after the end of her shift and then woken in tears from a dream she couldn't remember, heart racing. She felt slightly delirious. It had been some years since she'd been here and she'd forgotten the sounds of this place, the chimes and bells of machines, the voices and laughter. The slot machines, row upon row of men and women staring at screens and pulling levers, cherries and pineapples and bananas lining up and falling away before them. Beyond the slot machines she stood for a moment by the roulette table, watching the game. An impassive woman in a white shirt and black trousers spun the wheel, a dial of smooth heavy wood that gleamed under the lights.

This was what had caught her once, and held her here: once you stepped beyond the slot machines—and even these held a certain glinting allure—the casino was beautiful. White-and-gold ceilings arcing high between mahogany pillars, complicated parquet floors and thick carpets. When everything else around her had been squalid, there had always been this. This place had always held beauty even when it was killing her and the beauty reached her even now, even knowing what she did about how much could be lost here.

Sasha walked under mahogany archways into the hush of the poker room, where games were playing out at a dozen tables, bought into a no-limit game and sat with her chips in a small tower before her. After all these years of effort, of Gamblers Anonymous meetings, she was disappointed by an inescapable sense of homecoming.

The blinds were laid and the cards dealt. For a moment Sasha didn't want to look at her hand. She hesitated for so long that the man sitting beside her—a pinch-faced small person in a cowboy hat—glanced curiously at her. But she did look, finally, and it wasn't terrible. A jack and a nine, both hearts. There was hope there, or she could still fold and not have lost very much. Sasha raised a small bet and put in twenty, the first chips sliding away from her over the felt. She half-wanted to snatch them back and leave immediately before she lost anything important, but she forced herself to sit still. The flop was a two, a five, a queen. Nothing enormously useful, but the fourth card—the turn—was a ten of hearts and she felt the old quickening. It would be difficult, she realized, to hold on to herself here. She was thinking of *Delirious Things*, of northern lights and snow. She would go to Alaska! A half-formed idea that became a plan between the turn and the river card. She had always loved Florida but if her life was changing into something unrecognizable then she wanted Florida's opposite, she wanted winter and cold landscapes under northern lights. She would be alone there, but she was alone now. The river was the eight of hearts. She had the best hand and won three hundred dollars.

Her next two hands were useless and she folded, and after this she lost track of time. There was the smooth wood at the edge of the table under her fingertips, a faint scent of orange oil, the clicking of chips. She glanced up and the person next to her was now a large woman with a clipped northern accent. Sasha hadn't noticed when the man with the cowboy hat had left, or she'd noticed him leave but had forgotten it. There were tells and bluffs all around her, patterns in the cards. The stacks of hard disks by her hands rose and fell and rose again.

Her table was the nearest to the bar. She looked up and across the game and saw William Chandler watching her from a barstool, a jacket over his Parks Department uniform. He was sipping an amber liquid caught between ice cubes.

"I hoped I wouldn't find you here," he said. She wasn't sure if she'd heard him or if she'd read his lips, but she was certain of what he'd said to her. There was something unreal about the room now, the lights too bright, sound muffled.

"I know," she said. "I'm sorry." She knew she'd spoken aloud, but no one at the table glanced at her. The man across from her wore reflective glasses and a baseball cap, most of his face hidden. She couldn't tell where he was looking, so she tried not to look at him.

Sasha had a good hand, a king and a jack of spades, and the flop held a ten of the same suit. She held her breath. The turn was the nine of spades, the river was the queen and she'd just won, she realized, an extraordinary sum of money. The chips moved across the table toward her. She assembled them into careful towers. She was up two thousand four hundred fifty dollars. In the next game she lost seven hundred of this but it came back to her quickly. She couldn't remember having asked for a glass of water but one had appeared beside her chips, and she realized dimly that it was William who had set it there. Impossible to tell, in this room without clocks or windows, how long she had been here now. It had to have been a while, all these hands and the cast at the table around her still changing, the large northern woman with the clipped accent replaced by a larger red-faced man. She tried to remember all the hands she'd been dealt, but couldn't. William was watching her from the bar. She nodded at him in what she hoped was a reassuring way.

In her new state, she decided, Alaska or someplace else with snow, she would clean the wood of her home with orange oil. She liked the scent of it. The cards in her hands now were a two and a six, unmatched suits, so she folded and let her gaze slide over the room. This room was the promise: if you win enough at these tables you might move forever through rooms like this one, places with solid shining mahogany and warm colors, potted palm trees, high ceilings. All the interiors of your life might be elegant after this, opulent and always clean. Her next hand contained a pair of aces that brought towers of chips sliding over the table toward her and it was some time after this, although she wasn't sure how long, when she heard William Chandler's voice behind her.

"Sasha," he said, "it's time to stop."

His voice broke the spell. She looked at the pile of chips before her and realized, waking from the dream, that she was up a little over six thousand dollars.

"Fold," she said. The game was almost over. She watched the showdown, the dealer's hands sliding the stacks of chips toward the man with the reflective glasses, who broke into an exuberant grin. Her legs were unsteady when she stood. William took her elbow. He helped her cash out her chips and in the gray twilight of the parking lot they stood together by his car. She felt dazed and emptied out.

"Thank you, William." Her voice was hoarse. "What time is it?"

"Eight o'clock," he said. "You working tonight?"

"I got someone to cover for me," she said. "I don't have to be at work till ten. I didn't know how much time I'd need."

"What now, then?"

"Let's go to the ocean."

"The ocean?"

"I'm leaving Florida soon," Sasha said. "I don't know when I'll see it again."

"Okay, then, the ocean. You have a spot in mind?"

"There's an access point at the end of Cordoba Boulevard."

"Fine," he said. "I'll follow you."

She started her car. These mechanical motions, automatic pilot. William's headlights in the rearview mirror. She usually felt more sharpness and purpose in a car than elsewhere but now she drifted through the twilight, palm trees approaching and falling away in the windshield, her headlights a thin glaze on the half-dark streets. Stay awake. Stay awake. She had to remind herself to blink but she felt sleep crowding close around her, a chaotic darkness at the periphery. It would be easy to slide. She wondered where Anna was, but that thought was pure agony and she shied quickly away from it. The six thousand seventy dollars from the casino were divided here and there on her body, some in the zipped inside pocket of her jacket, some in her handbag, some in her sports bra between her breasts. These tropical streets where she'd lived all her life. The long passage down Cordoba and the darkened sea at the end. She parked the car and walked out on the sand in the still salt air. There were three condominium towers by the beach here, but the units hadn't sold. Almost all of the windows were dark, one or two lights shining high above.

"I'm going somewhere where the air's lighter," she said to William, when she heard his footsteps on the sand beside her.

"Where you planning on going?"

"I'm going to Alaska," she said. "Or as close to Alaska as I can get before my car breaks down."

"When?"

"Soon. Maybe tomorrow or the next day."

"Then I might not see you again," William said.

AT NINE forty-five Sasha was at the diner, reflexively checking the booths and tables for Daniel or Gavin as she walked to the staff room. Neither was there.

"Sweetheart," Bianca said, "you look like hell."

"I had insomnia." Sasha moved past her and locked the staff bathroom door behind her. She looked worse than she would have guessed. Her eyes were bloodshot and glassy, her stare unblinking. Her lipstick was gone. There was a shine of sweat on her skin, smudges of mascara at the corners of her eyes. She washed her face, stripped out of her uniform and gave herself a cold sponge bath with paper towels. She tried not to look at herself in the mirror. She dressed and smoothed out the wrinkles with a damp paper towel as best she could, combed her hair and pinned it up behind her head, carefully reapplied her makeup. When she was done she thought she looked presentable, except for the eyes.

"You'd tell me, wouldn't you, if something were wrong," Bianca said.

"No," Sasha said, "I think I've been enough of a burden."

The dinner rush was nearly over, a few stray customers here and there in the booths. Her apron and her bra were full of money, hundred-dollar bills warm against her skin. She stood by the cash register, listening to the muffled clatter of Freddy and Luis washing up from the dinner rush in the kitchen. She picked up dirty dishes and dropped off dessert menus, carried a towering slice of New York cheesecake that seemed to float before her across the room. Sasha admired the gleam of lights in melting ice cream as she set a banana split on a table. Her exhaustion was taking on the force of gravity. She drank cup after cup of coffee and it helped but her heart was racing, spots in front of her eyes when she turned her head too quickly. She was trying not to look out the windows, because it was possible that beneath the surface of the reflections she might see the man's face looking up at her from outside like a corpse in deep water. The idea of swimming. She went to the restroom to splash cold water on her hands. All this money pressed close against her body but the idea of going out on her own was terrifying.

"Where are your parents?" Bianca asked. They were standing together by the cash register, a momentary lull. The question was unexpected. It took Sasha a moment to compose her thoughts.

"I don't know anymore," Sasha said. "Why?"

"It would've been my mother's birthday today," Bianca said. "I've been thinking about parents, I suppose."

"What was your mother like?"

"She was kind. She worked hard. She raised five kids. Liked soap operas and calla lilies. Yours?"

"My mother isn't any good. I haven't spoken to her since high school."

"What do you mean, she isn't any good?"

"She just never was."

"Where's your father?"

"He doesn't talk to me," Sasha said. "I stole his car and sold it for gambling money."

"But you're better now, aren't you?"

"I don't know," Sasha said. "I'm trying to be better."

It occurred to her around midnight that this might be her last night here. The idea of departure cast the diner in a vivid light, a picture coming into focus. She felt suddenly awake, the fog lifted. The brilliant red banquettes and the gleam of chrome under the lights, pebbled Formica tabletops and all the sounds she barely heard anymore, the clatter from the kitchen and the voices of other diners and the passage of cars on Route 77. She looked around, blinking, she caught Bianca's eye and smiled.

"I just want you to know," she said, "I've always enjoyed working with you."

"Well, thank you, sweetheart." Bianca didn't smile back. "You sound like you're saying your good-byes."

"I don't know," Sasha said. "Maybe."

She moved like a ghost through the caffeinated hours.

Twenty-Eight

A brief history of the money:

A HUNDRED and twenty-one thousand dollars in a gym bag in a basement in Salt Lake City, destined to be taken to a sympathetic investment banker the following morning. Cameras in the basement caught the image clearly: Anna descends the stairs—"She looks kind of wild-eyed," Daniel said nervously, watching the footage with Paul in the hours after the theft was discovered, afraid for his life—and she unzips the bag at the bottom of the stairs, grabs it, and slips like a shadow back up to the first floor. The theft takes less than a minute. Careless to leave the money unsecured and Paul never did it again. He was still new in those days. He'd been in his profession less than a year.

A FEW hours earlier Anna had been lying on top of the sofa bed in the storage room at Paul's house, watching the movement of the fan on the ceiling above. A charitable organization at the hospital had given Anna an infant car seat, a package of diapers, a bottle and formula, some brochures. She threw out the brochure about adoption and read the others over and over again, trying to memorize everything. Paul's house wasn't home but she didn't know where else she could go, marooned as she was that night in the Kingdom of Deseret. She was alone in the storage room with her baby and she'd been putting Chloe to sleep in the car seat at night, because she was afraid of rolling over on her in the bed. Daniel was living in an upstairs room, not speaking to her. Sasha had wired her two hundred dollars. Anna took expensive taxis to the pharmacy for diapers and infant formula. She didn't know what she would do when the money ran out, if it would be possible to ask Daniel for more. Whenever she saw him in passing in the house he looked at her with such fury that words froze in her throat. She tried to avoid him.

How well did she know Daniel? Not well, when she considered the question, but who else did she have? There was Sasha far away in Florida, struggling. There was Gavin, but the thought of Gavin filled her with guilt and approaching him seemed unthinkable after what she'd done; she had ideas about honor and knew she'd transgressed. She wasn't sure what would become of her, or what Daniel would do. Every part of her ached with exhaustion. Days slipped into a week and then two and even music didn't soothe her. Chloe slept and woke, cried and made small noises, gurgled and kicked her feet. Anna had never imagined such an intensity of love.

On the night she took the money she was restless and ill at ease. When Chloe finally fell asleep Anna lay on her back on the sofa bed, fully dressed. Shadows passed over the ceiling from a branch blowing in front of the backyard light, and a cold wind came into the room. She stood to close the window, and this was when she heard them. Paul and

Daniel were in the backyard, far back in the shadows by the picnic bench under the tree. A woman's voice, Paul's girlfriend, a too-thin woman with blond hair whom Anna had seen only in passing. The faint smell of cigarettes. She didn't hear what Paul said—she caught her name and the word *responsibility*, nothing else—but Daniel's reply carried clearly on the breeze.

"I could kill her," he said. "That's how angry I am."

She stepped away from the window. Chloe was still sleeping. All she could think of as she left the room and slipped down the stairs to the basement was Paul beating that man in the backyard a few months earlier, the blood on the grass the following morning. You're judged by the company you keep, a social worker had told her once, you *are* the company you keep, and wasn't Daniel Paul's friend?

The bag wasn't heavy. She had no idea how much money weighed, but she was half-blind with fear and the thought occurred to her that this couldn't be more than a few thousand dollars, five thousand perhaps, she would take it and use it to get away from here and pay Paul back later and perhaps someday he'd even understand. Back in the storage room she was fast and silent, throwing everything she could see into her duffel bag. Cigarette smoke still drifted in through the window; she heard them talking, too quietly to hear, and the miracle was that Chloe didn't wake when Anna lifted the car seat and slipped out the front door. She half-walked, half-ran down the hill to the doughnut store where she'd worked, called a taxi, and bought a doughnut and a cup of coffee while she waited for the car to arrive. It wasn't until much later, waiting for the bus that would take her out of Utah, hiding in the ladies' room until the last possible moment, locked in a handicapped stall with Chloe and the two bags, that she looked for the first time at the money in the bathroom's harsh light and understood exactly how much trouble she was in.

. . .

IN THE small hours of morning Anna held Chloe wrapped in a blanket in her arms and they fell together into a fitful sleep, Utah passing outside the window. Mostly darkness, every so often a town in the distance. In the house in the suburbs in Salt Lake City, the theft had just been discovered. In the master bedroom where he'd set up his command center Paul was watching the footage from the basement camera over and over again, and Daniel was sitting on the bed with his head in his hands. Paul's girlfriend had been waiting, smoking and painting her nails in the kitchen, for a half-hour before she finally came in.

"I told you not to come in," Paul said, but he was distracted. The girl on the screen lifted the bag for the twelfth time.

"Tell me what's wrong," Paul's girlfriend said. "Why won't you just *tell* me?" But she was already moving toward the screen. She watched Anna slip quickly up the stairs.

"A hundred and twenty-one thousand dollars," Paul said, but this, after leaving the basement door unsecured, was his second mistake of the evening.

"Are you serious? That little girl?" She spoke with such derision that a decade later Daniel remembered her exact wording, the look on her face, even though he couldn't remember her name. "That little girl stole a hundred and twenty-one thousand dollars from you? Oh my God, baby, that's hilarious. You gonna let that slide?"

Paul stared at the screen and even though Daniel was far from the underworld, he'd seen enough movies to understand. Paul couldn't let this slide because the girl was a witness. Daniel assumed that if word got out that it was possible to get away with stealing a hundred twenty-one thousand dollars, then Paul was finished.

"Of course not," Paul said. He turned to Daniel, as he had a half-dozen times in the past half-hour; but now everything was different, because now someone was watching them. "I could hold you responsible," he said. Daniel hoped this was for the benefit of the girl.

"I told you I had nothing to do with this. I haven't spoken a word to her since the baby was born."

"Where would she have gone?"

"I have no idea," Daniel said.

"I might be willing to believe you," Paul said, "but first you have to tell me who her friends are." The girl was chewing gum, looking from one to the other.

"She doesn't really have—"

"Who did she spend time with before she came here?" Paul asked.

Daniel spent the rest of his life laden with guilt, but at that moment telling him seemed the only way out of that house. He gave him the names of the rest of the Lola Quartet. "But look, the only place she would go is Florida," he said. This bit of misdirection seemed the last thing he could do for her. In an hour he would call her and speak into her voice mail, he would tell her how sorry he was and how stupid she'd been and beg her to go anywhere but Florida. In two hours she would stand at a counter in a small town in Colorado and change her bus ticket to South Carolina. "She's never in her life been anywhere else."

Twenty-Nine

Ten years later in the city of Sebastian Gavin read the account of Paul's death and sat still for some time looking at nothing before he closed his laptop and continued on with his day. Later that evening he showered and shaved, put on his best shirt and drove to the address on the torn corner of newspaper. Driving was unpleasant and nerve-wracking with his bad arm, he didn't like having only one hand on the steering wheel, but he was tired of taxis. The address Deval had given him was another motel, even farther out than the Draker, a run-down place just within Sebastian city limits. It was late already, ten thirty p.m., and lights were on in no more than five or six motel-room windows. He parked his car and made his way toward the building.

A girl was jumping rope by the stairs that led up to the second story. He couldn't see her face, a blur of long dark hair in the shadows, but something in her movement arrested him. He sat down on a step and waited until she stopped.

"Hello," he said. The girl from the photograph stared back at him. Eilo's thin lips and straight dark hair, a dusting of freckles on her nose.

Traces of Japan in the shape of her eyes although her eyes were the color of Anna's, bright blue. "Is your mom around?"

"No," she said. There was something deerlike about her. She was winding the skipping rope around her hand, watching him, and her bearing suggested that she might bolt at any moment.

"Where's your dad?"

"I don't have a dad," the girl said. "He died before I was born."

"Really," Gavin said. "Before you were born?" He wanted nothing more than to stay in this moment forever, sitting here on this step with his daughter before him. Trying to imagine all the years he'd missed, what she'd looked like at nine, at seven, at two.

"My mom said it was a car accident."

"A car accident," Gavin said. "I'm sorry to hear that."

She shrugged. "It's okay," she said. "I didn't know him."

"Where's your mom?"

"She's at night school," the girl said.

"What time does she get home?"

"Late. Maybe eleven."

The desolation of this small motel. The dirty stucco, the paint coming off the doors in patches and strips. She dropped the wound-up skipping rope at her feet, raised her arms and did a slow back handstand off the cement walkway onto the grass, walked on her hands for a few steps, and pivoted to face him once she was upright. He applauded.

"I've been practicing," she said. He was watching her with tears in his eyes. A memory of Eilo doing backflips in a circle around the yard when they were little. A firefly sparked in the nearby air and she crouched down to look at it.

"I'm not sure what your name is," he said.

"Chloe." The firefly blinked out. She stood.

"Chloe Montgomery?"

"How did you know?"

"I know your mom," he said.

"But how did you know she was my mom?"

"You look like her."

"No, I don't," Chloe said.

"You have the same color eyes," he said.

"What happened to your arm?"

"Just a silly accident," he said. "It's getting better."

"How do you know her?"

"Your mom? We went to school together."

"How old were you?" Chloe asked.

"Older than you," Gavin said. "I guess I was fifteen when I first met her. She was fourteen."

"Were you her boyfriend?"

"Yes."

"Oh," she said. She was studying him closely.

"Why are you here at the motel?"

"I don't know," she said. A flicker of doubt crossed her face. "My mom said it was a vacation."

"A vacation?"

"She said sometimes people stay in motels for a while and that's what a vacation is."

"Oh," Gavin said. "You know, she's right, actually. That's exactly what people do on vacation."

"We keep going from motel to motel," Chloe said.

"Chloe, I have to talk to your mom."

"She gets home late," Chloe said. "I make my own dinner."

"What do you make?"

"Macaroni and cheese. 'Bye," she said abruptly, and went to the door of a motel room halfway down the row. She fumbled in her pocket for a key, unlocked the door and closed it behind her, and a light flicked on behind the curtain. He stayed on the steps for a long time, waiting, listening to crickets and muffled television noises, watching cars pass on the street. Two cars pulled up to the motel in the interval, people coming home with bags of groceries. This was a motel, he realized, where people stayed for some time, a place for people who didn't have houses or apartments anymore.

A third car pulled in, a small battered Toyota. The driver parked in front of the room that Chloe had disappeared into. It took him a moment to recognize Anna, hazy in the blue-white light. She had cut her hair short and dyed it. But she was wearing a sleeveless shirt that night and when she got out of the car he saw the bass-clef tattoo. She was less than thirty feet away.

"Anna," he said. She started and took a step backward, came up hard against the door of the car. He raised his hands.

"It's me," he said, "it's Gavin. Gavin Sasaki."

"Gavin. Christ." He remembered her smoking when they were teenagers, and understood from her voice that she'd never stopped. "How did you find me?"

"Deval gave me your address. I just wanted to talk to you. It's been years." He stood up slowly from the step. He didn't want to frighten her.

She looked at him for a moment, walked around the car to retrieve a bag of groceries from the passenger seat. She unlocked the door to the motel room, fumbling with her keys. "Why don't you come in," she said.

ANNA HAD a job as a file clerk, but she was studying to be a paralegal. She was twenty-six and looked older, pale when she turned on the dim light over the stove in the kitchenette. She was blond but he saw the dark roots of her natural hair. She lived with her daughter in a single motel room. Chloe was nowhere to be seen, but Anna raised a finger to her lips and pointed at a squared-off corner of folding screens, and Gavin understood this to be Chloe's room. There were two mismatched stools at the kitchenette counter, no table. The room had two beds; he could see the flattened-down space of carpet where Chloe's bed had been, before it had been pushed into the corner and hidden from view. Anna moved efficiently in the tiny kitchenette, putting groceries away. She took two bottles of beer from the fridge, popped both, and passed him one. He held the bottle briefly to his forehead.

"You haven't changed," she said. "Still can't take the heat."

"I never could."

"So what are you doing back in Sebastian?" She had the same quick bright way of speaking. Here she stood before him and he realized that he was still looking for her, trying to find the Anna he'd known in her face, in her movements, still searching for clues.

"It's a long, boring story."

"You were a journalist, weren't you?"

"I was," he said.

"Daniel told me you got fired. He said you lied in all your stories."

"Not all of them. The last few."

"Why did you lie?" Anna asked.

"I don't know, there was so much pressure at that place."

"Come on," she said.

"You come from nowhere, some suburb somewhere, there's such an expectation that you'll succeed, everyone back home talking about you—"

"Why did you lie?"

"I just came undone," Gavin said. "I wasn't expecting it."

She had nothing to say to this. She pulled herself up to sit on the counter and sipped her beer and in that motion he saw a glimpse of her as a girl—but had he ever actually seen her sit on a counter? Perhaps at a house party? Or was it just that sitting on a counter was something he expected teenagers to do? She was wearing sandals. Her toenails were painted a sparkly blue. He glanced around in the awkward silence that followed and saw that she'd gone to some effort to make the motel room look like home. A child's drawings had been Scotch-taped to the walls. One in particular caught his eye: a house with a child and two women beside it and a sun with spiked rays overhead, Chloe's name written carefully in a corner in rounded letters with a heart after it. There were pictures of acrobats executing squiggly backflips, suspended in the air with red and blue birds flying overhead. A dish and a fork were drying on a dish towel beside the sink, and a faint aroma of macaroni and cheese lingered in the air.

"You went to Utah," he said.

"I did." She was sipping her beer, expressionless, and he tried to imagine what her memories might be like.

"What was it like there?"

"What was it like? It was lonely. It was uncomfortable. Nothing terrible happened to me. I just spent whole days alone in the house, pregnant, whole days waiting in this unfamiliar house while Daniel was at work, and the rest of the time I was working at a doughnut shop. It's so long ago now," she said. "I don't think about it."

"You took some money," he said.

"I did." She regarded him for a moment. "Have you ever made a decision in a moment of panic and then regretted it for the rest of your life?"

"I've done regrettable things. Why did you come back here?"

"Back to Sebastian? It'd been three years. I'd broken up with Liam.

I wanted to be near Sasha again. We figured if anyone were still looking for us, they'd have found us by then."

"Anna," he said, "is that my daughter?"

"No," she said. "She's my daughter. No one else raised her."

"If I'd known she existed . . ."

"Then what? You would have stayed in Florida?"

"I don't know, Anna. I would have done something."

She shrugged. "Well," she said, "you didn't." A hardness in her
voice. He was looking at her and thinking, The robin's-egg-blue headphones. The way you listened to music. The way your hair fell over
your face while you did your homework. The way you stood before the
wall in the park and showed me the word you'd spray-painted over
and over again, NO for New Order. The girl he'd searched for, he realized, no longer existed. He was shot through with unease.

"I'm sorry," he said. "I came here to apologize. I think I knew you
were pregnant. There were all those rumors, and you said you had to
tell me something but you didn't, and then you disappeared. I didn't
really make inquiries. I didn't really look for you. I just took off for
New York and let you go."

"I didn't tell you," she said. "I left town before you did."

"But you know what? I should have known. You were always—
you were good," he said. "You deserved better than what I did."

She smiled. "Good? Is that how you remember me?"

"Yes." In the long silence that followed he tried to think of a way
of casually enquiring about the death behind the Starlight Diner, came
up short and opted for bluntness. "Did you give Deval my address?"
he asked.

"He insisted. He said he had to apologize to you." Her voice had
changed, her smile gone. "I told him he was out of his mind, going to
see you in the state he was in. He wasn't thinking clearly."

"He told me your troubles are over."

"One of them," she said. "The most dangerous one."

"What happens now, Anna?"

"Now?" She spoke quietly, contemplating the bottle in her hand. "Life continues. I get up and go to work every day. I'm going to move back in with my sister next week."

"And you're . . . someone died last night," he said. "Aren't you troubled by that?"

"Keep your voice down." Anna was peeling the label from her beer bottle, working sparkly blue fingernails under the corners. "I am," she said after a moment. "Of course I am. I know what I've done."

"But you're—"

"But I'm not wrecked by it," she said, "because there was nothing else I could do. Sasha's pretty torn up about it. Want to know something about Sasha? She's never gone anywhere or done anything, and it's made her naive. You know what people like Sasha assume? They assume every human life is equal."

He felt a touch of vertigo that he couldn't blame on his arm. "You think some lives deserve to end."

"He was a dealer who threatened my daughter." She was rolling the torn-off label into a tiny ball between her fingertips, a quick nervous motion. "I watched him beat a man almost to death once. Surely you don't wish he were still walking this earth."

"I think it isn't for me to decide."

Anna was cast in yellow by the stove-top light, a shine of sweat on her nose. "Think about it," she said. She wasn't nearly as calm as he'd thought, he realized. Her voice was strained now, tears in her eyes. "It was a hundred and twenty-one thousand dollars plus interest. None of us had money, or families with money, or friends with money, or the kinds of credit ratings that lend themselves to loans. Daniel thought he had an inheritance, but it fell through at the last minute. What were we supposed to do?"

"I don't know," he said. He was struck by a sudden mad thought that he was speaking with an impostor, but there was the bass-clef tattoo on her shoulder.

"You see? We didn't know either. What would have been the right thing to do, Gavin, under the circumstances?"

"I can't help but think . . ." He was short of breath. "I just think there's always another way."

"We couldn't think of one," she said.

"I just don't know how you move on from something like this," Gavin said.

"You mean, you don't know how *you're* going to move on from this." She set her half-empty beer bottle next to the sink and jumped down off the counter, opened the refrigerator and removed a bottle of ginger ale. She filled a glass with ice and they both listened to the cubes cracking as she poured the soda. She didn't offer him a glass. "Or are you implying that I've moved on from it? I haven't, of course I haven't. I will carry this with me for the rest of my life. But if you're asking how to keep going, what you do is you remind yourself of the truth," she said, "which is that there wasn't a choice. That's the difference between me and Sasha. I understand that and she doesn't."

"You could have turned him in. Cooperated with the police."

"You mean, help convict an *alleged* drug dealer for having had a hundred twenty-one thousand dollars stolen from him ten years ago in a distant state? Don't be stupid. I was the thief. The way I see it, the theft and the provenance of the money cancel each other out. How could anyone possibly prove that the money I found in his basement ten years ago came from dealing crystal?" Her eyes were shining. "You don't understand the position we were placed in," she said. "He found us, he forced our hands. He had someone take Chloe's picture at Liam's mother's house. Daniel went to talk to him about repayment, but then it turned out there was no money after all. None of us was even close. We could have done . . . *this*, we could've done what we did, or I could have disappeared again with Chloe, and Liam's mother would probably have been in danger. Sasha too, and Daniel's children. People like him, they come after your family and friends."

He looked away from her. His arm hurt.

"The photograph of Chloe . . ." he began, but couldn't finish. Not telling her, he realized, was the only kindness he could give her.

"I had to hide before," Anna said. She cleared her throat and continued in a steadier voice. "After I left Utah that time, when I was seventeen. I ran and hid for years, and I just couldn't do it again. You don't know what it's like. Always looking over your shoulder, looking out for strange cars, the way all the windows have eyes. This time there wouldn't have been any money, Gavin, this time we would've been in hiding forever, Chloe and I. New names, no friends, no more family, no money, and this time I'd be with a child who was old enough to understand and old enough to give us away, and the people we left behind would be in danger, like I said. There wasn't a choice."

Chloe stirred in her sleep and they were both silent for a moment, looking in her direction.

"I'm sorry," Gavin said. "I don't think you had to do what you think you had to do."

Anna said nothing. What were they capable of, Anna and Daniel and Liam? If you've gone all the way once, isn't it easier to do it again? He was chilled in the dim air of the motel room.

"It was your idea," he said, "wasn't it?"

"It wasn't anyone's idea." She sounded immeasurably weary. "We were talking about what to do, the three of us—"

"You, Daniel, Liam Deval?"

"Right. I can't remember anyone bringing it up, but the idea was there, in the room. We were talking and it was something we were skirting around. No one said it directly. It just . . . it slowly became something that had been decided on. If we hadn't done this," she said, and there were tears on her face now, "how much danger would we have been in? What might have happened to Chloe, to Sasha, to Daniel's kids? 'You pay with money or you pay with your family.' That's what he said to Daniel."

"But it was the wrong thing to do," Gavin said. "It's the worst thing anyone I know has ever done."

Anna had gone still. She was watching him intently. Could she throw something at him? Everything within her reach was suddenly a weapon; the toaster, the heavy glass in her hand, the hard bowl on the dish towel by the sink. Gavin backed away from her and opened the door. He was afraid to look away until he'd closed the door between them, and he glanced twice at the motel on the fast walk back to his car but the door remained shut, the curtain over the window unmoving.

Gavin drove to his apartment. He hadn't accumulated much. He made a neat stack of his clothes and bedding in the backseat of his car, working quickly. His socks and underwear went into a cardboard box behind the front passenger seat. He hid his laptop under a pillow on the backseat and packed a plastic bag with half a loaf of bread and some peanut butter, all the bottles of water from the fridge, an unripe banana and an orange. The kettle, which was of course easily replaceable but was his favorite of all the kettles he'd ever owned, a pleasing fire-engine red. His magnificent 1973 Yashica and the gold pocket watch he'd found at a stoop sale in New York, the glass dog stolen from his mother, the photograph of Chloe. When he was finished all that remained was the sofa that had been there when he moved in, a cheap bed and dresser and coffee table from Ikea. On the way out he dropped the apartment key through the mail slot.

H E D R O V E to the Starlight Diner and parked in the shadows by the back door. No trace remained of the crime scene. The diner was quiet at this hour, a midnight lull. When he came in Sasha was standing by the cash register with another waitress, the older blond woman with turquoise eye shadow whom he'd met once or twice before. Gavin waved at them and sat in a banquette where he could see the parking lot.

"Will you sit for a moment?" he asked, when Sasha came to his table. She did, sliding onto the padded bench across from him. She looked worse than she had the last time he'd seen her, paler, dark smudges under her eyes.

"You look tired," he said. He realized it was a tactless thing to say as the words left his mouth, but she didn't seem to take offense.

"I was up all day playing poker." Something tugged at him when she said this—a long-ago conversation he'd had with her outside the school, money lost in a high school poker game—but the memory was fleeting and vague.

"Where's Grace?"

"I don't know. I drove her home that night."

"Sasha, you told me once that you hated the plan."

She glanced at Bianca, but Bianca was across the room and couldn't hear them.

"I did," she said softly. "I do. Yes."

"Did you know what the plan was?"

"That's just it," she said. "I thought I did, but I think the plan was actually something different." Her hands were clenched on the table. "Did you know what the plan was, Gavin?"

"I didn't know anything."

"I thought it was just money." There were tears in her eyes. "Anna and Daniel, I thought they were just paying back a debt. I didn't know."

"Sasha," he said, "we were friends back then, weren't we? In high school?"

"That was a nice time," she said. He hadn't expected her to turn nostalgic on him. Her eyes drifted toward the window, and he saw how tired she was. She was losing focus, not as sharp as she had been a week or two ago, not even as sharp as she'd been in high school. She closed her eyes for just a moment and touched her fingertips to her forehead. "I'm sorry," she said. "I haven't been sleeping much. Do you ever miss the quartet?"

"We were good."

She smiled. "We were. You remember our last concert?"

"Behind the school. How could I forget? It was the only time I ever played in the back of a pickup truck."

"I think about it sometimes," she said. "Taylor singing, the fireflies, everyone dancing."

"Sasha," he said, "have you thought about going somewhere else?"

"I have." She was still gazing out the window. "I'm leaving soon," she said.

"When?"

"I don't know, I just want to get away from all this." She looked at him. "I can't go to the police," she said. "She's my sister. You don't know what she's done for me."

"I want to ask you a favor," Gavin said. "As a friend."

"What kind of favor?"

"Sasha," he said, "I want you to leave town tonight. Please. Don't tell anyone you're going."

"Tonight?"

"Will you do it?"

"Why . . . ?"

"Because you're complicit," he said, "and because I don't know if you're safe here."

"But you're not going to say anything about this, are you? What would happen to Chloe?"

The thought of his daughter made his heart seize up.

"Just say you'll do it, Sasha, please."

"Okay," she said, "I'll leave town tonight." A brightness in her eyes that he hadn't anticipated. She was frightened, he realized, but also excited. How many times in your life do you get to flee town? How often do you get to lose everything and start all over again?

GAVIN HAD already researched the boundaries of police precincts in this part of Florida and now he pulled out of the parking lot and turned right on Route 77. He crossed the first boundary within a few minutes—Fellever Road—and kept driving. It wouldn't hurt, he thought, to cover some distance. He stopped for gas and a road map. The suburbs were shining, glass and stucco and lights along the freeway and palm trees silhouetted along the edge of the sky. He was traveling north. He had a few thousand dollars, the savings from his work with Eilo. He would stop and call Eilo to explain and then keep going, up out of this land of palm trees and alligators, somewhere far. He was thinking about Chicago. He didn't think his life would be easier there but he was certain it would be different.

Gavin crossed the Sebastian city limits. The city-limits sign was in the middle of a long block between a shopping mall and an office park. He was entering the city of Cassidy, according to the signs, and now he'd crossed Alberly Street. This was yet another demarcation. He'd put at least six precincts between himself and Daniel. After some time had passed he saw a sign for a police station and pulled into the exit lane. The station was a massive square of cinder blocks in an ocean of parking lot.

Gavin parked the car and retrieved the photograph of Chloe from the glove box. Ten years old, standing by the window in an almost empty dining room. He put his hand on the car door, but he didn't open it.

He'd played the sequence of events over in his head so many times that it felt almost like a memory. I get out of my car and walk across the parking lot, I push open the glass doors of the police station and cross a threshold into a bright world of blue paint and fluorescent light panels humming, voices and the crackling of radios. I address myself to the police officer watching me from behind a high blue countertop, I say the words that change everything: *I have information about a murder.* I make statements, I name names. I do the technically correct thing, the right thing, the thing a law-abiding citizen does in the presence of a crime.

A knock on the driver's-side window made Gavin jump. He'd been too lost in the dream to register the police cruiser pulling into the lot, and now a police officer was looking at him through the glass. Gavin rolled the window down and the cool air of the car escaped.

"Can I help you?" the officer asked. His tone was unexpectedly friendly.

"Just getting my bearings." Gavin was grateful now for the map, open on the passenger seat. He gestured weakly at it.

"You need directions?"

"I'm trying to get on the interstate," he said. It came out a whisper. He was having trouble finding his voice. He cleared his throat and repeated himself. The photograph of Chloe was still in his hand. "Just pulled in here to take a look at the map."

"Where you going?"

"Chicago."

"You want I-95." Gavin tried to listen while the police officer described a series of turns. "Anything else I can help you with this evening?"

Gavin set the photograph of Chloe on the seat beside him. "Thank you," he said. "There's nothing else."

He pulled out of the police-station parking lot and left the town of Cassidy, lights burning all along the interstate, northward flight. His lips moving with the words of a letter that he would transcribe some days later in Chicago, a letter that he would write but never send: I wanted to find you, dear Chloe, I wanted to help, but in the end the best I could do for you was to leave you in peace. I love you. I'll never know you. I'll always wonder who you are.

On either side of the highway the suburbs continued uninterrupted, a continuous centerless glimmering of lights, shadows of palm trees on parking lots, malls shining like beacons and he was nowhere, this could be any suburb on the edge of any city but it seemed to him that none of the cities had edges anymore, just a long slow reach across landscapes. At four a.m. he stopped for food and coffee at a diner very much like the Starlight, left a long message on his sister's cell phone, and drove on toward Chicago, toward the north star and morning.

ACKNOWLEDGMENTS

With thanks to my editor, Greg Michalson; to Steven Wallace, Caitlin Hamilton Summie, Libby Jordan, Rich Rennicks, Fred Ramey, Rachel Kinbar Grace, and all of their colleagues at Unbridled Books;

to Kim McArthur, Devon Pool, Ann Ledden, Kendra Martin, and their colleagues at McArthur & Company;

to my wonderful agent, Katherine Fausset, and her colleagues at Curtis Brown;

to Sohail Tavazoie, for so graciously accommodating my book tour schedule;

to Gina Frangello, whose review of my two previous novels on The Nervous Breakdown influenced this work;

to Alexander Chee, for his help with titles;

to Jessica Lowery, for telling me about Chicago;

to Mandy Keifetz and Peter Geye for reading and commenting on early drafts;

and to Kevin Mandel, for being an early reader and for everything.